THE UNCERTAIN YEARS

Recent Titles by Beryl Matthews from Severn House

DIAMONDS IN THE DUST
A FLIGHT OF GOLDEN WINGS
THE FORGOTTEN FAMILY
HOLD ON TO YOUR DREAMS
THE OPEN DOOR
A TIME OF PEACE
THE UNCERTAIN YEARS
WINGS OF THE MORNING

THE UNCERTAIN YEARS

Beryl Matthews

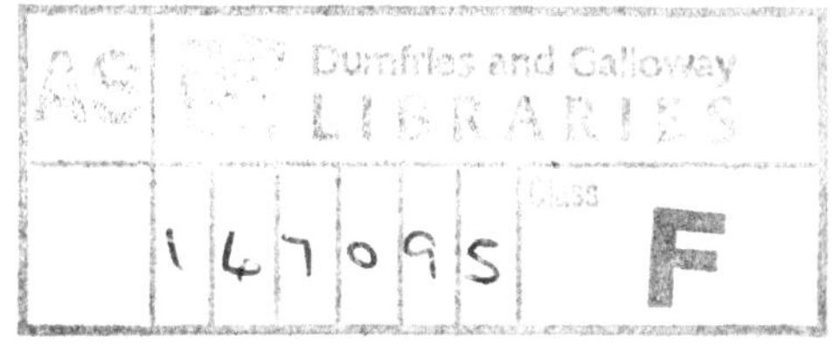

Dumfries and Galloway
LIBRARIES
147095
Class
F

This first world edition published 2010
in Great Britain and in the USA by
SEVERN HOUSE PUBLISHERS LTD of
9–15 High Street, Sutton, Surrey, England, SM1 1DF.
Trade paperback edition published
in Great Britain and the USA 2010 by
SEVERN HOUSE PUBLISHERS LTD

Copyright © 2010 by Beryl Matthews.

All rights reserved.
The moral right of the author has been asserted.

British Library Cataloguing in Publication Data

Matthews, Beryl.
The Uncertain Years.
1. World War, 1939-1945–England–London–Fiction.
2. Journalists–England–London–Fiction. 3. Stepney
(London, England)–Social conditions–20th century–
Fiction.
I. Title
823.9'2-dc22

ISBN-13: 978-0-7278-6891-6 (cased)
ISBN-13: 978-1-84751-228-4 (trade paper)

Except where actual historical events and characters are being described for the storyline of this novel, all situations in this publication are fictitious and any resemblance to living persons is purely coincidental.

Severn House Publishers support The Forest Stewardship Council [FSC],the leading international forest certification organisation. All our titles that are printed on Greenpeace-approved FSC-certified paper carry the FSC logo

Typeset by Palimpsest Book Production Ltd.,
Grangemouth, Stirlingshire, Scotland.
Printed and bound in Great Britain by
MPG Books Ltd., Bodmin, Cornwall.

One

Stepney, London, 3rd September 1939

The friends stood silently outside their terraced houses, each deep in their own thoughts. The news they had just heard would change their lives in ways they could hardly imagine.

Rebecca Adams – Becky to her friends – glanced at her brother Will's tense expression, and saw the same look on Bob Walker and Jim Prentiss. They had been talking about the possibility of this happening for a long time now, but like everyone else, they'd been hoping a solution would be found. It hadn't, and now they were at war with Germany.

'Well, that's it then!' Bob Walker was the first to speak. 'I'm going in the navy. You coming with me, Jim?'

'No fear! I'm going to keep my feet on firm ground. It'll be the army for me. What about you, Will?'

William Adams grimaced. 'No one's going to take me.'

'Course they will. They're going to need everyone they can get.'

'Not me, Jim. They don't want cripples.'

'You're not a cripple!' Becky glared at her brother. 'Your left arm's three inches shorter than the other, that's all. It doesn't even draw attention, and you're as strong and capable as any man.'

'I'm only stating the truth, Becky. The medical is strict and they only want the fittest.'

It hurt to hear her brother talk like this. At twenty-one he was tall with dark hair and gentle grey eyes. She adored him. 'There'll be something you can do. You've got more brains than the rest of us put together. News will be very important, and the paper you work for are going to need you.'

'I'm little more than an errand boy,' he laughed.

He looked relaxed, but she knew him well enough to realize this was far from the truth. The disappointment showed in his eyes and she wasn't going to see him depressed about this. 'Don't be daft. Of course you're not.'

'Everything's going to change,' Bob said, wanting to offer his friend encouragement. 'They printed your piece about Hitler after Chamberlain came back and said there wouldn't be a war. You said the Nazis couldn't be trusted, and you were right. They're going to lose a lot of their reporters, and you'll be badly needed, Will.'

'I suppose you're right, but I'm going to hate being left behind.'

'You won't be alone.' Jim's smile was teasing. 'Becky will be here.'

'No I won't! I'm joining the ATS.'

The three boys burst into hilarious laughter.

Standing with her hands on her hips she glared at them, her expressive hazel eyes glinting. 'What's so damned funny? If you lot think I'm staying at home knitting socks, then you're very much mistaken!'

'We're going to need socks,' Jim spluttered, not able to control his amusement.

That was too much for her and she lashed out, just missing Jim as he ducked. He'd done a bit of boxing and knew how to move. 'How can you stand out here in the street laughing when we've just been told we're at war? Mum's worried sick because Dad might still be young enough to be called up – and I bet your mums are in the same state. You're acting like kids instead of twenty-year-olds. But I tell you what, once you're in the forces you're going to have to grow up quickly.'

'Don't upset yourself, Becky.' Her brother ruffled her short dark hair. 'Our messing about is just in reaction to the devastating news, that's all.'

'That's right, and we're sorry,' Jim told her. 'I expect the women's army will be pleased to have you. You'll make a good sergeant.'

'Don't start again,' she warned. 'And I don't care what you all think. I'm going to the recruiting office in the morning.'

Bob, the tallest of the group, studied Becky carefully, looking her up and down. 'Why don't you join the Wrens? You'd look good in navy blue.'

She gave an exasperated sigh. 'I'm not interested in looking good! I'll have more chance of doing something useful in the army.'

'Such as?' Jim asked.

'I don't know. I'll have to go to the recruitment office first and see what there is.'

'Well, it looks as if we'll all be joining up straight away.' Bob shoved his hands in his pockets, looking apprehensive.

'Hold on a minute!' Will stopped his friends talking. 'Don't you think you'd better wait for your call-up papers?'

'No.' Bob was shaking his head. 'If we volunteer now we'll have more chance of getting into the service we want. If we wait we'll probably have to go where they send us.'

'I agree,' Jim said. 'And the sooner we do it the better.'

'I still think you ought to wait,' Will continued. 'Both of you have only a year to do of your apprenticeship, and you'll be qualified toolmakers then. That will be something to come back to.'

'That doesn't seem important now.' Bob kicked a pebble up the empty road, frowning deeply. Then he shook his head. 'No, my mind's made up.'

'In that case you'd better go and tell your parents what you're intending to do.'

Both boys pulled a face. 'Did you have to remind us of that, Will?'

'Yes, I did, Jim.' He took hold of his sister's arm. 'And that's a job you've got to do right now. There could be a hell of a row; you know that, don't you, Becky? You're only nineteen.'

'You'll support me though, won't you?'

'Don't I always?'

She nodded. 'You're the best brother a girl could have.'

'Oh, compliments.' He grinned at her. 'Now I know you're really worried about telling Mum and Dad.'

'We'd better get this over with,' Bob said.

The friends waved as they all made their way to their own homes. They lived in a terraced block of houses right next door to each other, and had been firm friends from the moment they could toddle.

Becky was near to tears now, as realization of what they were facing hit her. 'We're going to be parted for the first time in our lives.'

'It's hard, but this sort of thing will be happening right across the country. It's something we've got to accept.' Will glanced down at his sister, his black hair shining almost blue in the sunlight. 'If you do go into the ATS, you'll have to get used to being with other girls. Lots of them.'

'Hmm. Hope they're not silly and giggle all the time. It's always been the four of us, and I'm more used to wielding a spanner than gossiping with other girls. Do you think Bob will let you have his old motorbike if he goes into the navy?'

'He might. I'll ask him.'

'Good, you'll find that useful – if you can get any petrol for it. That's bound to be in short supply soon.' They reached their front door and she hesitated. 'Mum's going to cry, I just know she is.'

Their parents were sitting at the large, well scrubbed kitchen table with cups of tea in front of them.

'Any tea in the pot?' Will asked as they joined them.

'Plenty, it's a fresh pot.' Mavis Adams gave her children a tired smile. 'I suppose you've all been deciding what you're going to do?'

Will poured two cups, pushing one over to his sister, and then nodded. 'There's nothing to worry about. Between us we've got this war won.'

'Ah, well, we can relax then,' Bill Adams laughed, lightening the tense atmosphere. 'When these four get together Hitler won't stand a chance.'

'We'd better tell him to surrender at once then,' his wife joked.

'What about you, Dad? You're still young enough to be called up, aren't you?' Becky was stalling, trying to delay the time when she had to tell her parents the decision she'd made.

Bill pursed his lips. 'I'm forty-three, so we'll just have to wait and see.'

'They won't take you away from your work.' Mavis looked anxiously at her husband. 'You're working on parts for that plane.'

'The Spitfire.' Will rested his elbows on the table, leaning forward. 'Mum's right. You're on vital work, and at your age you'll be more valuable helping to turn out fighters than being in the forces.'

His father's mouth turned up in amusement. 'Are you suggesting I'm too old for the forces, Will?'

'Of course not! Look at you, six feet four and as strong as an ox. You'd frighten the life out of the enemy. But you're also a damned fine engineer.' Will shook his head. 'No, you'll have to stay where you are. Those planes are going to be needed.'

Mavis nodded, relief showing in her eyes, and then turned her attention back to her children. 'So, what have the four of you been planning? You probably think this is very exciting, but war's a terrible thing, and all our lives are going to change beyond recognition.'

'We know that, Mum.' Becky took a deep breath, knowing she couldn't delay any longer. 'Bob's going to try for the navy, Jim for the army, and I want to join the ATS.'

'I thought you'd all want to stay together if you could.'

'That's impossible, Dad. For the first time in our lives we'll have to split up.' Becky was surprised there hadn't been instant opposition to her plans, but from her parents' resigned expressions, she knew they'd expected this to happen. She had grown up in the rough and tumbles of three boisterous boys, and had never been one to stand on the sidelines.

'What about you, Will?' his father asked.

'I don't know. The services won't take me.'

'How do you know?' Mavis asked.

'Because I've already seen all three of them and failed their medicals.'

'What!' Becky spun round to face her brother. 'You never told us you'd done that.'

'I knew this was coming and wanted to find out what my chances were. My left arm's too weak and I'd never be able to tackle an assault course, or hold a rifle.'

Her brother's usual placid expression was unchanged, but she knew how painful this was for him. It was going to tear him apart to see his friends join up and leave home. He had never let his slight disability stop him doing the same as the rest of them, and to be honest, they never even noticed his left arm was shorter than the other. It hadn't mattered before, but now it did.

'You've got a talent for words, and news is going to be vital,' Mavis told her son firmly.

'I've already told him that,' Becky said. 'He'll be more useful doing that than running around in a muddy field playing soldier. The rest of us have got to join up because we haven't got his kind of talent.'

'Quite right.' Their father smiled encouragingly at his son. 'I don't know where you got the brains from, but use them. If the forces won't take you then that's their loss. Stay at the paper and let's see what happens. We'll all have to do what we can if this country is going to survive.'

That was something they all agreed upon and so they made a fresh pot of tea. No one knew what they might have to face, and for the moment, all they could do was wait.

* * *

Later that evening when their children were fast asleep, Bill turned off the wireless, his brow furrowed with concern. 'I thought you'd object when Becky told us what she intended to do.'

'I wanted to, but what was the use? Our daughter is strong willed and will do whatever she thinks is right for her.' Mavis put down her knitting, swallowing hard to keep control of her emotions. 'And I know how unhappy Will is, but I'm relieved he won't be able to go into the forces. I know it's selfish of me, darling, but I'm also praying they won't take you either.'

Bill sighed. 'I wonder how many families are having this same discussion tonight?'

'Just about everyone, I expect. The last terrible war was only twenty years ago, and it still has vivid memories for many parents. There will be sleepless nights as we all force ourselves to watch children and loved ones going off to another war.'

As Bill closed his eyes, visions of his time in the army flashed through his mind. He'd only been a boy, younger than Will, and like everyone else, eager to join up. The horrors he'd seen had never left him, and he'd never spoken about them. And it was all about to happen again . . .

'Two wars in our lifetime. Is it going to be as bad as the last one?'

His wife's voice brought him back to the present, and he opened his eyes and looked straight at her. She was an intelligent woman and it was no good lying to her. 'I believe it will be a long, bitter struggle, and no one will be safe. If things get nasty I want you and Will to get out of London.'

'You know neither of us will run for safety and leave you here. Anyway,' Mavis gave a tight smile, 'you could be wrong and it might not last long this time.'

'That's what people said about the last one.'

'I know it's a vain hope, Bill, but it's all I have to cling on to at the moment. Don't volunteer, darling.'

'I promise.' He stood up and held out his hand. 'Come on, let's try and get some sleep.'

Two

The next morning it was chaos in the newsroom, and Will was pounced on as soon as he walked in the door. It seemed as if everyone was shouting requests at the same time.

'Hold it!' he bellowed at the top of his voice. 'One thing at a time. You'll never get anything done if you keep running around like headless chickens!'

A hush fell over the room as every head turned in his direction.

'Good Lord,' one man muttered. 'I never knew you could raise your voice, Will.'

'Sorry, but it was the only way I could make myself heard.'

'Don't apologize,' the chief said as he came out of his office. 'Come with me, Will, I want to have a word with you.'

Wondering why the boss wanted him, he followed him into the office and stood in front of the desk, waiting while the chief settled in his oversized chair.

'You said war was coming and you were right.' Ted Dunstan studied the tall boy in front of him. 'I'm going to lose a lot of my most experienced reporters. What are your plans?'

'I haven't any at the moment, sir. The forces won't take me because of my arm.'

'Ah, I can see you're disappointed about that, but I'll be honest with you – I'm pleased. I'm hoping you'll decide to stay with us. That was a fine piece of writing you did about Hitler. You've got a sharp mind and have the makings of a good reporter.'

'Thank you, sir.' Will was taken aback by such rare praise. 'I'd like to stay.'

'Good, good, you can go out with Andy for a couple of days, then you'll have to work on your own.' Ted Dunstan grimaced. 'This place is going to start emptying out quite soon and we'll have to take on some women. What about your sister, would she be interested?'

'She's determined to go into the ATS.'

The chief sighed wearily and nodded. 'Thank God I'm too old

for this one, but it's going to be hard for you to see your friends joining up.'

'It is,' he admitted.

'Don't be too down about it. The people are going to want news, and we'll be here to provide it.' He stretched his mouth into an unaccustomed smile. 'Didn't someone say, "The pen is mightier than the sword"?'

'Bulwer-Lytton, sir.'

'That's the man. Then let's prove him right, shall we, and fight our war from here.' He settled comfortably and waved to a chair. 'Sit down and tell me what you think is going to happen.'

'You're asking me?' He was stunned, but pulled up a chair and sat down. The chief obviously wanted to talk, and who was he to question that?

'Go ahead.'

'Well, no one really knows. All we can do at the moment is guess.'

'All right, guess.'

Will gathered his thoughts. 'I'll tell you what I think, but it could be completely wrong. I've watched the rise of Hitler and the Nazis and believe they want domination of Europe. They'll turn their attention to France, and if they can get a hold there they will throw everything they've got at us. Shipping is our life-line so they'll try to sink as many ships as they can. If he wants to invade us he'll have to cross the Channel, and that won't be easy without sustaining heavy losses.'

'So, what will he do?'

'Try to bomb us into submission before he invades. He's used that tactic successfully before.'

'And will France hold?'

'I expect so.' Will shifted uncomfortably, feeling he'd been talking too much, but he'd been studying what had been happening in Germany for the last few years. It was a subject he was passionate about. 'I've just outlined the worst possible scenario, but what worries me is that Germany has been re-arming for some time, and they're looking strong.'

'Are we ready?'

'No.'

The chief narrowed his eyes as he looked at the boy in front of him. 'Do you think the Nazis can be stopped?'

'Yes, but the cost will be high.' Will spoke with confidence. 'If we believe they can't then we might as well surrender now.'

'You're right about that, and the attitude this paper will take is that we can – and will – win.'

'I'm probably completely wrong about everything else, sir, and they'll be defeated before they even set foot in France. No one knows what direction this war will take.'

'That's true.' The chief stood up. 'Thank you for talking to me. It's been most enlightening; you've obviously given this a great deal of thought, and I'm convinced you're going to be valuable to this paper.'

'Thank you, sir.' Will stood up as well. Now he understood what the chief had been doing; he'd been finding out if he was up to the job.

'Didn't expect this many girls!'

The voice whispering in her ear made Becky jump, and she turned her head sharply. The girl grinning at her was expertly made-up, her blonde hair waved and shining, and her dress bright pink. She was quite lovely and completely out of place in the queue to sign on for the ATS. Becky could picture her as a model, but not in a khaki uniform.

'My name's Alice Henderson.' She thrust out a beautifully manicured hand.

'Er . . .' She shook hands carefully, hoping this elegant girl didn't notice her rough hands. 'I'm Becky Adams.'

'Nice to meet you. I thought I might be the only one here, but lots have the same idea. I expect it's a chance for some to get away from home.'

'Might be, I suppose. What are you hoping to do?'

'I'm a secretary.' Alice's smile widened. 'Perhaps I can wangle a job looking after the officers' paperwork. What about you?'

'Not sure yet. I'll have to see what's going.'

Their conversation was brought to a halt when Becky was called. The man sitting at the table was in uniform, but she didn't know enough to work out his rank. He was an officer of some kind, though, and had a pleasant face.

'Sit down, please.'

Hmm, nice voice too, she decided, feeling immediately at ease in his company as she sat opposite him.

After studying her intently for a moment, he said, 'How old are you?'

'Twenty,' she lied. Well, she would be in January. The rest of his questions she answered truthfully.

When he'd finished writing down the details he glanced up. 'Can you type?'

'No, and I don't want office work. I would like to do something useful.'

'Such as?' He laid down his pen, giving her his full attention.

She shrugged. 'I was hoping you could suggest something. I work in a shoe shop and haven't any office skills, but I'm quite handy with a screwdriver.'

'Explain.'

She was sure she saw the corners of his mouth twitch, but didn't care if he found her funny. 'A friend of ours has a motorbike and he's shown me how to repair it when it breaks down – which is often – so I've had plenty of practice.'

'Can you drive?'

'Not a car, but I have a go on the bike.' She was talking about her favourite subject now and her hazel eyes sparkled. 'There's a bit of spare ground near us, and I can go faster than the boys and still stay on.'

The officer looked down at the form on his desk as if it was the most fascinating thing he'd ever seen, but when he glanced up his expression was quite composed. 'You'd like a transport division then, would you?'

'Oh, that would be lovely!'

'I can't promise that's where they'll put you, but I'll add a note of recommendation on your application.' He stood up. 'You'll be hearing from us, Miss Adams.'

As she left the room she was sure she heard a roar of laughter, and she didn't care. A transport section would do her nicely.

'You've been a long time.' Alice was waiting for her. 'How did you get on?'

'All right, I think. What about you?'

'I only had to tell them I could type and do shorthand and that's all they wanted to know. What are you going to do?'

'Transport.'

Alice looked horrified. 'You'll get your hands dirty.'

'I hope so!'

They burst into laughter and Alice slipped her hand through Becky's arm. 'Oh, I like you. Let's go and find a nice tea shop somewhere. I do hope we end up at the same camp.'

After telling her mother the exciting news, Becky rushed next door to see if Bob was there. She found him and Jim tinkering with the motorbike.

'They're going to put me down for transport!' she exclaimed. 'How did you get on?'

The boys wiped oil from their hands and Jim tossed her a spanner. 'You'd better get in some practice and have a go at the bike then. Bob wants it in good running order so he can give it to Will later.'

She caught the tool deftly. 'Give me a chance to change first. I'm still wearing my best frock. Now, tell me, have you both signed up?'

'Yes, but I've got to wait and see if the navy will take me,' Bob told her. 'If they won't then I'll try for the RAF.'

'What about you, Jim?'

'Same thing. We've put our names down, and it's just a matter of waiting.'

'How long do you think it will take before we hear?'

Bob smiled, shaking his head, making a strand of light brown hair fall over his eyes. 'Impatient as ever. It will take as long as it takes, Becky. We've done all we can – now it's up to them.'

'I suppose so, but I hope they don't take too long. Now I've made up my mind I don't want to hang around.' She studied the spanner in her hand for a moment. 'I'll change my frock and then have a go at the bike. I've got a lot to tell you. I met the most amazing girl today.'

'Hurry up then.' Bob took the spanner from her. 'Once it's running smoothly we'll take it for a spin on the spare ground.'

'Oh good!' She tore off, dark hair bouncing as she ran, eager for the chance to ride the bike. She knew a lot of the local girls thought she was odd, messing around with machines, but she loved it. And she saw the longing glances they gave the boys and that amused her.

'Where are you off to in such a hurry?' her mother called when she was halfway up the stairs. 'Tea will be ready in an hour.'

'We're going to work on the bike. Bob wants it in good order so he can give it to Will when he goes into the navy.'

'That's kind of him.'

Something in her mother's voice stopped her, and she came down again. 'This is hard for you, isn't it, Mum? But you must try not to upset yourself too much. I'm sure Dad won't be called up, and Will can't go into the forces anyway.'

'I know, but I remember the last war, and I'm scared. Not just for us, but for all of our friends. Bob and Jim's parents are putting on a brave face, but those boys are their only children, and they're devastated to see them signing up so soon.'

'We're only doing it now because it's the best way of getting into the service we want.' She laid a hand on her mother's arm. 'We'll be fine.'

Mavis Adams took a deep breath and wiped the worry from her face. 'Of course you will. Now, you'd better get on with repairing that old wreck of a bike.'

'Don't you let Bob hear you call it that!' She laughed. 'It's his pride and joy.'

Her mother laughed with her. 'Off you go. I'll put tea back for six o'clock.'

'Oh, ta.' She ran lightly up the stairs, relieved her mother seemed all right now.

Within half an hour Becky was riding round the spare ground, listening intently to the sound of the engine. She pulled up by the boys and nodded. 'Sounds all right now.'

'All right?' Bob looked scandalized, patting the bike as if comforting it. 'She's purring like a kitten.'

Jim burst into laughter. 'Some kitten! The noise is enough to deafen anyone within half a mile.'

'More like a mile.' Will strolled towards them, grinning. 'I didn't have to ask where you were, I heard you. Stop messing with that now. I want to hear how you all got on today.'

After propping the bike against a tree the friends sat on the ground, their expressions serious as they related the events of the day. There was silence for a while as they contemplated the momentous steps they were about to take.

'Our families think we've rushed into this without giving it proper thought,' Jim remarked. 'But Will's been sure for a long time that war was inevitable, and I believed him. I've spent many sleepless nights coming to this decision.'

'Me too,' Bob agreed. 'We know the future ahead of us is going to be rough and dangerous, but we have to do what we feel is right. We'll get called up anyway, so we might as well do it now while we have some kind of a choice. It's a bloody mess, isn't it, and Hitler can't be allowed to win.'

The friends all nodded, in complete agreement.

Three

The postman was three doors away when Becky ran to the gate to wait for him, shivering as the cold wind hit her. Christmas was nearly here and it was turning out to be a strange kind of war. Nothing was happening.

Well, that wasn't true really. There were troops and planes in France, but here at home the waiting was driving her to distraction. After volunteering, the three of them had soon been called for medicals, which they all passed A1. Jim was the first to go, followed four weeks later by Bob.

Stamping her feet in an effort to keep warm, she scowled as the postman became involved in a lengthy conversation with one of their neighbours. Her reaction when she had waved goodbye to Jim and Bob had shocked her. She had never thought she would be so upset. There had been tears in her eyes, but she'd managed to wipe them away quickly before the boys had noticed. How embarrassing. But how she missed them. She was still waiting for her own call-up papers, and it seemed as if they would never come.

'Hello, Becky.' The postman finally reached her. 'What are you doing standing out here in the cold?'

'You know darned well why I'm here.' She peered into his satchel. 'Got anything for me today?'

'Hmm, let's see.' This was a game they'd been playing for some weeks.

As he searched through the letters the hope faded from her eyes. 'Nothing again.'

'Don't think . . . Ah, what's this?'

Grabbing the envelope he was holding up, she tore it open, then gave a whoop of delight.

'I take it that's the one you been waiting for?'

'Yes! They've accepted me.' She did a pirouette, stopped in front of him and reached up to plant a resounding kiss on his leathery cheek. 'Thank you, Stan.'

'You take care, young Becky. There's a lot of tough and rough men in the forces.'

'Oh, Stan,' she laughed. 'That won't bother me. Don't forget I've grown up with three boys, and can take care of myself.'

'That's as may be, but you still be careful.' He smiled sadly, his sparse grey hair ruffling in the wind. 'But I'm glad the letter has made you happy. I'm afraid I won't always be delivering welcome news in the future.'

'Were you in the last lot?' she asked, studying him carefully.

'I was, and I remember what it was like.' He sighed, patted her arm, and continued with his round.

'Becky!' her mother called. 'Was there any post?'

She waved the letter and ran towards the house. 'I've got to report on the seventh of January.'

'But that's your birthday.' Mavis shut the front door as soon as her daughter was inside.

'I know.' She grinned. 'Some birthday present, isn't it? Well, I told them I was twenty, so I didn't lie after all. We can celebrate my birthday at Christmas. I wonder if Bob and Jim will be able to get home?'

'We can only hope so. Come into the kitchen where it's warm and I'll make us a pot of tea. Then we can read your letter properly.'

By Christmas Eve, Becky had given up hope of seeing the boys, as she had so wanted to before she went away. There was no telling when they would all be able to get together again. It was no good fretting about it, because this was how life was going to be from now on. She began to turn away from staring aimlessly out of the window, but as she moved something caught her attention in the road, and she spun back, nose pressed against the cold glass.

Was it . . .? As the figure strode closer she let out a yell of delight. 'Mum! Mum! Jim's home.'

The front door crashed open as she hurtled out, waving frantically. 'Jim!'

He dropped his kitbag, laughing as she threw herself at him. He lifted her off her feet and spun round with her.

'Why didn't you let us know? How long have you got?' she asked, as soon as he put her down.

'It was an unexpected four-day pass.'

Jim's mother reached them, smiling with joy as she greeted her son. Mavis also arrived with Bob's mother so Becky stepped back and studied her friend. He was thinner and his features more finely chiselled. He'd always been a strong, athletic boy, but now he looked fit and healthy. In fact he wasn't a boy any longer – he was a man.

'Come on, Becky, let Jim have some time with his family.' Her mother took hold of her arm. 'You can see him later.'

'Yes, of course.' She waved at Jim. 'I want to hear all your news when you're ready.'

Hoisting his kitbag on his shoulder he nodded. 'Any sign of Bob?'

'No, afraid not.'

'That's a shame. See you later, Becky.'

She went back indoors with her mother. 'At least Jim's made it, and that will please Will. He misses them terribly.'

'And so do you.' Mavis put the kettle on for tea.

'I know, but at least I'll be joining up myself soon, but Will has to stay behind. He never complains or shows his disappointment, but he's not happy about being left out.'

Mavis smiled sadly at her daughter. 'You mustn't worry about Will, darling. I know you feel protective towards him, but he's had to live with his disability all his life. It's made him strong and determined though. He'll deal with anything he has to, and find himself a useful role in this war.'

'Course he will. He's got more courage than all of us.'

'And I thank God for giving him that quality.' Mavis's expression was a mixture of pride and sadness for the son she adored.

The tea was made when Bill and his son walked in.

'My goodness, you're early,' Mavis exclaimed.

'Well, it is Christmas, even if there is a war on.' Bill kissed his wife on the cheek. 'And we might as well make the most of this one because there's no telling what the next one will be like.'

'Jim's home,' Becky told them, 'so I think we should have a party.'

'Oh, that's marvellous!' Will was on his feet in an instant and heading for the back door. 'I'll nip round and see him.'

'Any sign of Bob?' Bill asked, as his son disappeared.

'No, but he might still turn up.' Mavis poured the tea. 'Even Jim didn't know he was coming until the last moment.'

'It would be lovely if we could all be together.' Becky's expression was wistful, and then she brightened again. 'But we can still celebrate Jim's leave and my birthday, can't we?'

Before anyone could answer, the back door swung open and

the two boys came in, laughing and obviously happy to see each other again.

Bill smiled. 'It's good to see you, Jim. You look well. How's army life treating you?'

'Tough.' He grimaced as he sat down and accepted a cup of tea from Mavis. 'Dad said we should all go to the pub tonight and sink a few pints of beer.'

'Only lemonade for Becky.'

There was a stunned silence for a few seconds as all eyes turned to the tall sailor standing in the doorway. Then pandemonium broke out.

'Bob! Now we really can have a party!' After hugging her friend, Becky gave him a playful punch. 'And I'll have something stronger than lemonade. I'm almost twenty.'

'Well, seeing as you're soon going to be a soldier we might let you have a shandy.'

They all laughed at the usual teasing between the two of them, and they all had to squash up as the boys' parents also crowded into the small kitchen. Happiness glowed on every face. Whatever happened in the future they would all be together this Christmas.

'Right, all the men in the front room.' Mavis began to organize the milling crowd of neighbours. You've got to make room for us women to get you something to eat, then we'll go to the pub and have a night to remember.'

The boys' mothers hurried off to find contributions to the tea and Mavis began slicing bread. She caught hold of her daughter's arm to stop her following the men. 'You'll have plenty of time to talk to them later, Becky. We need your help here.'

'Of course.' She was longing to ask the boys a million questions, but it would have to wait. She was so happy she couldn't stop smiling. 'Shall I butter the bread? Isn't it wonderful to have them home, and don't they look smart in their uniforms?'

Her mother nodded. 'Brings home just how grown-up they are now. They're not boys any longer.'

'No, they're not, and our carefree days are over.' Becky had to swallow hard as the reality of what was happening swept away her happiness for a moment. But her smile was back in place when the others returned with armfuls of food.

'My goodness!' Mavis exclaimed as they put tins, biscuits and other items on the kitchen table. 'Where did you get all that?'

'Bob and Jim came home with their bags full of tins.' Sally Walker grinned. 'Bob's kitbag must have weighed a ton.'

They all set to work and soon had plates piled high with ham, cheese and salmon sandwiches.

There were roars of laughter coming from the men, and Jim's mother, Pat, grinned. 'Sounds like they're telling tales not fit for our ears.'

Once several pots of tea were ready, it was all put on trays and taken into the front room.

When the debris was cleared away, they grabbed coats, eager to get to the Red Lion for a celebration.

The place was packed and they had to push their way in. Becky's father made straight for a corner of the saloon bar and started gathering enough chairs for them all, but progress over to him was slow. The boys were instantly welcomed, with neighbours wanting to buy them a drink. There were plenty of others there in uniform as well, all intent on having a riotous evening.

They finally made their way over to Bill. 'How did you manage to get here so quick?' Jim gasped. 'This place is heaving!'

Bill grinned. 'I'm too big for them to argue with.'

In no time the table in front of them was full of drinks. The noise was deafening, and it was almost impossible to hold a conversation. By the time someone began pounding on the piano and the place erupted into song, they gave up trying to talk to each other, and just sat back and joined in the fun.

Bob placed a shandy in front of Becky and they grinned at each other. She'd have her chance to talk to both of them tomorrow, but for this evening she would just enjoy being with them again.

After giving a sharp knock on the back door, Becky bounded into the kitchen. 'Happy Christmas, Mr and Mrs Walker. Where's Bob?'

'Still in bed.' John Walker peered at her through half closed eyes. 'Where we should all be after the night we had.'

'It was fun, wasn't it?' Becky was bouncing with pleasure.

John groaned and rubbed his head. 'Sit down, Becky, you're making me dizzy. And don't shout.'

'Oh dear, you do look rough.' He winced as she dragged a chair from the table and sat down. 'Have another cup of tea.'

'I've had six, and Sally's had four. How's your folks?'

'Don't know. I haven't seen them yet, but Mum must have got up because the chicken's in the oven. I expect she went back to bed, and Will's still asleep.'

'Wise man.'

'Hmm.' She pushed away from the table. 'I'll go and see if Jim's up.'

'He won't be.' Sally motioned her to sit down again. 'I know you're eager to see them, Becky, but let them sleep in this morning. They've both been dragged out of bed at the crack of dawn during basic training, and this is a treat for them.'

'But they've only got four days,' she protested. 'They can't waste it in bed. I haven't had a chance to talk to them yet.'

The back door opened slowly and two dishevelled characters crept in, sat at the table and reached for the teapot.

'Want some toast?' Sally asked.

They nodded silently.

Becky stared at her brother and Jim for a moment, and then shook her head in disbelief. 'If this is what happens when you've all had a few beers, then I'm glad I don't drink.'

'Don't shout,' they both whispered.

'Oh, you can talk then? And I'm not speaking loudly.' She began to see to the toast, as Bob's mother didn't seem to be able to concentrate. 'What you all need is a good breakfast. Have you got any eggs, Mrs Walker?'

'Don't you dare start cooking things like that. Our stomachs won't take it.' Will glared at her. 'Toast will do.'

'I'll have some scrambled eggs, Becky.'

'Ah, someone's feeling normal this morning.' She beamed at Bob who was leaning against the door he'd just come through, and then she raised her eyes to the ceiling. 'I take that back. You sure you want scrambled eggs?'

'Of course, I'm starving!'

'He always did have a cast-iron stomach.' Jim stood up, holding on to the table for support. 'I'm just going to stick my head under the cold tap, and then I'll be back when Bob's finished eating.'

'Try having a shave while you're at it,' she said, as he lurched towards the door.

'Told you,' he muttered. 'She's going to make a perfect sergeant.'

Unable to stand the smell of cooking, everyone else disappeared, leaving Becky alone with Bob. 'Right!' she said after putting a plate of eggs in front of him. 'Tell me what it's like.'

'Hmm?'

'Concentrate, Bob,' she demanded. 'I'll be joining up myself in a couple of weeks, so I want to know what happens when you arrive at the camp.'

'I don't know about the women, but the men had to strip off, stand in line to have needles stuck in them, then given uniforms, and spend the next few weeks marching around a parade ground.' He cleared his plate, sighed, and sat back.

'What else?' She leant on the table, eager to hear more.

'That's about it. The rest you'll find out for yourself.' He stared at her thoughtfully. 'Don't expect it to be easy.'

'It certainly isn't.' Jim rejoined them, looking more awake and respectable. 'But Becky's no weakling. She'll take it in her stride.'

When Bob nodded in agreement she was touched by their confidence in her, making her determined not to let them down.

The rest of their leave went in a flash, and it was just as hard saying goodbye again. Once 1940 arrived it would be her family and friends waving her on her way. Now the time was close the prospect was a little scary, but she wouldn't let them know she felt that way.

Four

'I wish you'd tell me how you can still manage to smile?' Jane Greenwood, from the same hut as Becky, eased herself on to the bed and scowled at her.

'A sense of humour helps.'

'What the hell's funny about square bashing? I joined up because I wanted to do something useful in this blasted war, but what have we done? Nothing! I'm afraid to take my shoes off. I think my feet are frozen to the leather. It's snowing, for heaven's sake, and they've still had us marching around for hours.'

'Only just over an hour this morning. I think the sergeant took pity on us.'

'Pity? Come on, Becky, they don't know the meaning of the word. I think you've enjoyed all this. You're not human, do you know that?'

'Stop grousing, Jane. We're almost at the end of our basic training. We should get some leave soon.'

Jane sat up, the scowl draining from her face. 'Hey, you're quite right. I'd forgotten that in all my pain. Now I know why you're smiling.' She began to unlace her shoes. 'How long do you think they'll give us?'

'No idea. We'll find out after they've done our assessment and given us our new postings.' Becky couldn't wait. She was hoping to be sent to a transport section, but nothing was certain. Look what had happened to Jim. He'd wanted tanks and had ended up in the paratroopers. If they put her in clerical, she'd just keep putting in for a transfer. That's what she'd told Jim to do, but he wouldn't. Always the tough bloke, he'd do whatever was asked of him. She was proud of him – proud of all her boys.

Jane had removed her shoes and was inspecting her feet. 'Oh, dear. My feet were so cold I didn't realize I had so many blisters. Have you got any plasters, Becky?'

'Nope.' She leant over and peered at the damage to Jane's feet. 'You'll have to see the medical officer and get those blisters seen to, if you want to wear fancy shoes on your leave.'

'I'll wear them, even if it's agony. I'm determined to dance the nights away once they open those gates and let us loose.' She glanced up, smiling now. 'What you going to do?'

'I don't know. Jim's in the army, Bob's in the navy, and I don't expect Will to have much free time. If I can get my hands on the motorbike, I'll tinker with that. I expect it needs a good tune-up by now.'

Jane's mouth had dropped open in surprise. 'Have you got three boyfriends?'

'What? Oh, no, of course not. Will's my brother, and we've all been friends since we were little.'

'Only friends?'

Becky nodded. 'They've always treated me like one of them. They don't think of me as a girl.'

'Don't they like girls?' Jane eased her shoes back on.

That question made Becky laugh. 'They like them very much, and some of the local girls gaze at them with longing. They're an interesting bunch.'

'Got any pictures?'

'Hmm.' Becky rummaged in her kitbag and found a couple of dog-eared photos. She handed them to Jane, and leant over so she could explain who they were. 'That's my brother, Will. The tallest one is Bob, and the one next to him is Jim.'

'Wow! No wonder you hang around with them. Is that the motorbike you were talking about?'

'Yes.' Becky sat on the bunk next to Jane, her expression wistful. 'They let me ride it on some spare ground near us, and Bob taught me all about the engine.'

'Ah, that's why you're hoping for a posting to transport.' Jane was still examining the pictures. 'You look like your brother. Has he joined up as well?'

'No, he wanted to, but he's got a slight disability, and they wouldn't take him. His left arm's slightly shorter than the other one, and it's not as strong, but his right one makes up for that. He's got a grip like iron, and can do anything with that arm. He was terribly disappointed, but he's a reporter, so he'll be kept busy.'

Jane nodded, not taking her eyes off the boys in the pictures. She pointed to Jim. 'This one's in the army, you said?'

'That's right. They've put him in the paratroopers.'

'Really? I'm not surprised about that. He's a tough looking man.'

'He is. He's always been someone you could rely on. If any of us had problems, he'd wade right in and sort everything out for us. Bob's quieter, and has a gentle way with him for such a big man.' Becky took the pictures back and held them in her hands for a moment. 'I do miss them so much.'

'Adams!'

Becky winced and shot to attention. Their sergeant might be a woman, but she had a piercing voice.

'You're wanted outside. Move!'

It hadn't taken long to learn that when told to move, it meant at once. Becky ran to the door, making the sergeant step aside smartly.

Once outside, she stopped and looked around, puzzled. No one was waiting for her. 'Who wanted me, Sergeant?' she asked. But when she looked back there was no sign of her. Well, she wouldn't have been called for nothing, so she had better find out what this was all about. That corporal with his head under the bonnet of an officer's car might be able to help. He seemed to be the only one around at the moment.

She marched over and tapped him on the shoulder, making him come up so quickly he bashed his head on the open bonnet.

'Bloody hell! Did you have to creep up on me like that?'

'I didn't creep, I marched, but the snow must have muffled the sound. Sorry. You having trouble?'

'Damned thing just died on me. My officer's not going to be happy if I'm late picking him up.' He stepped back, rubbing his head. 'Suppose I'd better go and find a mechanic.'

'Hang on a minute. Let me have a look.' She couldn't resist messing about with an engine again. 'I can strip down a motor-bike engine and put it back together again, but I've only had a look at cars a couple of times. Still, an engine's an engine. I might be able to help.'

'Go ahead then.' He stepped out of her way.

'It didn't take her more than half a minute to spot the trouble and, furious, she spun round, hands on hips. 'All right. Who put you up to this? I know you men think it's a great joke to tease us girls, but you really didn't think I was daft enough to fall for this, did you? Hand them over.'

'What?'

'Don't play the innocent. You know what I mean.'

'Are you looking for these?' a quiet voice said from behind her.

She recognized the cultured tone, and turned slowly. Without a word, she took the spark plugs from his hand, ducked under the bonnet and put them where they belonged, then slammed the [illegible]

When he tossed them to her, she got in and started the car. Leaving it running, she climbed out and faced the officer, and as much as she wanted to give him a piece of her mind, she knew she must be careful what she said.

'There you are, *sir*. No need for you to be late now you've had your fun.' She was so hurt it was hard to curb her tongue. 'If you'd wanted to make a fool of me, you should have made it a little more challenging. Sir!'

'That was not my intention,' the officer said, his eyes alight with amusement.

'Really?' She could hear the corporal trying to stifle his laughter and she was angry – and hurt. She'd liked this man the first time she had met him, and had talked freely about herself – and now he'd played this prank on her. Their sergeant was obviously in on it, and goodness knows how many others. Oh, they were all going to have a good laugh in the mess tonight.

Upset that he had been trying to make a fool of her, she turned and, without saluting, marched back to the hut, not giving him a chance to say anything else. Men! Did they never grow up?

'Oh-oh,' Jane said when she saw Becky's face. 'You look furious.'

'I am. These bloody men think we're a joke, but when this war really gets going, they're going to need us.'

The other girls gathered round, wanting to know what had wiped the smile from Becky's face. She told them, in great detail, giving release to her anger. Quite a few of them had had jokes played on them, and were sympathetic.

'They didn't make a fool of you, though, Becky.' Jane gave her an admiring look. 'I wouldn't have known what was missing from that engine, but you did. I'd say their little game backfired on them.'

Becky sighed, her anger seeping away. 'I know, and if I hadn't seen that particular officer there, I'd have probably joined in the joke. It hurt to think he was trying to make a fool of me. He was the officer I saw when I went to sign on, and I liked him.'

'Nice, was he?'

'I thought so . . .'

'Make yourselves decent,' their sergeant bellowed from the doorway. 'There's an officer present.'

The girls scrambled to stand to attention by their bunks. The sergeant nodded her approval and turned to someone standing behind her.

'Please don't take us back on the parade ground,' Jane groaned under her breath.

Becky kept her eyes straight ahead, and listened to the firm footsteps echoing on the bare hut floor. They were coming straight for her – she just knew it. She was in trouble. You didn't cheek a colonel and then march away without permission. She should have joined in the joke and laughed. Fool, fool! She'd thrown away any chance she had of getting the posting she wanted.

The officer stopped in front of her, just as she knew he would. Well, she would accept her punishment, and apologize if she got the chance, even if it did go against her nature. She met his gaze steadily, and kept her mouth shut.

'Do you have a decent frock with you? Something feminine.'

That threw her into confusion. She had braced herself for a reprimand – and he was asking about a frock? 'I don't do feminine, sir.' The words came out without thinking.

'In that case, do the best you can, but no uniform. My driver will collect you at six o'clock.'

'Pardon, sir?' She cast a quick glance down the hut, and knew all the girls were straining to hear their conversation.

'I thought my instructions were quite clear. You will wear civilian clothes, and we shall dine together this evening.'

She couldn't believe she was hearing this. What was he up to? He was breaking every rule in the book! She leant forward and whispered, 'Full blown colonels don't date privates.'

'This isn't a date. I'm going to give you a chance to tell me exactly what you think of my behaviour. And then I shall explain why I arranged that little test.'

'Test?'

'That's what I choose to call it. We shall both be out of uniform and able to speak freely. If you try to tear me off a strip now, and I know that's what you are itching to do, I'll have to put you on a charge for insubordination. So, obey my order now, Private Adams, and you can safely let rip this evening.'

'Yes, sir.' She spoke clearly, and then lowered her voice. 'You don't know what you're letting yourself in for – sir.' She tacked that on for safety.

'Oh, I believe I do.' He turned on his heel and marched towards the door, smiling. 'At ease, ladies.'

'We're here, Miss,' the corporal said as he opened the door for her.

'I'm not going in there.' She folded her arms and refused to move.

The corporal stooped down to look in the car. 'I'm told it's a very good restaurant.'

'I'm sure it is.' She smoothed her hand over the skirt of her simple dark red frock. 'Is he in there?'

'Yes, and waiting for you.'

Becky gave him an imploring look. 'Would you go and tell him I haven't got the right clothes for a place like this.'

'You don't have to worry about that. You look just fine.'

'Oh, come on,' she snorted. 'I'm a tomboy, and have never been near a posh place like this in my life. I'll embarrass him.'

'No, you won't,' a quiet voice told her. 'Stop putting yourself down, Rebecca. You are an attractive and intelligent young woman. I shall be proud to have you join me for dinner.'

She gave a resigned sigh and clasped the proffered hand, allowing him to help her out of the car. 'I can see you've been trained well in the art of being a gentleman. What school did you go to?'

'Eton.' He tucked her hand through his arm.

'I might have guessed,' she muttered, and wiggled her fingers over the fine material of his sleeve. This certainly wasn't a ready-made suit.

'Thank you, Corporal,' the colonel said to his driver. 'Come back for us in three hours.'

'Begging your pardon, sir, but isn't that leaving it a bit tight? We've got a way to go and you mustn't be late.'

'Of course you're right,' he said on a regretful sigh. 'Collect us in two hours.'

'Yes, sir.'

'Come on, Rebecca, let's eat, I'm hungry.'

The head waiter greeted them as they entered, all smiles, and led them over to a secluded table in the corner of the most sumptuous room Becky had ever seen. It was all gold and royal blue with subdued lighting. She felt completely out of her depth, and wondered if he'd done this to intimidate her. Another glance at his superb suit was enough to wipe that idea from her mind. No, they were here because this is what he's used to.

A menu was placed in her hands and she found herself looking at a lot of meaningless words.

'What do you fancy, Rebecca?'

Not prepared to show her ignorance, she closed the menu and placed it on the table. 'I'll eat anything. You choose for me, please.'

While he was ordering their meal she studied her dinner companion. He was a very attractive man of around thirty, she guessed, and this was the first time she'd seem him in civilian clothes. He looked marvellous.

'I've ordered a dry white wine to go with our meal. Will that be all right for you, Rebecca, or would you prefer something else?'

'I've never had wine with a meal before, but I'm sure it will be all right.' She smiled, for there was no point pretending she was something she wasn't. 'I don't know what I'm doing here. It's ridiculous. I don't even know your name.'

'David Hammond.'

'Everyone calls me Becky.' Why hadn't she noticed before that he had the clearest blue eyes she'd ever seen?

'I prefer Rebecca.' He sat back. 'Now is your chance to tell me what you think about that little stunt I pulled on you.'

'I can't do that in here. Anyway, I'm not angry now, but I would like to know why you did it.'

'I've been away, and when I arrived home on leave I enquired about you. Your basic training is almost over, so I decided to see if I could help you get the posting you told me you wanted. But before I put in the recommendation for you, I wanted to find out if you really did know anything about engines. I was intrigued when you came to the recruitment office. You were the only one who showed an interest in anything mechanical.' He lifted his hands in apology. 'It was a poor test, but I wanted to see how long it would take you to see through the deception. It was only a matter of seconds, and I was impressed.'

'Did you think I'd lied to you about my interest in engines?'

'I thought you might have exaggerated. Many do to get what they want. I needed to be sure of my facts before putting my recommendation in writing. I wrote the letter before coming here.'

This was too much to take in. Officers didn't go out of their way to help recruits like her – unless they wanted something, of course. She eyed him with suspicion. 'Why on earth are you doing this for me?'

'It's my way of apologizing for such an ill advised test. I should simply have asked you to look at an engine for me, but fun has been sadly lacking in my life for a while, and I couldn't resist.' He studied her expression and gave a wry smile. 'Don't worry, Rebecca, I'm not trying to seduce you. Not that I wouldn't like to, but I haven't got the time. I'm trying to help you because I was intrigued when I met you. I want to do this. Do you object?'

'No, no, of course not. I'm very grateful.' She breathed out a silent sigh of relief. She was too inexperienced to handle a man like this. 'Thank you so much.'

'Don't thank me yet. The decision isn't up to me, and you still may not get the posting you want.'

'I know, but I'll have a better chance now, won't I?' She gave him an impish grin. 'A recommendation from a colonel must carry some weight.'

'Let's hope so,' he said laughing.

Their first course arrived. The soup was delicious, though Becky had no idea what it was. The wine wasn't bad, either.

'Do you like it?' he asked when she'd taken a sip from her glass.

'It's quite nice,' she grinned. 'But I'd better not drink too much of it. I'm not used to drinking.'

They were enjoying their main course when he asked, 'Will you write and let me know how you're getting on? My leave is up and I won't be around for a while.'

'Of course I'll write. Where are you going to be stationed?'

Without answering her question, he handed her a sheet of paper with an address on it. 'That will find me.'

The address told her nothing. Mail went to a central depot and was then forwarded on to the troops wherever they were.

They enjoyed the rest of the meal, talking about anything but the army and the war. Becky had relaxed and was really enjoying herself, and was disappointed when it was time to leave.

The driver was outside and drove them back to the camp. David opened the car door for her, and she shivered when she got out.

'Wrap up warm,' she told him, 'wherever you're going.'

'I will. Thank you for your company, Rebecca. It has been a

lovely way to spend my last evening before returning to duty.' He kissed her gently on the cheek. 'I expect the Channel will be quite choppy this time of the year. Goodbye, and good luck.'

'You too.' She watched him get back in the car and drive away, feeling incredibly sad. He'd just told her where he was going: France.

Five

Jim Prentiss leant his head back and closed his eyes, wondering how on earth he'd ended up on this plane waiting to throw himself out into thin air. He wanted tanks or even the Royal Engineers, but he'd been transferred to the paratroopers. It had all happened so quickly he couldn't be sure how it had come about. One minute he'd been tackling a tough assault course and thoroughly enjoying the challenge, and before he'd got his breath back he'd been practising a parachute landing.

He opened his eyes and glanced along the row of men. The noise from the engines made it impossible to hold a conversation, but the expressions on the faces told him a great deal. Some were white as sheets; others had adopted an air of nonchalance in an effort to kid the rest of the men that they weren't scared. But they all were. Soon the order would be given and they would have to throw themselves out of the plane and rely on a thin piece of material to keep them alive.

Jim's stomach did an unpleasant lurch. *Control your nerves*, he told himself firmly. *Run over the routine and concentrate only on that.*

The man next to him, Stan, gave him a nudge and mouthed, 'Not long now. You all right?'

He replied with thumbs up, and they grinned at each other. Jim mimed floating down, rolling up the parachute, and then downing a large drink.

'You're on,' Stan shouted in his ear. 'The first drink is on you.'

A couple of the officers were jumping with them. They were old hands at this, having jumped many times. Just having them there helped to bolster the first-timers' courage.

The door was opened and the cold air rushed in. They all stood up on the signal, and the sergeant moved along the line to check that no one had made any mistakes.

The men began to disappear, and then it was Jim's turn. He took a deep breath, and as soon as he felt the tap on his shoulder he stepped out.

It seemed an age before his parachute opened, but of course it wasn't. Those first few seconds had been terrifying and exhilarating at the same time. As he floated down he relaxed enough to look around. It was cold, but the morning was bright with clear skies, and the view was incredible. Below the landscape stretched like a patchwork quilt of many shades.

Suddenly the ground was rushing towards him and he turned his whole attention to landing safely. The last thing he wanted to do was break something, because he would like to do this again. Oh, boy, did he want to do this again! Perhaps that officer had been right when he'd told Jim that he was just the type they wanted in the paratroopers. He landed heavily, but safely, with Stan not far from him, grinning in triumph.

They gathered in the barracks afterwards, all smiles and jokes now the first jump from a plane was over. The officers marched in and they snapped to attention.

'At ease.' Captain James swept his gaze over the assembled men. 'I can see you're all feeling pleased with yourselves, and no doubt planning a bit of a celebration this evening. But I'm about to spoil your fun. The booze-up will have to wait, because you're going to do it all again tomorrow morning.'

There were some quiet mutters, but the officer ignored them. 'I want you to have your kitbags packed ready for you to collect after we've had another jump. Then we're getting straight back on the plane and going for a little trip.'

'Where would that be, sir?' Stan asked.

'You'll find out when we get there. Now go and get some lunch. I expect some of you didn't feel like eating breakfast.'

There were a few sheepish grins, and the officer nodded. 'You did well today, and your training is officially over. You've all been issued with your wings and are now part of the Parachute Regiment.'

As soon as the officers had left the room, Stan grabbed Jim's arm. 'Come on, let's get something to eat. I'm starving.'

'Where do you think they're sending us? And why by plane?' Jim asked Stan as they headed for the mess.

'No idea. I expect we're being transferred to another part of the country and it's quicker to get us there by plane. After all, this is just a training camp, and I expect they need to make room for the next batch. We're paratroopers now, and have the badges to prove it.'

Jim's smile spread as they sat down with a welcome plate of sausages and mash. 'I never dreamt I'd end up doing this, and enjoying it.'

'Me neither.' Stan tucked into his meal with gusto, speaking in between mouthfuls. 'Though we mustn't forget that it won't be so much fun when we have to jump over enemy territory, and that's what we've been trained to do.'

'True, but we'll face that when we have to. I hope we can stay together, Stan.'

Stan nodded. 'That would be great.'

The clear weather held, and the jump the next day went smoothly. Afterwards they were flown to their permanent posting and, much to their delight, were greeted with friendliness by the regiment they had been assigned to. And that evening they were herded to the mess by the regulars so they could all get to know each other better.

It turned out to be hilarious as they listened to the stories they were told, and they soon found out that many of them were on leave from Norway. Jim and Stan didn't ask what had happened to the men they were replacing.

'What's it like out there?' Jim asked a man called Frank Singleton who had just come up with drinks for them.

'Cold, but it could turn out to be a hot spot quite soon.' He downed the pint in one go and held up his empty glass. 'Come on, you're lagging behind. Drink up and have another one.'

'I'll get them.' Jim and Stan stood up together.

Jim pushed his friend down again. 'These are on me.'

By the time he got back with a tray of drinks, someone was playing the piano and they all joined in the singing.

'Good Lord,' Stan shouted in Jim's ear after he'd handed round the drinks. 'We're never going to be able to keep up with this lot. I think they've got hollow legs.'

'They certainly can drink, and they know how to enjoy themselves,' said Jim with a laugh.

'And I bet they know how to fight.' Stan was suddenly serious. 'They haven't said what they've been up to, but I've got a strong impression they've been in the front line somewhere. They're just letting off steam tonight. We've got a lot to learn from them.'

'And we will.' Jim slapped his friend on the back and raised his glass. 'You know I didn't want to be a paratrooper, but I'm glad it's turned out this way now.'

'So am I.' Stan chuckled. 'And I volunteered for this lot.'

'You did? Good Lord, you're a brave man.'

They grinned at each other and settled back to enjoy a riotous evening, feeling quite at home already.

The next morning they didn't have time to worry about a hangover, as they climbed into a plane and flew to Scotland.

For the next week they climbed mountains in freezing conditions, and ploughed through the snow in mock battles, until they were exhausted.

Stan slithered over to Jim's position on his stomach. 'Captain says there's a gun emplacement on that ridge, and he wants us to put it out of action.'

'Just us?'

'Yep.' Stan grinned. 'But he said not to worry because they'll be right behind us as back-up. They're toughening us up. Do you feel tough?'

'All I feel is cold and hungry.' Jim studied the terrain. 'Let's get this done. There's more cover to the left, and we might have a better chance of getting up there without being seen.'

'Good idea.' His friend pursed his lips thoughtfully. 'Mind you, they'll be expecting an attack from that direction so why don't we try to get behind them, then we might take them by surprise.'

'Let's give it a go and hope we don't make fools of ourselves.'

Much to their delight and relief, their plan worked. They were aware it had been a test, and both of them were desperate not to fail. If this had been a real situation then their lives would have been at risk, so they moved as if that was the case.

With manoeuvres over for the day, they piled into the trucks and went back to camp. After a shower, change of clothes and a good meal inside them, their fatigue was forgotten.

After drinking down a pint as if they hadn't had a drink for weeks, Jim laughed. 'We're learning, Stan. Not only how to relax when we have a chance, but more importantly we're finding out how to survive in harsh conditions.'

'I've no doubt that's something we're going to be able to put to use quite soon.' Stan didn't look too disturbed about the prospect.

Jim merely nodded, wondering just what was ahead of them and how Bob was getting on.

* * *

The ship Bob boarded in Liverpool dock hadn't looked as big as he'd expected, and it was even smaller inside as the crew found bunks and stowed their gear. Still, she was built for the job she had to do, and he was glad to have been assigned to the destroyer.

'Hey, Bob.' Reg pushed his way over. They'd been together since the first day and had become good friends. 'She's a bit cramped, isn't she, but we won't all be in here at the same time, thank goodness. Hope you're a good sailor because this is going to roll about like mad once we get into the Atlantic.

'The only boat I've ever been on was on the Thames. What about you?'

'Same here.' Reg grinned. 'As soon as we get under way we'll find out if we've got the stomach for it.'

At that moment the tannoy barked out orders, and there was a scramble to get fell in on deck.

They were soon on their way to meet up with a convoy making its way from America. Their ship was to take the place of a destroyer sunk two days ago. They weren't given details, and didn't ask. It was a tense time for Bob and the new members of the crew.

Once out and in open water the sea was very rough, but Bob was relieved to discover that the constant rolling and dipping of the vessel didn't trouble him at all. That wasn't the case for a few of the others, and even a couple of the experienced sailors were afflicted with seasickness. Evidently this was quite normal for them, and they soon recovered.

It took them two days to reach the convoy, and it was great to see sailors waving to them as they skirted the edge of the merchant ships to check for stragglers.

'Nice to know we're welcome.' Reg joined Bob on his watch. He had also been unaffected by the motion of the ship, and both men were feeling quite pleased with themselves.

An officer joined them. 'Keep your eyes peeled,' he told Bob. 'You know what to look for. The news is that there could still be submarines in the vicinity.'

'Right, sir.' Bob held the binoculars to his eyes and began to scan the surface of the sea for any sight of a periscope. He had been given this job because of his exceptional long sight.

The journey back to England was uneventful, much to everyone's relief. There was no time to relax though, as within three hours they were under way again, this time to rendezvous with a convoy making its way back to America. They were then to escort another one back to England.

'Hope we get a chance to go ashore in New York,' Bob said. 'It'd be a shame to go all that way and not see something of the place.'

'We might have to wait until the convoy is ready to sail. It would be nice to relax, because we're going to find out what it's really like to be at sea with an enemy trying to sink you all the time,' Reg remarked as they relaxed on a short break from duty.

'I tell you what, I'd rather be on this destroyer than one of the merchant ships.' He gulped down his tea. 'Especially the tankers.'

Reg shuddered. 'Damned brave men – all of them.'

'I agree. At least we have the chance to fight back.' Bob refilled his mug. 'But these convoys are vital. Without them England wouldn't survive.'

Reg nodded. 'Let's hope we can help get the next one, and ourselves, back safely.'

'Amen to that.'

Six

The wait was agonizing, but eventually Becky was told where she was being posted. It was a transport division based in Hampshire, and she was delighted. She wished David were here so she could thank him personally, because she was sure his recommendation had helped.

The girls she had been with during the basic training were being dispersed to various camps, and it was unlikely she would see them again. They had been a good lot, but she was too excited to feel sad about the parting. It had seemed strange at first to be with a load of girls instead of the boys, but she'd got used to it.

With her bag packed, she gave one last look around the hut, and with all the goodbyes said, she headed for the door. There were seven days' leave ahead of her, and she couldn't wait to see her family. It would be wonderful if the boys had leave as well, but she knew just how unlikely that was. Still, Will would be there, and she could hear all his news.

The week's leave flew by. Becky's father had borrowed an old Austin Seven from a friend and had spent every moment he could teaching her to drive. She'd tuned up the bike, and as she packed to return to duty, she felt she was well prepared for her new posting. The only disappointment was that Jim and Bob hadn't been home.

Will and her mother saw her to the train. The station was packed with service men and a few women in uniform, and she didn't miss the brief flash of regret in her brother's eyes. It hurt to see that his rejection by the armed services still lingered, and she hoped the paper would make good use of his talents. His great need at this time was to feel useful.

The train pulled out and she waved frantically for as long as her family were in sight. Then she sat back and wondered what was ahead of her.

It didn't take long to report in and stow her few belongings. The billet was better than the last bare hut she had shared with the girls, and there were only six bunks instead of twelve. Luxury indeed.

Then she made her way to the mess for her evening meal. After such a busy, exciting day, she was starving.

Much to her delight the first person she saw was Alice Henderson.

'Becky!' Alice rushed towards her, smiling with real pleasure. 'I was hoping you'd turn up here. You got what you wanted then?'

'I had a lot of help, but I'll tell you about that later. What about you?' Becky asked as they sat down.

'I'm working for a Major at the moment, but I'm aiming for a General before this war's over.'

'And I'm sure you'll find one,' Becky said laughing.

'I'll have a darned good try. They'll be hard pushed to find a better secretary.'

That remark reminded Becky why she'd found Alice so likeable. She oozed self-confidence, but not in a stuck-up way.

They spent the rest of the meal catching up with each other's news.

Becky hardly noticed the time passing. Slipping the spanner into her pocket, she straightened up and lifted her face to the warm May sunshine. She had spent hours with her head stuck in engines and books. With added responsibility came her first stripe. She excelled in anything to do with engines, and her abilities had been quickly recognized.

She wrote to David regularly, but she had only received two short letters from him, and nothing over the last four weeks. She loved what she was doing and had settled into army life with ease. Her happiness would have been complete if it hadn't been for the worrying news. It seemed as if the German army was unstoppable. David was somewhere in France, and maybe Jim was too. No one knew where Bob was at any one time, and shipping was being sunk at an alarming rate. Becky had never been a regular churchgoer, but she had taken to saying a prayer at night for all those she loved, and everyone else in danger. She had no idea if it did any good, but it made her feel better to remember them all in this way.

There wasn't any point dwelling on it, though, because if France fell then this country, and everyone in it, would be in the front line.

* * *

'Something's happening!' Will cried as he burst into the chief's office one day without pausing to knock. 'Someone's just told me anything that will float is being requisitioned by the navy. There are boats of all shapes and sizes making their way to the coast.'

'Well, don't just stand there.' Ted Dunston was on his feet and moving towards the newsroom. 'Go and find out what the hell they're needed for. Charlie! Go with Will. Find out what's going on and get back here quickly! Will, you stay with this until you have the full story. And take a camera with you.'

'Right.'

The two boys ran and didn't stop until they reached the Thames. Gasping for breath they watched the flotilla of assorted boats in amazement.

'Where are you going?' Will called to a man steering a fair-sized cabin cruiser.

'Sheerness Dockyard,' he shouted back.

'Why?'

'No idea, mate. We've been told to take our boats there. The navy wants them for some reason.'

'Can I come with you? I'm a reporter.'

The boat eased over to the bank, and Will pushed Charlie. 'Run back and tell the chief I'm going with one of the boats. I'll report back as soon as I can.'

Charlie took off as fast as his legs would carry him, and Will leapt on to the boat. 'Thanks. My name's Will Adams.'

'Doug Wilkins.'

'Pleased to meet you, Doug. Will you tell me what happened?'

'First thing I knew was the navy blokes banging on my door saying they wanted my boat. It was chaos where I moored her. They gave us petrol and asked if we'd take our own boats to the coast at once.'

'And that's all they said?'

'Only that it was vital they had everything that could float.'

'What on earth can they want such an ill-assorted collection of boats for?' Will gazed around, unable to believe his eyes. There were navy personnel on some of the boats.

'I don't know what's happened, but I've got a nasty feeling we must be in terrible trouble.' Doug's mouth was set in a grim line. 'This operation looks like an act of desperation to me.'

Will had to agree with that. 'Do you think they'll tell us at the dockyard?' he asked, as he took several photos.

'They'll have to if they want to use my boat. I'll want to know where she's going before I hand her over.'

Will put the camera back in the case. It would be easy to snap away, but he must keep plenty of film for later.'

'Going in the forces yourself, are you?'

'Afraid not. I tried, but they wouldn't take me.'

'Why not? You look a fit young man.'

Will stretched out his arms. 'Because of this.'

'Ah.' Doug nodded. 'I never noticed that. Never mind, lad, you stick with me and we'll find out what they want with us. Whatever it is, I want to stay with my boat if I can.'

Will's eyes shone with excitement. 'Would you say I'm part of your crew so I can come with you?'

'Sure.' Doug grinned. 'Glad to have you aboard, Will. Want to have a go at steering?'

'Yes please!'

For the rest of the journey Doug taught Will how to handle the boat, and anything else he might need to know about the vessel.

Doug took over again when they reached their destination, and Will gazed around in wonder at the sight that met them.

'My God!' Doug gasped as he edged the boat to the dock.

Everywhere was crowded with boats, and more were steaming in all the time, passing others already heading out to sea. The navy was clearly in charge, and as they tied up, a sailor ordered them over to a hut.

Will caught two men who had already reported in. 'Do you know what this is all about?' he asked.

'Our army's trapped on the beaches at Dunkirk, and they want anything that will float to go over and rescue them. The navy tried to give us train tickets home, but we ain't having that. Where our boat goes, we go as well. Just about all the others feel the same, and to be honest, I think they're only too relieved to have the help.' The man looked at Doug. 'What about you?'

'I'm the only one who is going to take the wheel of my boat.' Doug clapped Will on the shoulder. 'You don't have to come any further, lad. Take your pictures and write the story.'

Will's face dropped with disappointment. 'Let me come with

you. Please! You're going to need someone else on board. This trip will be too much for one man.'

'It's going to be dangerous.'

'I know that, but I can do a much better story if I'm actually there.'

Seeing the eagerness on his face, Doug gave a reluctant nod. 'Phone your editor and let him know what you're doing.'

As soon as they'd reported to the sailors taking names, Will managed to find a telephone, and got through to his editor.

The chief listened carefully to what Will was able to tell him, then said, 'This sounds dangerous. Are you sure you want to go?'

'I'm sure, Chief. The *Lucky Lara*'s a sound vessel and the owner is an experienced sailor. But if anything should happen, would you tell my parents?'

'Of course, but you be sure you don't put me in that unpleasant position. They'll never forgive me for allowing you to go on this crazy trip. Let's pray that boat you're on lives up to her name. Good luck, Will.'

'Thanks. I'll be in touch as soon as I can.' Will replaced the phone and ran to join Doug on the boat, his heart pumping with excitement – and more than a touch of fear, though there wasn't time to dwell on that.

'My God!' Will gasped as they got under way. 'There's a destroyer coming with us.'

'They're calling on everything to help with the rescue. We've got to get our army off those beaches, or we're finished.' Doug's expression was grim, as he concentrated on steering the boat.

'How many men can we take?' Will asked, wondering how on earth these small boats were going to cope with thousands of men.

'Twelve, at the most.'

The sight that met them at Dunkirk was beyond belief. There were navy vessels with smoke pouring out of them, small boats wrecked along the shoreline, and thousands of men on the beaches.

'There's a line of men in the water over there,' Doug yelled above the sound of gunfire from German planes overhead. 'Let's start picking them up and take them to that destroyer.

As soon as they reached them, Will began pulling men into the boat, blessing the fact that his right arm was extra strong.

'That's enough. We'll be right back, boys,' Doug called as he manoeuvred the seriously overloaded boat towards the navy ship.

They lost count of how many trips they made, but eventually Doug called a halt. 'We're getting low on petrol. Collect ten only, Will, and we'll head back to Dover.'

There was an almighty explosion that dangerously rocked the *Lucky Lara*, as two boats near them received a direct hit. The carnage around them was sickening.

Without a word Doug headed out to sea with the few exhausted soldiers on board. Dover would be a welcome sight for all of them.

As soon as they arrived back in Dover, Doug was asking for more petrol. 'I'm going back, lad. I'd be glad of your help, but you don't have to come. You've done enough.'

'You're not leaving me behind,' Will said without hesitation. 'I'll phone in my story while you're refuelling.'

Seven

There was a sense of urgency running through the camp as Becky jumped out of the truck. She had just passed her driving test, but her elation faded as she noticed the grim faces all around her.

'What's happening?' she asked as Alice came to congratulate her. There were lorries springing into life all around her.

'Don't know,' she replied, stepping out of the way as the convoy began to move towards the gates.

'Get back in that lorry,' a sergeant yelled at Becky, 'and follow the others.'

'But I've only just passed my test, Sergeant.'

'I don't give a damn. You can drive, so bloody well drive! And you.' He glared at Alice. 'Go with her. You're going to be needed as well.'

'But I'm just about to go on leave,' Alice protested.

'All leave's cancelled,' he snapped. 'Now do as ordered.'

The girls didn't argue or speak, but clambered back in the lorry. Becky had to put her foot down to catch up with the others.

'He might have told us where we're going,' Becky muttered, concentrating on finding the gears without making a mess of it. 'I wonder what's caused the need for so many lorries?'

The convoy halted for a moment, and a corporal jumped in, pushing Alice along to make room for himself.

'Where are we going?' Becky wanted to know. 'I've only just passed my test.'

'Ah.' He leant forward to look at her. 'I'll drive if you're nervous.'

'I'm not nervous!' she exclaimed, not caring for the smug expression on his face. 'I'm more than capable of driving this thing. All I want to know is where are we going.'

'Dover. Our army's trapped on the beaches at Dunkirk, and transport is needed for some of those being brought back.'

'Oh my,' Alice murmured. 'How bad is it?'

'About as bad as it can get. France is about to fall, and then Hitler will be able to see us across the Channel.'

Becky, like everyone else, had been aware that things were not going well in France, but this news was horrifying. She knew David was over there, and maybe Jim, as well. 'Do you think Hitler will invade us now?'

'He will if he's got any sense,' the corporal replied, his tone as grim as his expression.

'Ah, we'll be all right then.' Alice sat back and folded her arms. 'We know he hasn't got any sense, don't we?'

Despite the seriousness of the situation, they laughed at Alice's feeble joke.

For the rest of the journey Becky concentrated on her driving, not wanting to lose contact with the other vehicles.

On arrival at Dover they were escorted to a parking place by the combined efforts of the navy and army. They jumped out of the cab and gazed around in utter disbelief. Boats were coming in loaded with men; there were medical staff helping the wounded, and WVS handing out tea and sandwiches. The army were gathering the more able men together and putting them on various modes of transport. The girls could only gaze at the scene before them, completely lost for words, but they were in no doubt about the seriousness of this disaster.

'You stay by the lorry,' the corporal ordered, 'while I find out what we've got to do.'

Alice and Becky watched him stride away, their hearts pounding in dismay. A navy destroyer was edging in, smoke pouring out of her from somewhere, and listing drunkenly.

'Look at that!' Alice gasped. 'It's packed solid with soldiers. How on earth has it stayed afloat?'

A lump came in to Becky's throat, and she fought to keep herself calm. The dock was a seething mass of people with only one purpose, and that was to get the soldiers off the ships and cared for.

'Poor devils.' Alice took a shuddering breath. 'Got any cigarettes on you, Becky? I've only got one packet, but those men must be gasping for a smoke.'

She dived in her pocket and held out a full pack of twenty. Alice grabbed them and immediately disappeared into the crowd, while Becky continued to study the faces around her. Was David in amongst these tired and battle-weary men, or was he still on the beaches? The questions and fears continued to race through her mind. Was Bob on one of the navy ships? And what about Jim – where was he?

She dipped her head in anguish. What must the men be suffering as they waited to be rescued? It didn't bear thinking about. The only glimmer of comfort she felt was for the fact that her brother would not be involved in this desperate and dangerous situation. It was obvious that every effort was being made to get the men home, and all they could do was wait and hope the rescue mission was successful.

She continued to scan the faces, looking for anyone she might know, but all she could see was a mass of weary men. Alice came tearing up to her at that moment, quickly followed by a sergeant.

'Get ready to leave,' he shouted, as a column of soldiers marched towards their vehicles. 'Once the men are loaded we're taking them back to Aldershot.'

Becky clambered back into the cab of the lorry and started the engine. Alice tumbled in after her. They waited, not speaking, as they heard the men jumping in the back. It didn't take long before the lorries began to move. Becky slotted into the middle of the convoy and concentrated on her driving.

'I went right down to the dock,' Alice said, lighting a cigarette. 'You ought to see the assortment of boats coming in, all overloaded by the look of them. You remember that photo you showed me of your brother? Well I thought I saw him jumping into one of the boats. I wanted to go and ask him, but they were already heading out to sea when I got there.'

'You must have been mistaken,' Becky said, shaking her head. 'He could be here after a story for his newspaper, but there's no way he would be able to join in the rescue.'

'I guess you're right; it's just about impossible to recognize anyone in amongst that crowd.'

'Blimey! We've got a couple of girls here, lads. You got any fags? We're gasping back here.'

Alice turned round, smiled at the face peering at them, and handed over her packet. 'There's only five left, but you're welcome to them. Have you got any left, Becky?'

'Try my right-hand pocket, there might be some there.'

Alice dived in the jacket pocket and pulled out a crumpled packet. She counted them, and then handed them to the soldier. 'Only six. That's all we've got, boys.'

'Thanks, we'll break them in half.' The face disappeared.

'Hey, Jack, what they like?' one of the men said.

'Real beauties.'

There was a lot of scuffling in the back as the men took turns to have a look through the gap at them.

'Be careful,' Alice laughed. 'You're rocking the lorry, and my friend has only just passed her driving test today.'

'Bloody hell! We've been bombed, shot at and nearly drowned, only to find ourselves at the mercy of a woman driver.'

Alice turned until she could look at the men in the back. 'Not just any woman driver. This one's better than most men, and if we break down she can fix anything mechanical.'

'In that case, Miss, we could have done with you on our boat. I didn't think the poor old thing was going to make it, and I didn't have the energy left to row the rest of the way.'

The banter continued, and Becky relaxed, leaving Alice to do her best to make the men smile. Something her friend had said niggled at her, though. Had she really seen Will jumping into a boat? It was the kind of crazy thing he would do. She shook her head slightly, dismissing the worrying idea. It was highly unlikely. Still, she would get in touch with her parents as soon as she could, just to set her mind at ease.

Dover was crowded with ships, and Doug had to steer expertly to reach the open sea without colliding with larger vessels. They'd only been going for about an hour when they came across a tug wallowing helplessly without power. It was packed with troops all waving frantically at them.

Doug steered close and shouted, 'What's your trouble? Are you out of petrol?'

'No, we've got enough, but the engine's packed up and we can't get it started again.'

'Does the captain know what's wrong?'

'He ain't aboard, mate. He got killed when he went on to the beach. Only got a young lad here, and he can drive this thing, but don't know nothing about engines.'

'Hell,' Doug muttered before turning to Will. 'Know anything about engines?'

'A bit, but if my sister was here she'd soon sort it out. She's the mechanic in our family. I'll give it a go, though, if you can get me close.'

It wasn't easy, but with a lot of help and shouts of encouragement from the soldiers, Will managed to tumble on to the tug. After taking a look at the tug's old engine, Will was at a complete loss. He really did need his sister, he thought wryly. These men had to get home so he'd better try and fix the thing, because the *Lucky Lara* couldn't possibly take all these men. Pulling a handkerchief out of his pocket he began by wiping away some of the grease, and tightening anything he could see with a spanner from a nearby toolbox.

'What do you think, lad?' A soldier pushed his way through the crowded boat and hunkered down beside him.

'Well, there doesn't appear to be much wrong.' There was no way Will was going to admit that he didn't know what the hell he was doing. These men were so close to home, and somehow they had to make that last little bit. One look at their faces was enough to tell him how desperate they were. 'Perhaps the petrol isn't getting through. I'll check that.'

Fifteen minutes later Will sat back on his heels and shouted, 'Try it now.'

The engine coughed and spluttered, but refused to start.'

'Nearly,' the soldier said. 'Keep at it, lad.'

Will was losing heart. This was like nothing he'd ever tackled. 'It must be the fuel intake,' he said, hoping it sounded as if he knew what he was doing.

He lost track of the time as he struggled. If he couldn't make it work then they would have to take the men off a few at a time and ferry them back to Dover. The poor devils had suffered enough. They couldn't just leave them here hoping someone else would come along who was able to help.

'Again!' he called, not holding out much hope.

After several belching coughs and puffs of black smoke, the engine roared into life. Will was so surprised he could only stare at the engine in disbelief as the men cheered.

'Well done!'

He was hauled back on deck, slapped on the back, and surrounded by smiling faces. It was nothing short of a miracle that he'd been able to get the engine started again, but he didn't care how it had happened, he felt so good. He was relishing being in the thick of things.

'You haven't far to go now and you should be all right.' He grimaced as he looked at Doug. Both boats were tossing about. 'All I've got to do now is get back to my boat.'

Doug took a chance and came as close as he could. Will didn't hesitate – he leapt over and landed on his hands and knees on the deck.

'You take care over there,' one of the men called out. 'It's bloody dangerous.'

They waved as the tug resumed her journey, then Doug headed towards the French coast once again.

The situation was as desperate as the last time they'd been here. There were still thousands of men waiting to be picked up, and they immediately began ferrying men over to a navy ship. Suddenly all hell broke loose as planes screamed in, firing on the beaches and boats near the shoreline.

Will continued pulling men into the boat when he heard Doug gasp and fall backwards. With one mighty heave, Will dragged the man he was holding into the boat, then rushed to Doug's side. He was clutching his right arm trying to stop blood from flowing.

'Something hit me,' he gasped.

'I'll go ashore and see if I can find a medic.' Will was scrambling to his feet when Doug stopped him.

'They've got enough to do, lad. I'll be all right. Just find something to bind my arm.'

'He's right.' One of the soldiers already on board joined them. 'It'll be desperate on the beaches after that attack. 'Let's try and patch him up ourselves.'

Grateful for the man's calm help, Will removed his jacket and shirt, then began tearing the shirt into strips for bandages. It was a nasty wound, but thankfully the bleeding eased once the arm was bound.

With a grunt of relief, Doug sat up, wiping the sweat from his face. 'Get ten men on board, Will, and we'll head back. You'll have to steer. You all right with that?'

'I can do it.' Will nodded to the soldier who had helped him. 'Thanks; you seemed to know what you were doing.'

'I've had a deal of practice lately. My name's Alan, by the way.'

'Let's get back to Dover as quickly as possible, Alan. Doug needs medical help.'

They set about pulling men from the water and soon the boat was about full. 'Room for one more,' Will said, holding his hand out to an officer.

'I've still got men on the beach.' He lifted one exhausted man on to the boat, and began wading back to the shore.

'Good luck, Colonel Hammond,' Alan shouted. 'See you back in Dover.'

Will had a lump in his throat, sad to leave so many men behind, and couldn't help wondering what chance that officer had of surviving. Very little, he guessed. From the determined look on his face he was obviously going to stay until all his men were safe.

Knowing there was nothing else they could do, Will started the engine and headed out to sea.

It didn't take them long to realize that Doug wasn't the only casualty of the attack. They were taking on water. Again Alan came to the rescue by organizing the men, and the tin hats were used to bail out the boat. It wasn't too bad, but these men were exhausted, and Will didn't think they would be able to keep it up all the way back.

'We'll get it fixed,' Alan told Doug. And, taking one man with him, he began tracking down the leak.

Doug joined Will at the wheel, his face pinched with pain, but a smile on his face. 'We'll be all right, lad. I don't think the damage is bad.'

'To you or the boat?' he asked dryly.

'Both.' He sighed deeply. But this is the last trip this poor old boat will be able to make, unless we can get her patched up.'

Will glanced at him in amazement. 'The only place you're going is to hospital.'

'I guess you're right.' He pulled a face and gripped his arm. 'But I hate leaving those men behind.'

'There are other boats here, and more arriving all the time.' Alan stood beside them, wiping his hands. 'You've done enough. I know this isn't your first trip because I saw you before. We found a leak and have plugged it. With luck it will hold until we get back.'

The water had stopped coming in and the men spread out, trying to catch some sleep. With Doug navigating and Will at the wheel, they made it safely back to Dover. The men were immediately taken care of and Doug whisked off in an ambulance.

Exhaustion hit Will suddenly, and all he wanted to do was find a bed and sleep, but he shook off his tiredness. He had a story to write.

Pulling a notebook and pencil out of his pocket, he wandered the dock, talking to soldiers, sailors, relief workers and medical staff. He lost track of time completely, and it was only when his book was filled up that he thought about making his way back to London.

The journey back was just a haze. Will remembered being on a train crowded with soldiers, but not much else. Almost as if he was in a dream, he walked through the doors of his newspaper and into the newsroom, making straight for his desk.

'Will!' The chief rushed up to him. 'Where the hell have you been?'

'Dunkirk,' he muttered, pulling the typewriter towards him and rolling in a sheet of paper.

'You've got blood all over you. Are you hurt?'

He shook his head. 'It isn't mine.'

'Good.' The chief studied the boy typing away like mad. He was dirty, with lines of fatigue around his eyes, and without a shirt under his jacket.

Ted called Charlie over to him, and spoke quietly. 'Get him tea and sandwiches, and then as soon as he's finished, clean him up and take him home. He's been gone for three days and I don't want his family to see him in this state.'

Then the chief turned, faced the room and shouted, 'Hold the front page!'

Eight

The last convoy had been a nightmare, and Bob didn't think he would ever be able to forget the horror of ships exploding as the torpedoes hit them. He drew in a deep breath as the scenes flashed through his mind in vivid colour. And when that tanker had gone up in flames . . . well, it was just as if all hell had descended upon them. The merchant seamen were well aware of the danger, but they didn't hesitate to go to sea time and time again, knowing that the cargoes they carried were vital to the survival of this country.

Hoisting his kitbag more firmly on his shoulder, Bob turned into his road, looking forward to a few days at home. Perhaps the peace and normality of being with family and friends would help. As he thought about this he realized that his perception of normal didn't exist any more. France had fallen.

Bob reached his gate and stood there for a moment watching the evening sun highlight the flowers in the garden. Early June had brought forth a riot of colour. The back had been dug over to grow vegetables, as had just about every garden in the country, but his mother clung on to this small patch for a bit of beauty, she'd said, and she was right. He felt as if the blooms were welcoming him home.

He swore under his breath as his vision clouded. He was getting soft, and that was not going to help him get through this war. All he had to do was remember those poor devils in the burning sea, and that would cure him of mooning over a few flowers.

'Are you going to stand there all night, Bob?'

Composing himself he looked up and smiled. 'Just admiring the garden, Dad. It's nice to see so much colour after looking at grey sea all the time.'

His father nodded, and Bob wondered how long he had been watching him at the gate.

'Yes, it's a picture, isn't it? Come in now, you're mother's putting the kettle on and is anxious to see you.'

He walked to the door and his father took his kitbag from him, nearly dropping it when he felt the weight. 'What on earth have you got in here?'

'I've collected a few things on my travels.'

'It feels like it.' His father studied his son for a moment, and then smiled. 'It's good to have you home, Bob. Are you hungry?'

'Ravenous!'

'I told you he would be.' His mother rushed out of the kitchen to hug him. 'Oh, it's wonderful to see you. How long have you got?'

'Let him get in the door, Sal,' John chided his wife. 'Let's have tea first, and then we can talk.'

They settled around the kitchen table with steaming cups of tea in front of them and a plate full of sandwiches. Bob downed his first cup of tea, hungrily finished two sandwiches, then took a deep breath of pleasure, ready to answer his mother's question now. 'I've got ten days while they carry out some work on the ship.'

'Oh, that's lovely.' Then his mother frowned. 'What kind of work?'

'You know I can't tell you that.' He took a bite of another sandwich, and changed the subject. There was no way he was going to let either of them know how dangerous the last convoy had been. They had taken a chance and stopped to pick up survivors, which was something they shouldn't have done, but they couldn't leave the poor devils in the sea. The damage they had sustained had not been serious, but it was enough to give them this welcome break. 'Tell me about Dunkirk.'

His father reached for newspapers piled on the dresser behind him. 'You've got to see these. Start on the top and work your way through. They are all in order. Will has had the front page right through the evacuation.'

Bob began to read, the sandwiches forgotten in his eagerness to learn more about this disaster. He'd been at sea while this had been going on, and the information they had received had been sketchy at best. He was delighted to see his friend's name on the reports. It looked as if Will was doing well.

By the time he was halfway through the papers, he stopped reading and glanced up, puzzled. 'These sound like first-hand accounts – as if Will was actually at Dunkirk.'

'He was!' His mother's expression was concerned. 'He jumped on a boat going up the Thames and sailed over with the owner.

He was gone for some time and we were all so worried, not knowing where he was. The newspaper said he was covering the evacuation, and that's all they would say.'

'He made two trips,' his father continued the story, 'but when the owner was injured and the boat damaged, they couldn't go again. Will stayed at the dock to gather as much information as he could, then staggered, exhausted, in to the newsroom and wrote his story. When he finally arrived home he slept for twenty-four hours.'

A slow smile crossed Bob's face. 'That's just like him. He was very disappointed when we all joined up and he couldn't. He's got a wonderful way with words, and it looks as if he's found his rightful place in this war now. He's really brought this whole thing to life.'

'Yes,' his father agreed. 'This is what he was meant to do.'

'Bob.' His mother reached across and laid a hand on top of her son's. 'Would you have a talk with Will? He's making plans of some kind, but he's keeping quiet about it. He's changed.'

'We all have, Mum,' he said gently.

'I know.' She squeezed his hand and smiled sadly. 'I can see that in your eyes. But we're sure Will's up to something and he won't talk about it. The fact that he's become so secretive is making his mum and dad suspicious. He'll talk to you, though.'

'I'll see what I can do, but you're probably all imagining it. The forces rejected him, but Dunkirk has proved to him that he's just as capable as anyone else. It must have boosted his confidence, that's all.'

'I expect you're right,' his father agreed. 'Now, what do you want to do this evening, go to the pub?'

'Not tonight, Dad. Do you mind? I'll enjoy that tomorrow after I've had a good night's sleep. I've been looking forward to sleeping in my own bed.'

'I expect you have. We'll all get together and have a drink tomorrow.'

'Your room's just as you left it.' His mother gathered up the empty dishes. 'You have a nice rest.'

'Thanks.' Bob stood up, and when he lifted his kitbag he put it on the table. 'I forgot. We stopped in New York and I've got a few presents for you.'

As he unpacked various tins of fruit and meats, packets of biscuits, and other strange luxuries, his mother gasped. 'My goodness, Bob, I've never seen anything like it! Would you mind if I shared this with our friends?'

'Do what you like with it, Mum.' He was about to head for the stairs when the back door shot open and Will stood there, grinning with delight.

'Mum saw you arrive. Oh, it's good to see you, Bob.'

Tiredness vanished in a flash as Bob greeted his friend, and he dumped his bag on the floor. 'You look good, Will. I hear you've had quite an adventure, and I want to hear all about it.'

John Walker stood up. 'Why don't you boys go into the front room? You'll have a lot to talk about, and you'll find some beer in the sideboard, Bob.'

'Thanks, Dad.'

Bob studied his friend as they made themselves comfortable. His mother was right. The change in Will was obvious. There was something different about him, though it was hard to fathom just what it was.

'How long are you home for?' Will asked.

'Ten days, while they do some work on the ship.'

'That's great!' Then Will's expression sobered as he noticed the lines of strain around his friend's eyes. 'Rough trip?'

'Not as rough as they're going to get now France has fallen. The U-boats won't have so far to go to get to us now.' Bob sat back and quickly changed the subject. 'Do you know where Jim is?'

'He's safe. He managed to get out of Norway just before the Germans invaded.'

'That's a relief. I was worried about him. How's Becky?'

Will grinned. 'She's fine. The army was daft enough to teach her to drive a truck.'

Bob laughed. 'That I would like to see.' Then, satisfied that his friends were all right, he said, 'Tell me about the evacuation of Dunkirk.'

The next hour flew by as he listened to his friend. Bob knew only what he'd read in the papers, but he was enthralled to hear a first-hand account of what it had really been like.

When he'd finished talking, Will got them another beer from the cupboard, then sat down again, elbows resting on his knees as he leant forward. 'I've told you what happened to me, now I want every detail of your last voyage.' As the shutters came down on Bob's expression, he reached out and gently punched his friend on the arm. 'Come on, talk! I need to know exactly what's happening on land, air and sea. There's only the two of us here, and it looks as if it would do you good to let your feelings out.'

Bob pulled a face. Will had always been good at picking up on their moods. They'd never been able to hide anything from him. He started with the lighter side of life on board ship, and had Will laughing. Then the grim part of the voyage began to spill out.

There was silence when Bob finished speaking, and he could almost see his friend's mind working overtime. 'If you're going to write about this, Will, you make sure you praise the merchant seamen. They're bloody heroes, every one of them.'

'As are the sailors who guard them,' Will said gently. 'We're really up against it now. Hitler's got to starve us into submission if he can, so he'll try to sink as much shipping as he can.'

Nodding in agreement, Bob asked, 'Do you think he'll invade while we're weak from our losses at Dunkirk?'

'That's what many expect.' Will pursed his lips. 'But I think he'll attack us by air first. If he can destroy our air defences, then he'll have more chance of crossing the Channel without huge losses.'

'Have we got an air defence?'

'Oh yes.' A slow smile spread across Will's face. 'We've got the Hurricane and Spitfire. Not enough yet, but Dad said they're better than the German fighters, and production is going on day and night – so is the training of new pilots. I believe we're in for a bitter struggle, but we won't give in.'

'So Churchill has told us. That man certainly knows how to deliver a rousing speech. 'We shall fight on the beaches, we shall fight on the landing grounds, we shall fight in the fields and in the streets, we shall fight in the hills; we shall never surrender.'

Will laughed at Bob's terrible attempt to imitate Winston Churchill. 'If Hitler tries to invade we'll just have to set Jim on to him. He always was a tough kid, but you ought to see him now. The paratroopers have turned him into an impressive fighting man. I'm glad he counts us as his friends.'

'Like that, is it?' Bob smiled as he recalled the good, carefree times they'd all had together. Then he remembered what his mother had asked him to do. 'After your experiences with Dunkirk, what are you going to do now? I can't imagine you'll be content to just stay at the paper.'

'I'm not.' Will leant forward and sighed. 'I haven't told Mum and Dad yet, but I've been talking to someone at the Ministry of Information. I've only heard today that I've been recruited as an official War Correspondent. I'll be in uniform, but not part of the fighting force. My job will be to report back, and they're going to teach me Morse Code, as well as the use of a radio. I leave to start my training next week.'

'You'll be in the front line of any battle you are sent to report on,' Bob pointed out.

'Just as you and Jim are.' Will's mouth set in a determined line. 'And the whole country is in the front line now. I'm well aware of the risks, but this is something I can, and want to do.'

'And you'll be damned good at it. Congratulations, Will. Hey, I wonder what Becky's going to say when she hears this?'

'She'll be pleased for me.'

Bob nodded in agreement. 'I'd love to see her drive a truck – from a distance, of course.'

Sally and John Walker listened to the hilarious laughter coming from the front room and smiled at each other. Their son had been tense and rather withdrawn when he'd first arrived home, which was not a bit like him, and time spent with his friend was just what he needed to help him unwind.

Nine

Two weeks after Dunkirk and Becky hadn't heard a word from David. Jim was safe, and so were Bob and her brother. Will had survived helping with the evacuation, the crazy fool, but she was desperately worried about David. If only she knew where his family lived she could contact them, but she didn't. In fact, she knew absolutely nothing about him. They'd only met a couple of times and hadn't had a chance to get to know each other properly. She had chatted on about her family, but he hadn't said a word about his.

Wiping the grease from her hands, she slammed the bonnet of the car down, her mouth set in a determined line. Their acquaintance might have been brief, but that didn't matter. He'd been kind to her, and she liked him. Not in a romantic way, of course. That was quite out of the question because he was out of her class, and an officer. But, damn it, she had liked everything about him – his easy smile, and the way his gentle eyes shone with amusement when he'd teased her . . . She had to find out if he was all right! Alice might be able to help.

'Does it work?'

Becky glared at the car's driver as he sauntered up. 'Of course it does, Corporal.'

He caught the keys she tossed to him, and grinned. 'What's upset you today? Where's that bright smile?'

'Mind your own business, and go and collect your officer. And go easy on the brakes and clutch. We've had to overhaul the clutch, and replace the brake linings.'

'Yes, ma'am!' he said, standing to attention, still smiling.

Her normal good humour surfaced again, and she laughed. 'Go on, off you go, and don't slam those large size tens on the pedals so hard. The poor old car can't take too much rough treatment.'

After giving a dramatic sigh, he got in the car and wound down the window, gazing at her with a pathetic expression on his face. 'Please, Miss, can I have a new car?'

'No you can't. You know the army had to leave all its vehicles and equipment in France. Everything's in short supply.'

The driver pulled a face, suddenly serious. 'They nearly bloody well left me behind as well.'

'Oh, I didn't realize you'd been there.' She felt contrite about ticking him off. 'How did you get back?'

'On a navy ship.'

She leant on the open window. 'My brother went over in one of the little boats.'

'Did he?' The corporal smiled again. 'They did a fantastic job, and saved a lot of lives.'

'He's a reporter,' she told him proudly, 'and his stories were on the front page for days. Er . . . did you happen to meet a Colonel David Hammond?'

'No.' He shook his head. 'Missing, is he?'

'I really don't know; that's what's so worrying.'

'Well, I expect they're still sorting everything out. It was chaos over there, and I expect it will take a while to get together accurate lists.'

'Yes, I expect you're right.' Becky stood up and watched the car drive away.

It was her lunch break so she'd find Alice first.

She was in luck. Her friend was just coming out of her building. 'I want to ask a favour, Alice. Do you have a couple of minutes?'

'I can manage that as long as you walk along with me.' She kept walking and Becky fell into step beside her. 'What's up? You look worried.'

'Is there any way you could find out if Colonel David Hammond was among those who were rescued from France?'

Alice stopped suddenly and frowned. 'Ah, I know that name. He's the one who interviewed you when we signed on. Do you know for sure he was in France?'

'Yes, he hinted at it when he took me out to dinner. He was leaving that very evening.'

'You never told me you'd been seeing him.' Alice looked offended.

'I only saw him a couple of times.' She nudged her friend. 'Anyway, you're a fine one to talk. I think you're going out with someone, and I haven't heard a word about him.'

'I was just waiting to see how it went. He's in the air force, and he's lovely. Now, let's get back to the matter in hand. What regiment is your colonel in?'

'I don't know. I never asked, or took any notice of the insignia on his uniform.'

'Too busy gazing into his eyes, I suppose.'

'It was nothing like that,' Becky protested. 'I like him, and we got on well together. He was kind to me and I'm worried about him. Can you help?'

'I'll see what I can find out,' Alice said, giving Becky's arm a comforting pat. 'My Major might know him. If not I'm sure he'll make enquiries – if I ask him nicely enough, of course.'

'He won't be able to resist you if you turn on the charm,' Becky laughed. 'But seriously, I'd be ever so grateful if you could find out if he's safe. I've written twice since Dunkirk, and haven't received a reply yet.'

'Leave it with me.' Alice glanced at her watch. 'Oops, I must dash. I'll meet you at seven in the NAAFI.'

'Thanks.' Becky watched her friend march away on her errand. Now all she could do was wait.

It was nearly eight by the time Alice joined Becky. 'Sorry I'm late; we've been so busy. Major Brent seemed to know who I was asking about, but he wants to see you in our office, now.'

'What? Am I in trouble for asking about David?'

'Of course not, but he wants to talk to you before giving out any information.'

Becky's insides clenched in dismay. 'Is the news bad, then?'

'I don't know, Becky. This is an officer we're talking about, and Major Brent won't give out personal details to someone in the ranks. Not even to me, and I'm his confidential secretary.'

'Of course, I should have thought about that.' Becky stood up and made sure her uniform was in order.

She followed Alice, and waited impatiently while she rapped on a door and disappeared inside.

Alice soon reappeared. 'Come in now.'

She stood to attention in front of the officer's desk, and had never felt so frightened in her life about the news she was about to be given.

He wasted no time. 'Tell me how you know Colonel Hammond.'

Her explanation was brief, and she realized that it was doubtful if the officer would tell her anything. After all, it was clear she hardly knew him when it was put into words, but she didn't feel like that. It was as if she'd known David all her life.

'We've been writing regularly, sir,' she hastily explained. 'And I haven't heard from him for a while. I'm worried, sir. Could you tell me if he's all right? Please, sir. That's all I need to know.'

Major Brent sat back. 'I'm afraid he's missing. That's all the information we have at this time.'

It took a few moments to compose herself, and then she said, 'I'd like to write to his family, sir. Could I have his home address?'

'No, I can't give out that information.' Major Brent stood up, bringing the interview to an end. 'I'll see you are informed if we receive any further news.'

'Thank you, sir.'

The word 'missing' kept ringing through her mind for the rest of the night, making sleep impossible. She knew many families were worrying themselves sick over the same word since Dunkirk. It could mean that they were alive – perhaps taken prisoner – or they had been killed. While there was some hope, the uncertainty would be crippling.

Unable to sleep, she got up and wrote a long letter to her brother, pouring out her fears for David, and deep sorrow that she was unable to write to his family. She longed to offer some comfort, however slight. She had always been able to talk to her brother, and after putting the letter to him in the post, she returned to the billet. All the other girls were out, either on duty, or enjoying themselves at a dance somewhere, but Becky was too sad at heart to be good company.

There was no one to see her, so she shed a few tears, and allowed herself to grieve for the man she had become so very fond of, praying that somehow, somewhere, he was safe.

It was five days before her brother's reply reached her. Opening it eagerly, she settled on her bunk to read it before going on duty. As usual it was pages long, and she smiled when he told her about Bob's leave, then followed up with all the family news. She missed them all terribly, but even if she was at home things wouldn't be the same, and she really enjoyed army life. It was stretching her talents, and she loved striving to improve her skills as a mechanic. It was much more interesting than working in a shoe shop.

Her smile faded when the tone of the letter changed, and she gasped, unable to believe what Will was going to do. He was going to be a War Correspondent! Her emotions were mixed – pleased that he had found something he wanted to do, and worry about the danger he would be in by doing such a job. But he was well qualified, and she was so proud of him. She had always supported and encouraged him to go for what he wanted, and he would have her wholehearted backing for this as well.

After reading the next few pages of the letter, she was scrambling to her feet. If she went without breakfast she might just have time.

With the letter clasped in her hand, she ran as fast as she could, muttering to herself, 'Please be there!'

Alice was already working when Becky burst through the door. 'Is Major Brent here?' she gasped. 'I must see him.'

Her friend didn't ask any questions, and disappeared immediately into the adjoining office. She was back again almost at once. 'Come in, Becky.'

'What's all this about?' the Major demanded the moment she stopped in front of his desk.

'Sorry to disturb you, sir.' Becky stood to attention. 'I've just received a letter from my brother. He went over to Dunkirk in one of the little boats.' Still breathless from her mad dash to get there, Becky held out the letter. 'It's the last three pages, sir. Read what he says.'

She waited impatiently as the officer read Will's account of how he'd tried to make an officer come into their boat.

He read it once, and then, much to Becky's frustration, he began again. She was anxious not to be late reporting for duty.

Unable to remain silent any longer, she said, 'I know it doesn't tell us what happened to him after that, sir, but it might give his family some comfort to know he was seen, and was trying to get his men to safety.'

'This is an excellent description of what it must have been like.'

'Yes, sir.' Becky's eyes shone with pride. 'He's a reporter, and is going to be a War Correspondent. Do you think Dav . . . Colonel Hammond's family would like to know my brother actually spoke to him?'

He carefully folded the letter, then looked at Becky as if seeing her for the first time. 'May I take this to show his parents?'

'Yes, sir.' She glanced at her watch. 'Can I go, please, sir? I'm on duty in five minutes.'

'Of course, and if you get into any trouble, refer them to me.'

'I'll run all the way.' She gave him a genuine smile, so pleased he'd liked the letter.

'Off you go then. And thank you for bringing this to me.'

Still smiling, she saluted smartly, turned and hurtled out of the room, determined not to be late.

Major Brent waited until the sound of running footsteps faded into the distance, then he turned his attention to Alice. 'I believe you're a friend of that young woman. What do you think was between them?'

'Well, if you ask Rebecca she'll tell you Colonel Hammond put in a good word for her, helping to get the posting she wanted, and she likes him. But I suspect that her feelings go deeper than that. She wouldn't admit it though, because she's aware he's upper class, and he's an officer. There's also an age difference of about ten years, but I don't believe that worries her. She told me there are eight years between her parents, and it has never bothered them.'

'Hmm.' Major Brent tucked the letter safely in his pocket. 'She seems a sensible girl, and rather appealing. I can understand David taking an interest in her.'

'If they'd had more time together I think it might have developed into more than just an interest, sir.'

'You could be right, but the way things are we might never know.'

'Do you think he's dead, then?' Alice asked.

'I pray not. David and I have been friends since we were at Eton together.' He stood up. 'I'll be away for most of the day. If anyone wants me put them off until tomorrow.'

'Yes, sir.'

Ten

'When are you off duty?'

Becky started at the sound of Major Brent's voice. She'd been so intent on making this car shine that she hadn't heard him approaching.

Spinning round, she saluted. 'Tomorrow afternoon, sir.'

'Mr and Mrs Hammond were pleased to see your brother's letter, and they would like you to visit them. I'll tell them you'll be there around three o'clock.'

It took her a few moments to recover, not sure from his tone if that was a request or an order. 'They want to see me?'

'They want to thank you personally for sending the news about their son.'

'Oh, but that isn't necessary. I was pleased to do it.'

Major Brent studied the girl in front of him, and, as if he could read her mind, said, 'They are very kind people, and you will be doing them a great favour by visiting them.'

'Of course, sir.' Still surprised that they had invited her to their home, she took a deep breath. 'Where do they live?'

'Locally.' He handed her the address. 'You'll be able to get the bus right outside the gates.'

Becky took the paper from him. 'Thank you, sir. Er . . . should I take something – flowers, or something?'

'Just take yourself.' He actually smiled. 'Wash off the grease before you go.'

'Cheeky devil,' she muttered when he was well out of earshot.

They'll live in a big posh house, Becky thought as she polished buttons, shoes, and anything else that needed shining. She never wore make-up, but today called for a touch of lipstick. She gave a final check to see that all the grease had been removed from her nails, and then headed for the bus stop.

It was only a short journey to Frimley, or so it seemed. She was rather nervous about meeting David's parents. He'd obviously had a good education, and came from a well-to-do family, but she'd never felt intimidated by him. She hoped his parents were easy-going like him.

Once off the bus she consulted the map she'd brought with her and started walking. It soon became clear that she was now in an affluent part of town, but that was only what she had expected. Any fool could tell from his accent and bearing that he wasn't from a working-class family. It was a puzzle why he had ever taken an interest in her, but she was glad he had. He was such a lovely man, and she prayed daily that he was alive and well somewhere.

Ah, this must be it. Pausing at the gate she gazed up the drive at the house. House! It was more like a mansion. The thought crossed her mind that she might have to curtsy, and giggled quietly to herself, feeling apprehensive.

This was ridiculous, she told herself sternly. They were only people, and she had always been able to get along with everybody. They were like so many parents grieving for the son they feared was lost to them. They had asked to see her, and she hoped she could bring a little comfort into their lives by talking about their son.

That settled her and the nerves fled. Head up, she marched up the drive and knocked firmly on the door.

A maid opened the door, and she said, 'I've come to see Mr and Mrs Hammond. My name's Rebecca Adams, and they are expecting me.'

'They are in the sitting room, Miss. Follow me, please.'

The couple waiting to greet her were smiling as she entered. Mrs Hammond was around the same height as Becky – five feet six, or thereabouts. She was dressed simply in a well-cut linen frock of navy blue, and her only jewellery was a string of pearls. Mr Hammond was tall and straight, as if he had a military background, and the resemblance to his son was remarkable. David would look just like this when he was older. The only indication of the stress they were under showed in the dark circles under their tired eyes.

'Rebecca.' Mrs Hammond stepped forward and shook her hand. 'Thank you so much for coming, and allowing us to read your brother's letter.'

'Yes, indeed.' Mr Hammond smiled. 'It was a comfort to know someone had seen our son during the evacuation.'

'I wanted you to know that, and to read my brother's account for yourselves. You can keep it if you like. Just ignore the chatter about family and friends.'

'That is very kind of you,' Mr Hammond told her, obviously pleased to be able to hold on to the precious letter. 'Your brother has given a vivid account of what it was like at Dunkirk, and we will treasure it.'

'My brother's always been good with words. He's going to be a War Correspondent.'

'I'm sure he'll make an excellent one.' Mrs Hammond indicated a chair. 'Sit down, Rebecca. We hope you can stay for a while?'

'I'm not on duty until tomorrow morning.' Becky sat in one of the large armchairs, and glanced admiringly around the elegant room. 'You have a beautiful home, Mrs Hammond.'

'Thank you. It has been in the Hammond family for four generations.' Mrs Hammond turned her attention to the maid who had just wheeled in a trolley of refreshments.

'Will you tell us how you met David?' Mr Hammond asked.

Becky took the cup of tea being offered her and placed it on a small table beside the chair, then feeling quite at ease she began to tell them about the day she had gone to enlist. Then the trick he had played on her with the car, smiling as she told them about the posh restaurant he'd taken her to by way of an apology.

'And what was the food like?' Mr Hammond asked, the same amused glint in his eyes as his son's.

'Very nice.' She pulled a comical face. 'I let David choose everything because I couldn't read the menu. It was an experience and I enjoyed every minute of the meal. He left immediately after, and we've been writing to each other regularly.'

'And is that all there is to your relationship?' Mrs Hammond asked gently.

'Oh yes. I must seem like a child to him, but he's been so kind to me, and I'm very fond of him.' She didn't mind admitting her affection for him, and there was no reason to take offence that they had asked. It was only natural they would wonder.

At that moment the door was pushed open and a little girl of around three years old came in. She was looking sleepy and clutching a rag doll.

'Hello, darling.' Mrs Hammond held out her hand. 'Did you have a nice sleep?'

'Yes, Grandma. I'm thirsty. Can I have a drink, please?'

'Of course. Tea, milk or orange juice?'

'Milky tea, please.' The girl's attention turned to Becky and she studied her with interest.

'Say hello to our guest first, Sara. This is Rebecca.'

Becky leant forward and smiled. 'I'm pleased to meet you, Sara. That's a lovely dolly you have there.'

The girl nodded. 'Grandma made it for me. You're in the army like my daddy.' Her bottom lip trembled. 'Why hasn't my daddy come home? He should have. Grandpa said the soldiers were brought home in boats.'

Startled, Becky shot Mr Hammond a questioning glance.

'Sara is David's daughter,' he explained, speaking quietly. 'Her mother died soon after the birth.'

After giving a slight nod, Becky slid off the chair and knelt down by Sara. She was a pretty thing, with curly blonde hair and large, troubled, blue eyes. 'Your daddy was helping his men get to the boats and wouldn't leave until they were all safe. He's a good officer, and you can be proud of him. He'll come home when he's found them all, but it might take some time.'

Sending up a silent prayer that she wasn't lying about him coming home one day, she gave Mrs Hammond a worried look, and breathed a sigh of relief when she nodded agreement.

'That's right, Sara. Rebecca knows because her brother saw him, and he's written a letter to tell us.' Mr Hammond took the letter from his pocket. 'See, here it is.'

'Oh.' Sara smiled at Becky then, obviously relieved to know someone had seen him. 'Daddy gave me a present before he went away. Would you like to see it?'

'I'd love to.' Becky stood up, pleased to see the distress no longer showing on the girl's face. She'd reached out to comfort and had spoken without thinking. There was no way she could tell this lovely little girl that her daddy might never come home.

Sara took hold of Becky's hand. 'Come on, it's in the kitchen, but we must be quiet.'

She allowed herself to be towed along a passage towards the back of the house. Then Sara placed a finger over her lips to indicate that they mustn't speak, and slowly pushed open the door.

The kitchen was large and the door to the garden was open, letting in a cooling breeze. Becky was wondering what the gift could possibly be when the girl pointed towards a round basket in the corner. Inside was a bundle of chocolate brown fur.

'It's a Labrador,' Sara whispered, 'but she's only a baby and needs her sleep.

A small face appeared and the puppy opened its eyes. A tail thumped with pleasure when she saw Sara.

'Ah, she's awake. We don't have to whisper now.'

'She's beautiful,' Becky said.

The girl sat on the floor, laughing, as a wriggling little animal clambered all over her in an effort to lick her face.

Joining them on the floor and receiving an equally enthusiastic greeting, Becky asked, 'What's her name?'

'Daddy said we have to call her Becky, because she's pretty and will probably get into lots of mischief.'

'Oh did he!' There was a smothered laugh behind her, and Becky turned to see Mr and Mrs Hammond standing in the doorway. Their son certainly had a wicked sense of humour, and it looked as if his parents shared that trait.

'Give Becky a drink, Sara, and then we can all go into the garden.'

Deciding to have some fun with them, Becky said innocently, 'I'm not thirsty, Mrs Hammond.'

'Not you,' Sara giggled. 'Grandma's talking about my puppy.'

'Is she? It's confusing because Becky's my name as well. In my home we have to call my brother Will, because if we shout for Bill, my father and brother both come. So, if you call Becky I'll answer as well.'

The little girl looked puzzled as she gave the puppy a drink. 'But your name's Rebecca.'

'I know, but all my friends call me Becky.'

'Oh, I see. But I'll have to call you Rebecca, otherwise I'll get in a muddle. Why did my daddy give the puppy your name?'

'I have no idea.'

As they all walked into the garden, Becky said dryly to David's parents, 'Just you wait until I see your son. I'll have a few words with him. I never get into mischief!'

As they all laughed, Becky realized they were no longer assuming that David might have died in France. He would come back. He had to.

It could be a false hope, but for the moment talking and laughing about him in a natural way had eased the pain of loss a little for all of them.

Eleven

July arrived without any news of David, and Becky was trying very hard not to give up hope. But it was hard. Also, the direction the war was now taking didn't help to ease anyone's worries.

On 30th June, German troops occupied Guernsey, then on 1st July they went into Jersey. And it had just been announced that tea was to be rationed. The allowance was only two ounces per person, per week, and in spite of all the gloomy news, that brought a smile to Becky's face. The kettle was always on in her house and she wondered how on earth her mother was going to manage. Such a small amount wouldn't last her for long.

'Lovely day, isn't it?' Alice came and stood beside her.

'Hmm.' They both turned their gaze skyward, watching the trails being made by planes weaving and diving. There was a battle going on up there. 'What does your boyfriend do in the RAF?'

Alice closed her eyes for a moment, then said, 'I expect he's up there.'

'He's a pilot?' Becky spun round to face her friend, concerned. Alice had been secretive about her boyfriend, talking only about the things they did on their infrequent dates, but never any personal details. However, she was certain this boy was special to her friend. To find out he was a fighter pilot made Becky sad. They were in the midst of a desperate battle. The Germans were determined to wipe out the air force before invading, and these pilots were equally determined to stop them. Everyone was aware of the great responsibility they had resting on their young shoulders.

Alice said nothing as she fingered a chain around her neck. Then she smiled. 'I came to see if you were free for lunch?'

Knowing her friend well enough not to pursue the subject, Becky smiled back. 'Give me five minutes to clean up.'

Only having an hour, they hurried towards the mess.

'How are the boys?' Alice asked as they sat down.

'Fine, as far as I know. If we can get leave at the same time you must come home with me, Alice. We might be lucky and one or more of them will be home at the same time.'

'Oh, thanks, I'd like that. But wouldn't your parents object to you bringing home a stranger?'

'You're not a stranger,' Becky laughed. 'They know all about you. We're great letter writers in our family.'

'I see, you've been gossiping about me, have you?' Alice teased.

'Of course. So, will you come?'

'I'd love to. We'll see what we can arrange.' She gave Becky a sympathetic glance. 'I'm sorry there hasn't been any news about your colonel. Have you been to see his family again?'

'I went last week while you were on leave. Last time I was home I found a beautiful doll I'd been given when I was about Sara's age, so I gave it to her. It was like new,' she hastily added. 'It was even still in the same box. I was more interested in playing with the boys' toys.'

'That doesn't surprise me,' Alice laughed. 'Did Sara like the doll?'

'Yes, she seemed very pleased with it, and was immediately pressing her grandmother to knit more clothes for it. Whoops!' Becky shot to her feet. 'I must get back. Are you going out tonight?'

'Yes, I'm meeting Anthony at the Red Lion – if he can get away.'

'Have a good time then.' Becky patted her friend's shoulder as she walked past, well knowing that it would be an anxious wait for Alice. Pilots didn't always appear after a day's flying.

She spent the evening writing letters to her parents, Will, Bob and Jim. She also wrote a chatty letter to David's parents. Although they hid it well, she knew they were half out of their minds with the lack of news.

Collecting up the pile of letters, she took them to the post room. Then as it was still only nine o'clock she went to the NAFFI to spend an hour or so with some of the other girls.

From a very young age Will had always had a quick mind. He absorbed information easily and retained it. His mother said he had been born knowing what was going on around him, and he now blessed that ability to learn easily. Although he wasn't going to be part of the fighting forces, he had to be able to take care of himself so he didn't put anyone else in danger. His job was going to be to report on the war, not make a nuisance of himself. Nevertheless, he couldn't wait to start doing his job – that was as long as they accepted him, of course. He knew what all this testing was about.

They had to be sure they were choosing the right people for the job, but he wished they'd put him out of his misery and tell him if he had a chance of being given the job.

As if in answer to his thoughts, the officer who had been his instructor in communications came and sat opposite him. 'You've done well, Adams.'

'Thank you, Captain.' Will drew in a deep breath. 'Does that mean I'll be accepted?'

'You will be receiving an official letter within the next week, but I can tell you now that you've passed the tests with flying colours.'

'Oh, that's marvellous!' Will smiled with relief.

'Go back to working for your newspaper, but it won't be long before you're sent for. You could be asked to cover any kind of operation, so I hope you're ready for the unexpected.'

'I am,' he said confidently. 'I don't care what I do or where I go.'

'That attitude has gone a long way to convincing everyone you're right for the job. But, while you're waiting for your first assignment, there's one hell of a battle going on in our own country. The Luftwaffe are determined to destroy our air defences before they launch an invasion fleet. If they don't they will be slaughtered as they try to cross the Channel. They've been attacking shipping, and are now intent on destroying our airfields, so you'll have plenty to keep you occupied until you're sent for.'

Will nodded in enthusiasm. Ever since Dunkirk he had been restless. There was so much happening and he didn't want to sit on the sidelines. When he'd applied to be a War Correspondent he'd had no idea if he stood a chance, but he'd managed to show them he was capable of doing the job. He knew that was no mean achievement. 'Hope they send for me soon.'

'I know you're anxious to get involved in the war, but you'll have your chance.' The officer's expression was grim. 'At the moment we are on the defensive. But eventually the tide will change.'

'You sound certain, sir.' Will studied the man in front of him. 'This country is alone, our shipping is being sunk at an alarming rate, and although the army was snatched off the beaches at Dunkirk, all their equipment was lost. The only thing standing between the Germans and us is our air force. The odds against us are high.'

'Indeed they are.' Suddenly the officer's face lit up. 'But I believe those very odds are helping. Many countries, including Germany, think we're finished, and it's only a matter of time before we're beaten into submission. They're wrong. We will never surrender!'

Will burst out laughing. 'So we've all been told by Churchill.'

'There you are then, it must be true.' He became serious again. 'We're in for a long hard struggle, and keeping the people informed is going to be vital. That's where you, and others like you, are going to be needed. It isn't going to be an easy task you've chosen, but you already know that.'

'Yes.' Will nodded. 'I saw how dangerous it could be at Dunkirk, but it's what I want to do.'

'And I believe it's something you are suited for.' He stood up. 'It's been a pleasure to meet you, Adams. Don't be too impatient. You'll be called upon soon enough.'

When Will arrived home that evening his parents were waiting anxiously for him.

'How did you get on?' his father asked as soon as he stepped inside the door.

'I've been accepted, but I've got to wait for an official letter.' Will dropped his bag on the floor, buoyant with a sense of achievement.

'I knew you'd do it.' His mother nodded proudly. 'What happens next?'

'They said they'd call on me soon, but in the meantime I can go and work on the paper again.'

'Tell us all about it,' his father urged, pulling out chairs from the table so they could sit down.

The tea was already made, and Will said, 'It's a very meagre tea ration, isn't it, Mum?'

'It certainly is. The only way I can make it last is to make the tea weaker.' Mavis grimaced as she poured them all a cup. 'We'll just have to get used to it.' She settled down and looked at her son expectantly. 'Now, we want to hear all your news.'

For the next half an hour Will told them about the different methods of communication he'd been shown, and how they'd been very thorough in testing to make sure he was up to the job. 'They won't send anyone out with the troops unless they're sure they can cope.'

'I expect your experience at Dunkirk helped to convince them.'

'I'm sure it did, Dad.' He drained his cup. 'Have you heard from Becky? I was wondering if her colonel has been found.'

'No, sadly, he hasn't.' His mother refilled his cup. 'She came home for a couple of days while you were away.'

'Oh, damn. We all keep missing each other. How is she?'

'She's worried about this man,' Bill Adams said, 'but apart from that I think she's enjoying army life. It seems to suit her.'

'She went to see his family and gave them your letter. They were very pleased to know someone had seen their son at Dunkirk and Becky let them keep it.' Mavis had sadness in her eyes as she asked, 'What do you think his chances are?'

Will closed his eyes for a moment, reliving the scene in his mind, and then he shook his head. 'He went back to the beach looking for the rest of his men. If no word has been heard from him by now, then I would say he probably died there.'

'Oh dear, I am sorry. She seems very fond of him.' Mavis began clearing the table. 'So much heartache. Men killed and missing, and those young pilots risking their lives every day. What's next, I wonder?'

Father and son gave each other a glance that said worse was to come, but neither of them put their fears into words.

'Anything from Bob and Jim?' Will changed the subject. It was no good alarming his mother with speculation. No one could predict the next move in this war.

'They write home when they can,' Bill said as he lit a cigarette. 'The last we heard they were fine.'

'Good.' Will stood up. 'Any hot water, Mum? I'd love a bath.'

'Yes, you go ahead while I make us a meal.'

Picking up his bag, Will headed for the door, stopped, and turned round, his expression pensive. 'It doesn't seem long ago when we were all messing around with the bike, and not a care in the world. How things have changed.'

Twelve

The battle in the air continued with increasing intensity. The pilots flew from dawn to dusk as the Luftwaffe attacked the airfields, and they were all aware of the importance of the fight. If Hitler could gain air superiority then he would invade. So much depended on these young men.

Becky knew Alice was worried because she saw it in her eyes in unguarded moments, but she never once spoke of her fears. All she had ever said was that they took each day as it came. They lived for each day, and in this perilous time that was all anyone could do. Wise words, but so hard to do when someone you loved was in danger every day, whether it was on land, sea or air.

August had arrived without any word that David was alive. Bob was at sea somewhere, and they had no idea where Jim was. The secrecy surrounding everyone's movements was frustrating, but necessary. It didn't help to ease concerns about family and friends though. Thankfully, her brother was still around and busy reporting on the home front.

'Hey! Anyone there?' Alice waved a hand in front of Becky's face. 'You were miles away.'

'Sorry.' She looked up and smiled. Alice never looked gloomy. There was always a ready smile for everyone. 'You going out tonight?'

'Not until nine o'clock. I've managed to cadge a lift to Kenley, so I'll wait in the pub there, but I'm not sure if Anthony will make it. The weather's been good, and if he's flown several sorties today, he might be too exhausted. I'll give him to closing time and then come back to camp.'

'Do you often have to wait and then come back without seeing him?'

'Now and again.'

'That must be worrying.'

'The pub's right by the airfield and news usually filters through if they've had a tough day. I wait just in case he can get away for an hour or so. I don't mind.'

'No, of course you don't.' Becky changed the subject. Her friend had said more than usual, and she didn't want to upset her by asking too many questions. If Alice wanted to keep her feelings to herself, then Becky respected that. Everyone had their own way of coping. 'Do you still want to come home with me if we can get leave at the same time?'

'I'd love to, but it might be a while before any of us have leave.'

'You're right. We'll keep it in mind.'

'I'd enjoy meeting your brother and friends. They sound an interesting group. Wouldn't it be lovely if we could all be on leave at the same time?'

'Very, but most unlikely. Perhaps in your exalted position you could arrange it with the War Office,' Becky teased.

'I'll see what I can do,' Alice laughed, then became serious again. 'Have you seen David's parents lately?'

'I went last weekend. Little Sara was pleased with the doll I gave her, but she's fretting for her father. I was glad I didn't go in uniform because I think that would have upset her even more.'

'Poor little scrap.' Alice sighed sadly. 'She's too young to understand.'

'And not knowing what's happened to him makes it even worse, and harder to explain to a child. It's all very distressing.'

'I know.' Alice squeezed her hand. 'But you mustn't give up hope yet. He might have been taken prisoner.'

'That's what I keep telling myself, but it's hard when I see his little daughter. It nearly breaks my heart. Thank goodness she has loving grandparents.' Becky gazed at her friend with troubled eyes. 'We've got to win this war, or else all this suffering is going to be for nothing.'

'Losing is unthinkable, but it's going to be a tough fight. I know we'll win through in the end. We have to believe that!'

'You're absolutely right, as usual. How did you come to be so sensible?'

'Just a gift I was born with.' Alice patted her hair smugly, and then couldn't keep a straight face. 'It's nice of you to notice.'

'You're incorrigible! My dad would love you. Anyway, back to the subject in hand. With Bob guarding the convoys, Jim with the paratroopers, my brother keeping the news flowing, and Anthony chasing the Luftwaffe away, there's no way we can lose. My dad says our planes and pilots are better than the Germans.'

'Of course they are.' Alice stood up. 'And talking of pilots, I hope there's one waiting in the pub for me.'

She watched Alice hurry away. She was right. No matter how bad things became, they must never entertain thoughts of defeat.

'Take cover!' Jim fell flat on his face and waited until the bombs had finished screaming down. Then he stood up, brushing sand from his uniform. 'What the hell are we doing in Alexandria?'

'Someone's perverse sense of humour.' Stan spat out some grains of sand. 'They issue us with Arctic gear and then send us to the desert so the Italians can drop bombs on us. I thought we were supposed to be fighting the Germans.'

'Don't worry. You'll get your chance.' The Captain walked over to them. 'They're here as well.'

'Ah, well, that's all right then, sir.' Stan grinned. 'But I'd rather be tackling them in their own country. How long we gonna be here?'

'Until we've pushed them out of North Africa.'

'A couple of weeks then,' Jim joked, making the men around them laugh. They numbered eight in all. After they'd managed to get out of Norway and returned home, their group had been singled out. This had been followed by a tough training session on explosives, and then being shipped out here.

'What are we doing here, sir?' Stan asked the question they all wanted answered.

'Report to the officers' quarters at fourteen hundred hours and you'll be told your mission.' He studied the group of tough-looking men. 'You are all hand-picked and are needed here. Now, get some lunch while it's quiet.'

The uncertainty about this posting didn't seem to curb Stan's appetite, making Jim shake his head in amusement as his friend cleared his plate for the second time. 'I don't know where you put all that food,' Jim told him, handing him a cigarette.

'Got to keep up my strength.' He drew deeply and blew the smoke towards the ceiling. 'I have a feeling we're in for a tough time, mate.'

'Let's go and find out, shall we?' Jim stood up. The fact that they were going to the officers' quarters and not the briefing room was unusual, and was making him highly suspicious about this whole business. They hadn't been able to get a word out of anyone until now, and he couldn't wait to hear what the hell was going on.

The house was large and on the outskirts of Alexandria. When their group of eight walked in they were surprised to see at least a dozen men already there. Jim studied them, wondering who they were, but their desert gear was lacking much in the way of identification. Excitement ran through him. What had they got themselves into?

'Oh, oh,' one of their group muttered. 'They look like a bunch of assassins.'

'Bet they're Special Forces.' Stan pursed his lips as he glanced at Jim. 'I wouldn't like to get on the wrong side of them!'

'You could be right.' Jim nudged his friend into a seat. 'This could be fun.'

There was no more time for speculation as the door opened and two officers marched in. Everyone jumped to attention.

'Good afternoon, gentlemen.'

Jim nudged Stan at that greeting. 'Never been called a gentleman before,' he muttered out of the side of his mouth.

The more senior officer gazed at them all in turn, his piercing look lingering now and again. 'Please be seated.'

When they were settled the other officer stepped forward. 'I'm Captain Allingham. Those of you who have just joined us must be wondering what you're doing here.'

'Too bloody right!' someone sitting behind Jim muttered.

'Well, you've all volunteered to join our little group.'

A mutter ran through the eight paratroopers.

'We don't remember doing that, sir,' Stan said, causing a ripple of laughter around the room. 'Unless we were drunk, of course.'

The captain's mouth twitched at the corners as he studied a piece of paper he'd picked up from the desk. When he looked up his expression was under control. 'It says here that you all volunteered to join this special unit.'

Jim chuckled. 'Then it must have been a hell of a party we had, sir.'

The regular members of the team were now enjoying the banter, and one of them turned round to face Jim. 'You enjoy a good party, do you?'

'As long as it's exciting.'

He winked at Jim and Stan. 'We can guarantee you an exciting time.'

They were then told about the covert work they were engaged in, and how vital it was. Jim and Stan listened intently, leaning forward, eager to hear every word.

'Any questions?' the officer asked when he'd finished speaking.

This was greeted with silence. It was quite clear what was going to be required of them, and it sounded highly dangerous.

Captain Allingham waited a few moments, and then gave a slight nod of his head. 'I bet you're all pleased you volunteered now, aren't you?'

'Delighted, sir,' someone quipped from the back of the room.

The officer smiled then. 'You will be split into four groups. The new members will be teamed with the experienced men. The list is on the board, so I want you to spend the rest of the day getting to know each other. Listen and learn from those who know what they are doing. And I want you all assembled here tomorrow at six hundred hours.' He glanced around the room. 'Sober!'

'Yes, sir.' They all stood to attention as the officers left the room.

'Do you think they'd tell us what happened to the men we're replacing?' Jim asked his friend dryly.

'Not a chance, mate. Let's see who we're teamed with.' Stan dragged Jim over to the board and scanned the names. 'Ah good, we're together.'

'You're on my team,' someone said from behind them.

They spun round to face the man who had been sitting in front of them.

He held up his hand when they started to introduce themselves. 'I know who you are. I've been watching you from the moment you arrived, and I asked for you to be assigned to my team. My name is Alan. We're quite informal here.'

'Right.' Jim could hardly contain his excitement. This was going to be very different from the paratroopers.

Alan beckoned to three more men. 'Meet Ted, Jack and Pete.'

They all shook hands, and Alan said, 'Now, let's get started. How are you at handling explosives?'

'We had a couple of weeks' special training before we came here,' Stan told him.

'What about unarmed combat?'

'That's a necessary skill if you're jumping out of a plane into enemy territory.'

Giving a wicked grin to his men, Alan said, 'Let's see just how good these two are, shall we?'

It didn't take long to find out that they needed to be very good indeed.

Thirteen

Over the next three months, Becky saw very little of Alice, whose every spare moment was spent with Anthony. During September there had been a sudden change of tactics as the Luftwaffe turned their attack to the civilian population. Bombs were now raining down on London. Night after night the drone of aircraft was heard, and the glow in the sky showed how the city was burning.

'Bad tonight.' Alice joined Becky and others as they watched the searchlights sweeping the sky. 'I'm glad my family have moved to Cornwall. And although it means I can't see them too often, at least I know they're out of this lot.'

Becky nodded. 'Mine have taken to sleeping in the Underground. Wish I could be with them.'

'I expect you do, but they will be relieved to know you're based outside London.'

'They've already told me that, but it doesn't stop me worrying about them.' Becky sighed. 'This change in tactic is giving our pilots a breathing space, and I expect you're pleased about that.'

'I am,' Alice replied. 'The boys said the fifteenth of September was the hardest day, but it was the day the tide turned. The Luftwaffe must have known they had failed, so now they are bombing our cities in the hope that it will make us crumble.'

'All they're doing is making us bloody mad,' one of the men said. 'And it's no good standing here worrying. Come on, girls, we'll buy you a drink.'

Later that night, Becky stared into the darkness, unable to sleep. After so many months, hope that David was still alive was fading. Some names were now known of those who had been taken prisoner, but David's wasn't among them. She had no idea where the boys were, and her parents were in constant danger from the bombing. At the beginning of the war many had predicted that it wouldn't last long, but they were under no illusions now. This was going to be a long conflict, with many dangers and heartaches to face. And yet people were still laughing, joking, going to dances and the cinema. She was impressed by the resilience and courage of the armed forces and the ordinary man in the street. Hitler had made a serious misjudgement. He was not going to be able to crash his way into this country as he had with others. The Channel was a serious obstacle to overcome without air supremacy. And that he didn't have.

She drifted off to sleep, comforted by these thoughts.

The next evening the planes came again.

'You can almost set your clocks by the buggers,' Pete muttered. 'You got family in London?' he asked Becky.

She nodded. 'They've been taking shelter in the Underground. I hope they're there tonight.'

'They'll be all right there. Want a drink?'

'Thanks.' Becky walked towards the mess with Corporal Pete Markham. He had been at Dunkirk and she'd become quite friendly with him. It was a comfortable friendship. He was happily married with a young son and another on the way. He treated Becky like one of the boys, and that suited her nicely.

'Any news of your colonel?' he asked, knowing she had been making enquiries about him.

'I'm afraid not.'

'Ah, sorry to hear that.'

'Me too.' She sighed. 'He's got the sweetest little girl, and I fear she's never going to see her daddy again. Her mother died soon after she was born.'

'Oh, that's sad.'

When they reached the bar, Becky insisted on buying the drinks. 'What you going to have?'

'Pint of bitter, please. I'll get the next round then.'

But they didn't even have a chance to finish the first drink. The door swung open as they were taking their first mouthful, and the sergeant marched in. His voice cut through the chatter like a knife. 'Medics, fire fighters and all transport personnel fall in at once!'

'What's up, Sergeant?' Pete asked as they lined up outside.

'London's on fire from a massive incendiary attack. They need ambulances and fire engines. Doctors and nurses are already here from the military hospital, so ambulance drivers get going! The same for all fire fighters – move! We've also got men lined up and waiting for transport to aid in the rescue, and I want the lorries loaded and out of here in ten minutes.'

Men were running in all directions, and with them were about five women. Becky wondered if they would be ordered to stay behind, but that didn't happen, much to her relief.

'Come on.' Pete grabbed her arm. 'You know London and I'm going to need you.'

The lorries were already full of soldiers, and Pete jumped in the first one he saw. Becky scrambled in beside him.

'Keep together!' the sergeant bellowed above the roar of engines. 'The ARP will direct you to where you're needed.'

The door next to Becky opened and the sergeant jumped in, pushing her over to make enough room for himself. He glanced at her briefly, and then turned his attention to Pete. 'Put your foot down.'

'I'm going to.'

The scene was one of organized chaos. Trucks and lorries were coming from all directions and heading for the gates. Men could be seen running to scramble on to the moving vehicles, and the blackout had been forgotten.

'Hope they have the sense to douse those lights once we're out of here.' The sergeant settled back, moving Becky over more so he could get comfortable. 'This could be nasty,' he told her.

'I know. My family are there.'

'Where you from?'

'Stepney.'

'Me too.' He closed his eyes. 'It's going to be a long night.'

No more was said until they were on the outskirts of London, where the smell of burning and the glow in the sky held them mesmerized. By the time they reached Hammersmith, Becky's insides were churning. *Please be underground*, she silently pleaded. It was about the only place her family would be safe in this mayhem.

They were waved on until they reached Wandsworth, where the police stopped them. The sergeant jumped out, ordering them to stay in the lorry. 'I'll see where we're needed.'

'Everywhere, by the look of it.' Pete peered through the windscreen trying to see just what was going on.

The ambulances and fire engines were soon on their way, heading towards the raging fires. Orders by other officers had the men jumping out of their lorry and piling into another one.

'Right.' The sergeant climbed back in the cab. 'We're heading for the docks. The all clear has gone and people are going to need all the help we can give them. Temporary centres are being set up in schools and church halls for the homeless, and our job will be to pick them up and take them there.'

'What are the troops going to do?' Pete asked, as he set the lorry in motion.

'They're going to be looking for any trapped in the rubble. It won't be easy getting to where we're needed. Roads are blocked by fallen rubble, and in places the fires are so fierce it will be impossible to get near them.'

Without saying a word, Pete backed and turned as he tried to find a way through, and Becky was relieved she wasn't driving in such terrible conditions.

The next few hours were a nightmare. Becky spent her time ushering people into the lorry, talking calmly to shocked families, and comforting frightened and bewildered children. Many were coming out of the Underground stations to find that their homes were no longer there.

Dawn arrived, and although Becky appeared outwardly calm, inside she was sick with worry. The three of them were tired and filthy as they accepted a cup of hot tea from a WVS van. The Women's Voluntary Service was out in force, offering refreshments to the exhausted rescue services.

The sergeant downed his tea in a couple of gulps, then said, 'Right, we've done all we can here. Let's see if we can get to Stepney. I'd like to see if my house is still standing. I expect you're anxious as well.'

Becky nodded. 'Thank you, Sergeant.'

After much turning, backing up and directions from Becky, they managed to reach the sergeant's street. 'Well, it's still here,' he said. 'Not a window left, by the look of it. Thank heavens my wife and kids are in the country.'

Pete then drove them to where Becky lived. It wasn't possible to get all the way, and she was soon out of the lorry, running as fast as she could, jumping and scrambling over rubble. It looked bad, and her heart was thumping.

When she turned the corner, she stood there clutching her sides in horror. There was a great hole where their three houses had been. She recognized bits of furniture scattered around, and even a fragment of her bedroom curtains. But it was the mangled pieces of motorbike that brought bitter tears to her eyes. What fun they'd had with that old bike. Her breath was ragged, unable to believe the scene in front of her. The destruction was so complete. Everything she had known all her life was gone.

Pete placed a hand around her shoulders. 'This your place?'

She nodded, still unable to grasp that their home was no longer there. But as devastating as that was, the fact that the bricks and mortar were no longer there meant little to her. Her thoughts were only for her family and friends who had lived there.

Through the mist of shock she heard the sergeant shout, 'Do you know if anyone was in these houses?'

A policeman came over to them. 'We've found two bodies at the moment, mate.'

Becky snapped back to awareness with a crash. 'What were their names?'

'Don't know.' The man gave her a sympathetic glance. 'You'll need to go to the church hall in the next street. They might be able to help you.'

As she spun round, intent on going to the hall, she saw four people in front of her. For a moment her mind didn't register who they were. Her eyes were full of moisture and she was so frightened it was hard to think straight. After wiping a hand across her eyes, she stared again. It was Bob's parents . . . and her own.

'Pat and Harry have been killed, sweetheart,' her father said as he hugged her. 'We've just identified them.'

'Jim's parents.' Becky almost doubled over in pain. 'What were they doing in the house during such a terrible raid?'

Her mother then held her tightly, both of them shaking. 'Pat wasn't feeling well. She kept being sick and said she couldn't possibly come to the shelters in that state. She said she was going to have a night in her own bed. Harry stayed with her, of course.'

'Jim must be told.'

'We've given the authorities all the necessary information, and they'll get in touch with him,' Sally, Bob's mother, said, her voice shaking with grief, 'We should be the ones to tell him – it would be kinder – but that's impossible. We don't even know if he's in this country. We'll go ahead and make the funeral arrangements, and hope the army can get Jim home in time.'

'What are you doing here, Becky?' her father wanted to know.

'We've been working in London all night,' the sergeant explained. 'This is my home as well, so we came here as soon as we were free. I'm dreadfully sorry you've lost your homes and friends. Is there anything we can do for you?'

'You can take us to the nearest rest hall where we can get something to eat, and try to sort out what we're going to do.'

'There will be people on hand to help you with temporary housing, and any immediate needs you have,' Pete told them.

Becky gazed at the place where their homes had once stood. The devastation was total. 'It's hard to believe everything's gone.'

'Things can be replaced, people can't.' Her father rubbed a hand over his face, looking exhausted.

'Come on, folks,' Pete urged. 'The lorry is just around the corner.'

'Move out of London,' Becky urged as they made their way along the street.

'We'll probably have to,' her mother told her. 'I don't suppose there's much left around here to rent.'

'I wish I could stay with you, but I've got to get back to camp.' Becky helped them all into the lorry. She squeezed her mother's hand. 'You'll let me know what you're doing and when the funeral will be, won't you?'

'As soon as we know ourselves.'

The sergeant scribbled a number on a piece of paper. 'You phone that number and we'll see your daughter gets any messages you leave with us. It will be quicker than the post.'

'Thank you, Sergeant, that's very kind of you.'

The centre they took them to was crowded, but they were given a warm welcome. Reluctantly, Becky had to leave them, but she knew they would help and support each other through this tragedy. They were lifelong friends, and it had always been the six of them.

Now there were only four.

Fourteen

'It's good of you to come, Alice. After all, you didn't know Jim's parents, but I'm glad to have you along.'

Alice slipped her hand through her friend's arm, well aware of the ordeal this was going to be. 'I feel as if I do know them. I've seen photos and listened to you talking about them.'

Becky smiled sadly. 'It's awful, but we're not the only ones dealing with tragedy. Just look at the place. I grew up here and I hardly recognize it. Mum said the church has lost most of its lovely stained-glass windows and part of the roof, but the Rector is carrying on as if nothing has happened.'

'That's all any of us can do, Becky.'

She nodded in agreement. It had been a difficult ten days, but at least her parents had found a house to rent in East Sheen, and were sharing it with Bob's parents. She would have liked to see them move further away from London, but her father insisted that he still needed to get to his work. The factory near the docks was still standing, by some miracle, and working day and night to turn out parts for the fighter planes. It wasn't going to be an easy journey for him, but at least he would be coming out of the danger zone at the end of his shift, and she was grateful for that.

'I hope the boys have been able to get home for the funeral.'

'They'll be here if they possibly can, Becky.'

She fought back the tears that were threatening to spill over. 'At least we're able to hold a proper funeral service for them. Not everyone is able to do that. Many just disappear . . .'

'That must be dreadful.' Alice took a deep breath, not mentioning David, as that would only upset her friend more. 'Oh, look, there's quite a crowd outside the church, and I can see army and navy uniforms.'

'Thank God! All the boys are there.' She glanced at Alice. 'This isn't how I wanted you to meet my family.'

'Never mind. I'll be pleased to meet them anyway.'

After quickly introducing her friend to her parents, Becky went straight to Jim. She had hardly recognized him. He was lean, tanned to a dark brown, and his expression showed anger simmering under the surface.

'Jim, I'm so sorry . . .' She reached out to him and was startled when he stepped back. Her hands dropped to her sides. They had always been such good friends, but now it seemed as if he didn't want to know her. She realized it was his reaction to shock and grief, but it still hurt her.

'This is Becky's friend, Alice,' her father told Jim, breaking an awkward silence.

Alice held out her hand until Jim had no choice but to shake hands with her. 'I'm sorry this is such a bad homecoming for you.'

Something seemed to snap in Jim, and he said angrily, 'Why don't you all stop mouthing empty words of regret? You've got no idea how I feel!'

'They're not empty words,' Bob told him. 'We all share the grief.'

'Like hell you do! You've got no idea.'

'Hold it there!' Alice stepped in front of Jim and had to tip up her head to look straight into his eyes. 'How dare you turn on people who love you?'

'And who the hell are you to tell me what to do?'

'I'm doing it because everyone else here cares too much for you to upset you any more than you are. Because I'm a stranger, I can see you as a great brute of a man who's hurting so much he's lashing out at the very people he should be thanking for their love and support.' She took a deep breath and didn't move an inch away from the towering, furious man.

'You don't know what it's like,' he snarled, hands curled into tight fists as if he wanted to hit someone.

Becky and the others watched in amazement as the lovely, diminutive girl took on Jim without flinching.

'Oh, I know exactly what it's like.' Alice pulled a fine gold chain from under her uniform and held it out for him to see. 'That's an engagement ring. I was supposed to be marrying a wonderful man, but he was killed when his Spitfire was shot down three weeks ago. And Becky's lost David. He disappeared at Dunkirk, and no one has seen him since. Don't you dare accuse us of not knowing the turmoil and grief you're going through. You're angry – we're all angry. You're not the only one suffering a devastating loss, and you'd do well to remember that.'

'Oh, Alice, you never said a word,' Becky whispered, distressed for her friend.

Jim was staring at the girl in front of him – then he did a surprising thing. He gathered her into his arms and rocked her gently, tears streaming down his face. 'Thank you, I needed someone to set me straight.' He glanced up. 'Forgive me. I'm so angry I lost my way.'

'No need to apologize, son,' Bill Adams told him. 'Alice is right, we're all bloody angry at this senseless loss of innocent lives.'

Becky's mother reached up and kissed Jim on the cheek. 'We love you like a son, and you'll always have a home with us.'

'Thank you.'

The hearse arrived then so there was no more time to talk. The streets had been cleared of rubble and the vehicle was able to get right up to the front of the church. Jim was still holding Alice's hand tightly as they followed the two coffins into the church.

'That's a very courageous girl you have for a friend, Becky,' Sally Walker murmured. 'I don't think I'd have had the nerve to face Jim down in the kind of mood he was in. She did just the right thing, though.'

Becky nodded, still stunned after hearing that Alice's boyfriend had been killed.

Bob edged his way to her side. 'Who's this David? First I've heard of him.'

'Someone who helped me when I joined up.' She didn't want to go into this now.

'Oh, special, was he?'

'Yes.' She glared at Bob. 'And don't refer to him in the past tense. He could still be alive.'

'Not after all this time.'

'Shut up, Bob,' she whispered, just loud enough for him to hear her above the sound of the organ.

He shrugged, placed her hand through his arm, holding her firmly at his side. 'Sorry, you're right.'

The church was quite full. It seemed as if all the neighbours from the street had come to say goodbye to Pat and Harry Prentiss. It was a sad occasion and Becky had to struggle to keep her composure. Her thoughts focused on Jim, knowing what an ordeal this was for him, and she was grateful Alice had come with her. She had her own grief to deal with, and although Jim had never met her before, they appeared to be giving each other comfort.

After the funeral they all went back to the rented house. It was the first time Becky had seen it.

'My goodness!' she exclaimed. 'It's huge.'

'We'll need the space,' her mother explained. 'We're all going to be living together, and if the four of you manage to get home at the same time we'll need every room in the house. And because we're bombed out the owners are letting us rent it at a reasonable price. Now, let's have a nice cup of tea. Who's staying the night?'

'Sorry,' Becky told her. 'We're due back at camp by six this evening.'

'But you'll never make it.' Her mother glanced anxiously at the clock.

'We've got someone picking us up, Mum. He should be here at any moment.'

'Is that allowed?' Will gave his sister an amused look.

'There are some advantages to being in the transport division. Also Alice works for an officer and he needs her back on time. Pete's got a London trip today and is collecting us on his way back.'

The words were hardly out of her mouth when the lorry rumbled to a stop outside the house.

After saying goodbye, they were just about to get in the truck when Bob pulled her aside. 'I'm sorry your boyfriend's missing. I didn't mean to upset you at the church.'

She smiled sadly and squeezed his arm. 'I'm sorry I snapped at you, and Colonel David Hammond isn't my boyfriend. As I said, he has been kind to me and I'm very fond of him.'

'Colonel?'

She nodded. 'And I'm as worried about him as I would be for any of my friends.'

'Ah.'

For some reason he looked relieved, and she studied him for a moment. 'I'm all grown up now, Bob, and I am allowed to have men friends, surely?'

'Of course you are.' He gave a lopsided grin. 'I keep forgetting that. In my mind you're still Will's little sister, who we all need to keep an eye on in case she gets into trouble.'

'I never get into trouble,' she protested, with a laugh in her voice. 'And I'm not so little any more.'

'No, you're not.' He gave her a hug. 'You take care now, and keep those letters coming.'

'And you do the same.' She turned and waved, then climbed in the lorry. 'Thanks for coming, Pete. Let's go.'

As they drove away, Alice nudged her. 'That tall sailor friend of yours is jealous.'

'Don't be daft!' Becky snorted. 'He still thinks I'm a kid who needs looking after.'

'And I think you're blind.'

'You're imagining things.' Becky changed the subject, too weary even to think about it. 'Why didn't you tell me about Anthony? You came to support me today; I could have done the same for you.'

'It happened when I was on leave. Major Brent extended my leave so I could go to the funeral. It was all over by the time I came back. I kept quiet because I just couldn't talk about it then.' Alice gave a ragged sigh. 'Jim's anger made me realize that was exactly what I was feeling, and it wasn't good to hold in all that grief. When he held me and shed tears, I did the same. It was what we both needed.'

Becky nodded, grateful Alice had been there and recognized Jim's anger for what it was – grief held under control until he was ready to explode.

'I like your family,' Alice said. 'And the boys are an interesting trio. Jim's a strong man and not one to be trifled with, but he has a gentle side to him as well. We can only hope this tragedy, and the army, doesn't knock that out of him. Bob now, he's harder to fathom. He keeps his feelings well hidden, but I get a feeling he's the kind of man who cares about other people.'

'Gosh, Alice!' Becky exclaimed. 'You've deduced that from one meeting? What about my brother?'

'He's the quietest of the three, but he's the most determined, and nothing is going to stop him from making his mark in life. He's going to do whatever he sets his mind to, and woe betide anyone who stands in his way.'

Becky turned and faced her friend, amazed by her evaluation of the boys. 'Will's always felt he had to prove himself capable of doing what everyone else does, but you've just described a very ambitious man.'

'That's what he is.'

'Well I never!' Becky sat back. 'If you're right then I really don't know them as well as I thought I did. And I'd never have said my brother wanted to make a name for himself.'

'Then you've underestimated him.'

'Hmm, well, only time will tell if you're right.' She still wasn't convinced. 'Have you always had this talent for summing up people?'

'I suppose so. Anticipating what people want is what makes me good at my job.' Alice smiled with satisfaction. 'I had you marked out as a good friend the moment I saw you.'

'And is this ability going to help you work up to a General?' Becky teased.

'After everything that's happened, that doesn't seem important now, does it?'

'No, it doesn't.'

Both girls were serious now, and finished the rest of the journey chatting about nothing in particular with Pete.

This brutal conflict had certainly changed their perspective on life. None of them were going to come out of this the same people they had been at the beginning.

Fifteen

Everyone had gone to bed leaving the three boys downstairs to enjoy a quiet beer together.

'I'm glad that's over.' Jim lit a cigarette and inhaled deeply, blowing the smoke out on a sigh. 'I knew London was taking a bashing, but I never imagined my parents would be killed. It's something you always think will happen to other people, but never you. I was so angry. They were good people and didn't deserve an end like that.'

'No, they didn't.' Will refilled the glasses. 'This is turning out to be a very bloody war. The loss of innocent lives is appalling, and it's only going to get worse.'

'It certainly is.' Bob downed his beer without stopping. 'The convoys are suffering terrible loses, and it makes you feel sick when you hear another explosion. The first time it happened and I saw those poor sods in the sea it tore me apart. I'm learning to deal with it in a hurry, because that's the only way I'm going to keep my sanity.'

'What have you been up to, Jim?' Will handed him a sandwich his mother had made for them to have with their beer. 'You didn't get that brown in this country. And I thought you were in the paratroopers?'

'I'm on temporary assignment to another regiment.'

'And you've been in a hot climate?' Bob probed, just as curious as Will.

'Hmm,' was all Jim said.

'Come on, Jim, you can tell us,' Bob urged.

'I bet I can tell you what our friend's up to, Bob. I'd say he's in the desert working with a special unit causing havoc on the enemy whenever they can.'

'Ah, that makes sense.' Bob leant forward, his gaze fixed on Jim. 'How close is he to the truth?'

'You know I can't talk about it. All I'm prepared to say is that Will is far too perceptive.'

'Aha!' Will looked smug. 'That proves I've guessed correctly.'

'You put that in one of your reports and you'll be in real trouble.'

'I'm not daft, Jim. My job is to report on aspects of the war that will inform, and hopefully lift the spirit sometimes, not give away secrets.'

'That's also something I'm curious about,' Bob said. 'Just exactly what are you doing, Will?'

Will was thoughtful for a while, and then his expression became animated. 'You'll all find out soon, but before I tell you I want your word you'll keep this to yourselves until it's over.'

'Promise,' Bob and Jim said together.

'I'm going on a bombing raid over Germany. We're going to make a newsreel to be shown in the cinemas.'

The boys glared at their friend in astonishment.

'Are you crazy?' Bob exploded. 'That's bloody dangerous.'

'And what you two are doing isn't dangerous?'

'When are you going?' Jim asked quietly.

'In three days' time – weather permitting, of course.'

'Well, for heaven's sake don't tell your mum and dad. They'll be sick with worry. Do you know how to use a parachute?'

'I've been on a quick training course, Jim, and have made a couple of jumps out of a balloon.'

'My God!' Bob handed round cigarettes. 'We turn our backs, Jim, and he's up to all kinds of dangerous things. Not satisfied with risking his life in a small boat at Dunkirk, he's now going to see what it's like to drop bombs while being shot at. I'm beginning to wonder if any of us are going to survive this war. I'm on the sea being hunted by U-boats, Jim's doing goodness knows what in the desert, and Will's about to climb into a bomber. I think we're all crazy!'

'Haven't we always been?' Will actually grinned. 'And we're all going to come through this, and when it's all over we'll go on a pub crawl around London. The drinks will be on me.'

'Now that's something we'll hold you to.'

The three boys sealed the promise by clinking their glasses together.

'Anyway, we have no choice. We've all got to come through this or Becky will never forgive us,' Bob said dryly.

For the first time that day they all laughed.

'Let me check your harness,' Andy, the navigator of the plane said.

'Thanks.' Will had needed help with all the flying gear they'd insisted he had to wear for the sake of his safety. He had spent the last two days with the crew he was to fly with. They should have gone last night, but the operation had been cancelled because of the weather. It looked as if it was on tonight, however.

'You're fine.' Andy patted him on the shoulder and smirked. 'Are you going to make heroes of us all?'

'You already are in my book.' Will was a seething mass of nerves. He didn't know how they did this night after night, and they were all so young. Their pilot was only twenty-one, and the rest of the crew around that age. It was incredible what this generation was doing.

'Do you get nervous before a raid?' he asked.

'Nervous?' Andy shook his head. 'I would say frightened, or sick to the stomach would be more appropriate words.'

'But not one of you shows it.'

'No point, chum. We always tell ourselves we'll be the ones to get back. Time to get on board. It's a long trip, so have you got enough film for your camera?'

Will took a deep breath and nodded. 'I've got more than enough.'

'You know,' Andy said, as they climbed in the lorry taking them out to the plane. 'You've got guts. You don't have to do this.'

'It's my job. The forces wouldn't take me, and I couldn't sit on the sidelines, so I'm putting my reporting skills to good use.'

'So you decided to become a War Correspondent.'

'That's right.' Will grinned in the fading light of evening. 'And here I am.'

The film crew had followed them out to the row of Wellington bombers and captured the scene of men clambering in. Will stopped under a wing and faced the cameras to record his introduction, and then allowed himself to be helped into the plane. From here he was on his own.

Once the door was closed the engines roared into life, and as they gathered speed for take off, Will wondered how something as big, and as loaded as this, could get off the ground.

But it did, and he saw how skilled the young pilots were. Once airborne all his nerves vanished, and he revelled in the sensation of flying. He settled down to enjoy the flight while he could, making notes and taking some pictures of the crew as they worked. The sight of the other planes was fascinating, and Will was determined to make this film report the best thing he'd ever done.

Their destination was Berlin, and that was why Will was on this raid. It was thought that the people at home would be heartened to see that Britain was striking back. He was so intent on capturing every detail that he quite forgot how long they had been in the air. He was jolted back to awareness when all hell broke loose.

'Five minutes to target,' came a voice over the intercom, and it was the longest five minutes Will could ever remember.

Suddenly, a searchlight caught them in its glare and the pilot had to turn and weave until they were free of it. One plane slightly in front of them had flames coming from an engine, and another was leaving a trail of smoke in its wake. Flack was all around them, but scared as he was, Will held the camera steady.

'Dear God!' Will gasped when their plane shook and, looking out anxiously, saw a plane just in front of them going down.

'Hold it . . . hold it . . .' The bomb-aimer spoke clearly and calmly.

Will held his breath as he filmed the fires burning on the ground.

'Bombs away!'

The plane banked and turned for home. As they straightened out there was an ominous crunching sound and the plane lurched.

Somebody swore, and a member of the crew – Will couldn't see who it was – was scrambling down the plane to try and see if there was any serious damage. He kept quiet, knowing he mustn't use the intercom when it might be needed urgently.

The crew member was soon back, and when he gave Will the thumbs-up, he saw that it was Andy.

'We've taken a hit near the tail, Skipper. It doesn't look too bad. How does she feel?'

'All right, as long as the tail doesn't fall off.'

The quiet laughter Will could hear over the intercom brought a lump to his throat, and he knew this was something he would remember for the rest of his life.

'You all right, Will?' the skipper asked.

'I'm fine, Skipper.' He addressed him the same way as his crew. He was honoured to have shared this night with them, even if it had been a terrifying experience. Of course, they weren't back yet, but they were away from the flack.

'We're a long way from home,' the skipper continued, 'so if the damage causes any trouble I want you to obey me without hesitation. If I order you to jump, you get out as quickly as you can. Is that clear?'

'Yes, Skipper.'

'Good.'

They made it back without mishap, and Will almost shouted for joy as they landed safely.

The first thing they did was to inspect the damage. There was a hole large enough to put your fist through, and several smaller dents covering quite a large area.

The skipper nodded. 'Just shrapnel damage. They'll soon be able to patch that up.'

Will used the last of his film on getting a good picture of the damage, then said, 'I thought from the noise that we'd taken a direct hit.'

'No, you would have been bailing out if we had.' Andy slapped Will on the back. 'Go and get some breakfast. We'll join you as soon as we've reported in.'

Other crews began to wander in while Will waited, and he studied their faces. Some were talking, some were quiet, but when he looked closely he could see the signs of exhaustion. It had been a long, dangerous mission, and these same crews were probably going to do the same thing all over again in a few hours.

When the crew he'd flown with finally joined him, he braced himself to ask the one question he needed to complete his report. With a notebook open in front of him, and pen poised, he said, 'I saw one plane go down and another seemed to be in trouble. How many didn't make it?'

It was the skipper who answered. 'Two. One we know bought it over Berlin, but we're not sure about the other one. They might have landed at another airfield, but that's doubtful. We should have heard by now if they had.'

Will concentrated on writing all this down; relieved to know it wasn't more, though goodness knows, that was bad enough! It was hard to believe any of them had survived. He also noted down his impression of what it was like to see the empty places at the tables already laid out for the incoming crews.

'Have you got all the information you need?' the skipper asked.

'More than enough.' Will stood up and shook hands with each

of them in turn. 'Thank you for putting up with me. It has been quite an experience.'

'You're welcome.' Andy pumped his hand. 'You let us know when the newsreel is being shown. We'll all go to the pictures that day.'

'I'll see the base gets its own copy, so you can have a private showing.'

Will walked out to the car waiting to take him back to London, and wondered if any of them would be alive to see themselves on film.

He really hoped and prayed they were.

As tired as he was there was a spring in his step. He'd been on a bombing raid over Germany.

And he was still alive!

Sixteen

It was only three weeks to Christmas, and Becky couldn't believe how fast the months were going, but she couldn't drum up any enthusiasm for the festive season. Nobody knew where the boys were. The Blitz was still going on, and she didn't feel a bit like celebrating. Everyone wanted passes at Christmas time, and both Alice and herself had been given four days' leave. It wasn't like her to be so downhearted, and she told herself to be more positive and count the blessings. For the moment Hitler had abandoned his plans to invade. Against all the odds this island was still holding out, and that was certainly something to be happy and proud about. And it would be lovely to see her parents. It was some time since she'd managed to get home, and she wondered if Will would be there. She knew he would if at all possible.

She started to sing quietly to herself, her mood lifting quickly, as it usually did. Her mother had always told her to count her blessings if she was ever depressed, and it was sound advice, for it always worked. Yes, going home for the holiday was something to look forward to, and now she'd see if any letters had arrived for her.

There were five, and she hurried to find a quiet spot to read them.

For the next few minutes she chuckled as she read amusing letters from her parents – they always wrote separately so she received more letters. The next two were from Will and Bob. She slit open the next one without looking at the handwriting, expecting it to be from Jim. Much to her surprise it was from David's parents, asking if it would be possible for her to visit them before Christmas.

Knowing this was going to be a difficult time for them, she was determined to find the time. David was now listed as 'Missing, presumed dead' by the War Office, and it was terrible to realize that they might never know what had happened to him.

Not one to waste time, Becky went at once to see when she could leave the camp for a few hours. And then something must be found to put under the tree for Sara. The little girl needed cheering up because she had been told about her father and was naturally heartbroken.

Becky was pleased she had given Sara the doll because it would have been lost when bombs had destroyed their house. The destruction had been so complete it hadn't been possible to salvage anything, and her parents had just walked away. She knew it had broken their hearts to lose everything they had lovingly gathered together over the years, but she had never once heard them complain.

The next day she was knocking on the door of the lovely house in Frimley, a small present tucked safely out of sight in her bag for Sara. There hadn't been time to find the little girl something, so she was giving her a silver charm bracelet. It had been a gift from her parents on her fourteenth birthday, but she was sure they wouldn't mind. It was the only suitable thing Becky had left. It would be too big for Sara, but she would grow into it, and hopefully, it would give her pleasure looking at the various charms.

'Rebecca!' Mrs Hammond opened the door herself, smiling with pleasure. 'We are so glad you've come. Come in and get warm.'

She stepped inside and waited for Mrs Hammond to close the door. 'I'm sorry to come without giving you notice, but this was the only time I could get off.'

'Don't apologize, Rebecca. You are welcome in this house anytime you feel like it.'

'That is very kind of you.' She held out the brightly wrapped parcel. 'That's a small present for Sara. I didn't know what to give her, but I think she'll like that.'

'Oh, I'm sure she'll be delighted.' Mrs Hammond popped the package in the hall cupboard. 'We'll put that under the tree for her to open on Christmas Day.'

'I'm sorry I had to come in uniform, Mrs Hammond, but these are the warmest clothes I have now. I hope it isn't going to upset Sara.'

'Don't worry about it, Rebecca, we do understand.'

Becky breathed a sigh of relief. The last thing she wanted to do was upset them at this difficult time, but all she had at the camp were summer clothes.

There was a lovely wood fire burning in the lounge, and the room felt warm and welcoming. A large Christmas tree was in the corner and covered in decorations. The rest of the room was also decorated with streamers and holly. Becky's heart went out to this family when she saw how determined they were to make it a bright Christmas.

The only person in the room was Mr Hammond, and he rose to greet her, smiling broadly. 'Ah, you've made it. It's good of you to come so quickly, Rebecca.'

David looked so like his father that it always gave Becky a jolt when she saw him. She hardly had time to shake hands when the door burst open and the dog threw herself at Becky, nearly knocking her off her feet.

'My goodness,' she gasped, fending off the excited animal. 'Look how you've grown, Becky!'

'Indeed you have, and not a trace of grease.'

She stilled at the sound of the voice, all the air rushing out of her lungs in shock. That sounded just like David's teasing tone, but it couldn't be. Steeling herself for disappointment, she turned to face the door.

At first she didn't recognize the man standing there. He was gaunt and leaning on a stick, but Sara was beside him, clutching his other hand, and her brilliant smile said it all.

'Daddy's home!' Sara jumped up and down in excitement.

'David,' was all she managed to say.

'You said he would come back one day, and he did!' Sara was bubbling with joy. 'I told him you came to see us, and showed him the dolly you gave me. He said it was a beautiful gift, and it is because I love it. Grandma's made more clothes for it and now we're going to have a happy Christmas because my daddy will be with us. He can't go back to work yet. He's got to rest . . .'

'Sara.' Mrs Hammond laughed at her granddaughter's antics. 'Stop gabbling and let Rebecca say hello to your father.'

The girl giggled and rushed over to hug Becky. 'Grandma says I talk too much.' Then she turned and tore back to her father. 'Sit down, Daddy. You know you mustn't stand up for too long.'

David ruffled his daughter's hair. 'And you stop bouncing around and give me a chance to thank Rebecca for being kind to all of you.'

'Sorry.' She was still smiling as she went to sit with her grandmother.

Speechless, Becky watched the scene, not being able to believe her eyes. The little girl obviously adored her father even though he was away for long periods at a time. But the grandparents were wise; there were photographs of him all over the place so that his daughter wouldn't forget what he looked like.

'Oh, where have you been?' she managed to say at last, determined not to cry, knowing instinctively that he wouldn't like that. 'You've given us such a lot of worry.'

'Is a reprimand the only kind of welcome home I'm going to get?'

His eyes were shadowed with exhaustion, but they still held the glint of amusement she remembered, and she was happy to keep this meeting light-hearted. Although he was in casual clothes, she was in uniform, so she snapped to attention and saluted smartly. 'I'm very relieved to see you home safely, Colonel . . . even if you have given us a terrible fright, sir.' His laughter was infectious, and she stood there smiling. 'Oh, it's wonderful to see you again. As you're not in uniform can I hug you?'

He reached out his hand and pulled her towards him, and then she reached up and planted a quick kiss on his cheek. 'Welcome home, David,' she said quietly.

'Thank you for looking after my family while I've been away.'

'I was pleased to do what I could. They're lovely people.' When he released her she stepped back and turned towards his parents and Sara. 'I'm so happy for you all.'

'Thank you, Rebecca.' Mr Hammond looked years younger. 'You've been a tower of strength to us during these worrying months, and at a time when you've had your own heartaches and losses to cope with. You have a generous heart.'

'Losses?' David frowned. 'What's happened?'

Mrs Hammond urged her son into a chair. 'Rebecca's house was bombed and two of their close friends were killed. The bomb completely destroyed their houses and they've lost everything, but she never once stopped caring about us, or you.'

'That's terrible.' David's mouth set in a grim line. 'Where are your parents now?'

'They've found a house to rent in East Sheen. They're sharing it with our next-door neighbours.'

'You tell me if they need anything.'

'Thank you, but there's no need. They've settled in the new house, and are coping well.'

'Can we have tea soon, Grandma?' Sara couldn't stay still for much longer. 'Rebecca must be hungry, and Daddy's got to eat lots.'

'In a few minutes.' Mrs Hammond smiled at Becky. 'Can you stay for a while?'

'I'm not on duty until tomorrow morning. She was bursting with questions, but she knew the subject of his survival would not be discussed in front of the little girl. And David might not even be able to talk about it at all. Many who had traumatic experiences were never willing to talk about them.

Tea was a lively affair, with Sara making most of the conversation. At seven o'clock, Mrs Hammond and David disappeared to put Sara to bed, and Becky took her chance to speak to Mr Hammond alone.

'How badly is he hurt?' was her first question.

'He's had bullet wounds to his side and leg. We've managed to glean some information from him, but he's not willing to go into detail. After the last of the boats left Dunkirk, he avoided the advancing Germans and made his way inland. He speaks fluent French, which was a help, and a family gave him civilian clothes and helped him move across the country. Of course being out of uniform was highly dangerous, because if the Germans had caught him he could have been shot as a spy. He won't talk about the journey, but from the look of him we can assume it was very arduous. It was right on the border with Switzerland that he ran into a German patrol and nearly got caught. The men helping him managed to get him across, even though he was injured. He doesn't remember much after that, and as he wasn't carrying any identification no one knew who he really was, not even the people who had helped him. All anyone knew was that he was a British army officer. The next thing he was aware of was being on a plane. He was taken to Aldershot Military Hospital, and being so close to home, he refused to stay.'

'He still looks very weak.' Becky was awed by his courage. 'When did he arrive home?'

'Three days ago. We wrote to you at once.' Mr Hammond's smile spread. 'A taxi arrived at the door, and I went to see who it was. Then David got out, hardly able to stand, and all he said was, "Hello, Dad. Pay the taxi for me, I haven't got any money." It took me back to when he was a teenager. He used to do the very same thing.'

They were both smiling when David came back. 'You both look amused.'

His father laughed. 'I was just telling Rebecca about the times you used to come home in a taxi and ask me to pay the fare for you. Is Sara asleep?'

David nodded. 'All the excitement has worn her out. She has grown over the last few months, and that puppy is going to be enormous.'

'She's been a brave little girl.' Mrs Hammond joined them. 'She's been fretting because you didn't come home, but Rebecca and the puppy have been such a help.'

'Oh, I didn't do anything,' Becky protested.

'But you did, my dear,' Mr Hammond insisted. 'We had that lovely letter from your brother, and you've visited whenever you could. But most importantly, you talked to Sara, giving her hope and comfort. And don't forget you gave her that beautiful doll, which I suspect was a treasured possession.'

Becky was embarrassed by the praise. 'I was glad to do it.'

'This is the first I've heard about a letter.' David was frowning again.

'David, you need rest so we haven't bothered you with too much information,' his mother told him. 'The letter was from Becky's brother to her, but she very kindly allowed us to keep it.'

'I'd like to see it.'

'Why not leave it for a while until you're stronger? It will bring back painful memories of Dunkirk.'

When David glared at his father, Becky could see the steel in his character. It was something she hadn't noticed before, but guessed he was probably alive today because of that trait.

Mr Hammond obviously knew his son wasn't going to back down, so without another word, he stood up and retrieved the letter from the bureau. Then he handed it to his son. 'The last four pages contain William's account of Dunkirk; the rest is a personal letter to Rebecca.'

'Thanks, Dad.' David turned immediately to the relevant pages. When he'd finished reading he looked up at Becky. 'That young boy in the boat was your brother?'

'Yes, he's a reporter and jumped on a boat to help the owner. They made two trips, but had to give up when the owner was injured and the boat damaged. They got the men safely back though.' She spoke with pride. 'He's a War Correspondent now.'

David took a deep breath. 'Those men in the little boats saved a lot of lives. I would like to know more about your brother, so would you allow me to read the rest of his letter?'

'Of course, if you'd like to. It's only family chatter though.' She watched his expression as he read, wondering what on earth he could possibly want with news about people he didn't know. When she heard him chuckle, she knew. It was ordinary life, and that was something that he had been missing over the last few, dreadful months.

'Your brother writes well, and I like the sound of your friends.' He folded the letter carefully and slipped it into the top pocket of his jacket. 'So, tell me how you're getting on.'

'Quite well.' She pointed to the stripe on her sleeve and grinned. 'I can drive lorries now, and I've learnt a lot about engines. Army life seems to suit me.'

'You've done well, but I knew you would.'

'Thanks.' Noticing how exhausted he looked, she stood up. 'I ought to be getting back.'

Mr Hammond also got to his feet. 'I'll drive you back.'

'Oh, there's no need, Mr Hammond. I can catch the bus.'

'I insist.'

David hauled himself out of the chair. 'You'll come again? I shall be disappointed if you stop visiting now I'm home.'

'Of course I'll come, but it won't be until the New Year. I'm spending Christmas with my family.'

'In that case . . .' Mrs Hammond took a parcel out of the bureau and handed it to Becky. 'This is from all of us, with our thanks for your kindness.'

'Oh, thank you.' She smiled at them all in turn. 'I know you'll have a lovely Christmas now. And you take it easy, Colonel, you need plenty of sleep.'

He smiled broadly and leant down to kiss her cheek. 'We'll see you after the holiday. And I promise to spend most of the time sleeping and eating.'

Seventeen

Although the house they were living in didn't seem like home to Becky, she couldn't have been happier. Bob had arrived on Christmas Eve, and so had her brother. 'It's a shame Jim couldn't make it.'

'I think if Jim was offered leave he wouldn't have taken it,' Bob said. 'I don't suppose he wanted to come here. It would have been very difficult for him without his mum and dad.'

Becky's father agreed. 'He'll probably feel better staying with his army friends. There won't be so many painful memories that way. He needs more time to get over the death of his parents.'

'You're quite right, dear,' his wife said. 'Goodness knows the loss is hard enough for us to come to terms with, but he wouldn't want us to be miserable. We must count our blessings. Becky, Will and Bob are here.'

'And I've got some wonderful news.' Becky had only arrived home two hours ago and hadn't had a chance to say anything. 'David is alive and well. He just turned up in a taxi one day.'

'What? He survived?' Will was sitting bolt upright with interest. 'Where has he been all this time?'

They all listened intently to Becky, and the good news helped to cheer them all up, and set the tone for the holiday. No matter how bad things were at times, it was lovely to know that good things were happening as well.

They talked long into the night, and no one bothered to get up until the middle of the morning. Then the men went off to the pub for a drink while Becky stayed at home to help prepare the Christmas lunch.

After the dishes had been cleared, they all sat down with a nice cup of tea and gave out the presents. By necessity the gifts were modest this year, as they were still trying to recover from the bombing. Clothes had had to be replaced, and it was expensive, so the gifts were useful things like socks, gloves and scarves. Except for one bulky parcel with Becky's name on it.

'We've all clubbed together to get you this, darling.' Her mother smiled as she handed the package to her daughter. 'You won't always want to be in uniform.'

She opened it and pulled out a winter coat in a lovely shade of red, which suited her dark colouring. 'Oh, it's beautiful!' she exclaimed. 'Thank you so much, but you really shouldn't have bought me such an expensive present.'

'We couldn't have our girl going out on dates not looking her best,' her mother said fondly. 'We chose a nice cheerful colour as well.'

'It's perfect.' Becky then went round the room and gave everyone a hug. 'I love it.'

'We knew you would. As soon as we saw it your father said that was the one we must buy.'

'Perfect taste, as always, Dad.' Then something her mother had said struck home. 'What dates?'

'You're surrounded by men,' her father teased. 'Are you telling us you never get asked out?'

'And now your colonel's home . . .' her mother persisted.

She could see the way their minds were working and knew she had to put them straight on the subject. 'It's not like that, Mum. You know he helped me get the posting I wanted, and I've been visiting his parents and his little daughter. They were grateful for Will's account of Dunkirk. It gave them some comfort, and I just tried to help them, that's all.'

'So you've said before.' Her mother clearly didn't believe there wasn't a romance between them. 'You've got another parcel here. Who's this from?'

'Mrs Hammond gave it to me from all of them.' Inside was a hand-knitted cardigan in cream. The wool was so soft Becky held it up to her face. 'I'll be lovely and warm with this under my new coat.'

'That's beautifully made, and the wool must have cost a fortune.' Becky's mother looked in the box. 'There's something else in there.'

It was a child's painting of the puppy, and Becky laughed in delight, holding it out for them all to see. 'Meet Becky. David named the puppy after me because it was bound to get into mischief.'

'He's right about that,' Will smirked. 'How old did you say his daughter was?'

'I never asked, but I would say she's between three and four.'

She held out the drawing to get a better view of it. 'Sara's done well; it does look like the puppy. I'll stick it in my locker at camp.'

She missed the knowing looks being passed around the others as she began to clear up the wrappings littering the room. 'What have you been up to, Will? You haven't said much in your letters.'

'They're keeping me busy,' he said evasively.

'Doing what?'

'At the moment I'm recording a commentary for a news report.'

'Is it going to be on the wireless then?'

'Hmm.'

'This is the first we've heard about a recording.' His father gave Will an enquiring look. 'When's it going to be broadcast?'

'I don know yet.'

'What's it about?' his father persisted.

'I can't tell you that, Dad. You know how things are.' Will was obviously uncomfortable discussing the subject. 'You'll find out when it's released.'

'All this secrecy is frustrating,' his mother declared. 'We just don't know what our children are up to.'

'No, we don't.' Bob's mother stared pointedly at her son. 'And they never say a word about where they've been, or what they're doing. Anyone would think we were spies.'

Bob grinned and stood up. 'I think I'll walk off some of the Christmas lunch, to make room for tea. You coming, Will? Becky?'

'Don't stay out too long,' his mother scolded. 'There's a nasty north wind blowing today.'

'That should wake us up.' Will shot to his feet, and pulled Becky out of her chair. 'Come on, lazy bones.'

The three of them disappeared, glad to get away from all the probing questions.

'Phew! Thanks, Bob.' Will wiped his forehead in mock dismay. 'I'll spoil their Christmas if I tell them what the programme's about.'

Becky grabbed her brother's arm, suspicious. 'What have you been up to, William Adams?'

'You'll have to wait like everyone else.' He continued walking and winked at Bob. 'She always was inquisitive.'

'Don't I know it!'

Becky wasn't about to give up, so she started on Bob next.

'You're keeping very quiet. Do you know what this crazy brother of mine has been up to?'

'As a matter of fact I do. And believe me, you don't want to know.'

Now she was worried. 'Come on, Will, you can tell me.'

'Nope.' He shook his head, determined.

Knowing she wasn't going to get them to talk, she sighed. 'You boys!'

It was a week into the New Year before Becky was able to visit the Hammonds again. She had written a long letter thanking them for the lovely present, and praising Sara for the drawing. Mrs Hammond had replied, but not a word from David. She hoped he was all right.

She pulled the collar of her coat up as she walked towards the house. 1941 had brought cold winds with it and she was grateful to have her new coat. At least she wouldn't have to visit in her uniform. The only frock she had now was a summer one, but the cream cardigan went with it nicely.

'Rebecca!' Sara rushed to meet her as soon as she stepped inside the door, but the dog beat the little girl and nearly sent Becky flying.

'Careful.' Mrs Hammond caught the animal. 'We're really going to have to teach this wriggling tornado some manners. Come in, Rebecca.'

There was no sign of David in the lounge, but she didn't have a chance to ask about him. Sara was waving her arm to show the bracelet on her wrist.

'Thank you for my lovely present. It was too big but daddy made it fit. I wear it all the time.'

'I'm pleased you like it, and it looks lovely on you. Your drawing was excellent, and I've put it in my locker at camp, and thank you Mr and Mrs Hammond for the beautiful cardigan. It's just what I needed.'

'It was our pleasure.' Mrs Hammond turned to her granddaughter. 'Take the puppy into the kitchen and give her a drink, darling. She's panting from all the excitement.'

'All right. Come on, Becky.' The two of them tore out of the room.

'Is David all right?' she asked, as soon as they were alone.

Mrs Hammond's expression clouded. 'He insists he is, but he's restless and often irritable. I don't think he's sleeping too well either.'

'That's only to be expected, my dear,' Mr Hammond said to his wife as he helped Becky out of her coat. 'It's going to take him a while to adjust to normal life again, and he's anxious to return to his regiment. He's been to the hospital and only arrived back a few minutes before you. He'll be down in a minute, and I hope to goodness the doctors have given him good news.'

Mrs Hammond nodded agreement, then smiled at Becky. 'The cardigan looks lovely on you. Did you have a nice Christmas?'

'Very, thank you. My brother and Bob managed to get home. Bob's the one in the navy,' she explained.

'Ah, Rebecca, you've finally made it.' David walked into the room without the aid of a stick.

The censure in his voice stung her. 'This is the first opportunity I've had. I have to wait for permission to leave the camp – as you well know.'

'Yes, of course, and you are right to remind me.' He smiled then, looking much more like his old self. 'Get your coat. We're going out.'

'But I've only just arrived and haven't had a chance to talk to your parents or Sara yet,' she protested.

'You can talk all you like when we get back. Where's your coat?'

'I've put it in the hall closet,' his father told him. 'Where are you going?'

'Just out.' David disappeared to collect her coat.

Becky gave his parents a startled look.

'Go with him.' Mrs Hammond spoke softly. 'A couple of hours with you might settle him.'

Becky nodded in agreement as he came back into the room. 'Nice coat,' he said, as he helped her into it. 'Christmas present?'

'Yes. It was a joint present from family and friends.'

'Lovely colour.' David turned to speak to his mother. 'I've told Sara we'll be back in time for tea.'

'Fine.' His mother gave Becky a grateful smile. 'Enjoy yourselves.'

She nodded as David ushered her out of the house and towards the garage.

'You'll have to drive. I'm not allowed to yet.'

Her eyes lit up with pleasure when she saw the Rolls Royce. 'Oh, my . . .'

'Not that one,' he told her. 'We'll use the one over there.'

She walked around the Rolls and saw a small MG sports car the other side. It had been completely hidden by the larger one.

David ran a hand lovingly over the bonnet. 'It's been a long time since I've had a ride in her. I checked her over yesterday and she's still in good working order. Get in.'

He was still good at giving orders, she thought wryly, but there was an edginess about him that hadn't been there before. She started the car and carefully backed it out of the garage. 'Where are we going?'

'To the cinema.'

'Oh, what's on?'

'I don't know, and I don't care. I just want to sit in a cinema and watch a film. You're the driver, Rebecca, so go anywhere,' he told her irritably.

'Yes, sir!' The nearest one was only a short drive from the house. She'd seen it from the bus, so she'd go there.

After parking the car they walked into the foyer, and it was only then that Becky noticed what was showing: *The Wizard of Oz*. She was about to point out to him that this wouldn't be to his taste, but quickly changed her mind. He was buying the tickets, and didn't seem to care.

They were soon settled in the stalls, and David appeared to relax. The short Laurel and Hardy film had them both laughing. The newsreel then followed this, which, of course, was all about the war. A special report came on, and as soon as it began Becky sat bolt upright, then surged to her feet, wide-eyed with shock. 'That's my brother!' she gasped.

'That's very interesting, Miss,' a man behind her said. 'If you would sit down we could all see your brother.'

'Oh, sorry.' She plopped down again, never taking her eyes off the screen.

When scenes were shown of the inside of the bomber and the raid over Berlin, Becky was gripping on to David's hand with all her might. 'The crazy devil,' she gasped. 'No wonder he wouldn't tell us what he'd been up to.'

She felt quite rung out when the film ended and the lights came up for the interval. David never said a word; he just squeezed her hand, and then left his seat. She was still sitting there trying to grasp what she had seen, when he returned with a drink for her.

'Are you all right?' he asked, handing her the soft drink.

She nodded, and turned round when the man behind tapped her shoulder. 'Which one was your brother?'

The War Correspondent.'

'Phew! He's got some guts.'

The lights began to dim for the main feature, but she didn't even notice it. She had always known her brother had a determination to prove he could do anything, in spite of his slight disability. But had this bombing trip been just guts, as the man behind had said, or was it recklessness? She took a deep breath. No, that wasn't a part of his character – he'd always thought everything out carefully before taking action. But there was no denying that he had changed since Dunkirk, and perhaps that taste of danger had brought to the surface a side of him hidden until now. There were men who craved excitement and danger. Jim was one of them; they'd seen that in him from a young age, but she'd never believed Will was like that. Now she was seeing a very different side of her brother and it was quite a revelation . . .

Completely lost in thought, she paid no heed to what was going on around her as she replayed Will's report over and over in her head. Her pride for what he had achieved almost took her breath away. Whatever the dangers, there was no denying it had been a masterly report, and he had carried out the mission with calm professionalism. He wasn't just good at this kind of thing – he was brilliant!

The lights went up and David gave her a wry smile. 'You didn't even look at the film, did you?'

'Oh, I'm sorry.' This afternoon at the pictures was supposed to help David adjust after his ordeal in France. 'I've been poor company. Please forgive me.'

'There's nothing to forgive. I understand your distraction. Come on.' He led her out of the cinema. 'You need a strong cup of tea.'

'That isn't necessary,' she protested. 'We mustn't be late back.'

'They'll wait, Rebecca. I'm not letting you drive my precious car until you've calmed down.'

She stopped suddenly and glared at him. 'I'm perfectly calm.'

'Don't argue, Rebecca. We're going to go in this café, sit quietly for a few moments while we enjoy something to eat and drink. And that's an order.'

'Typical officer,' she muttered.

He ignored her remark, led her to a table by the window and ordered a pot of tea and home-made cakes.

'I don't want anything to eat,' she told him. 'But you're right, the tea would be welcome.'

'You have whatever you want, but I'm hungry and I've got a lot of lost weight to put back on.' He reached across and caught hold of her hand. 'This has been a shock to you, but you have a very brave and talented brother.'

'Yes, I have.' She smiled back at him, and saw the understanding in his eyes. 'I'm sorry for snapping at you.'

'Stop apologizing, Rebecca. I understand how you must feel discovering your brother is doing dangerous things. But he's a War Correspondent, and he will be in all sorts of campaigns during this war – often in the front line with the troops. It's something you will have to accept. The Ministry of Information will seize on a talent like his and use him to the utmost.'

'I've always been proud of him.' Her face lit up with a brilliant smile. 'But now I'm fit to burst with pride.'

'So you should be.' David's eyes took on a faraway look. 'I remember that boy at Dunkirk urging me to get in the boat. It was bedlam and I was impressed with his calm demeanour then; I'm even more so now, and I'd like to meet him. Do you think you could arrange it for me?'

'Of course, and I know he'd love to meet you as well. I'll write to him tonight.' She poured their tea and even helped herself to a slice of plain Madeira cake. 'Did you enjoy the picture?' she asked, feeling much more composed.

'It was quite good.'

'Hmm.' She couldn't help laughing. 'I didn't think you'd want to see something like *The Wizard of Oz*, but you just bought the tickets and marched in, so I didn't bother to question it.'

'I didn't care what the picture was, and Judy Garland was very good in it. It was something that took me away from everything else. It was light-hearted nonsense and just what I needed. Along with your company, of course.'

'That's all right then.' She poured him another cup of tea, and watched him devour a second slice of cake. He was certainly more relaxed, and it was lovely having this short time alone with him. It reminded her of the dinner they'd had together just before he'd left for France. 'This is nice. I'm glad you insisted we come in here.'

He sat back and sighed deeply. 'I've been unbearable to live with since returning home. The first few days I just revelled in the pleasure of finally being home, but that soon vanished, and I have been finding it hard to adjust, being disagreeable to the people around me, which they don't deserve. This inactivity is driving me crazy and I need to get back to my regiment. I've persuaded the doctors to declare me fit, and I'll be back in uniform by the end of the month.'

'That's wonderful; I'm so pleased for you.' Her smile was bright, but she knew exactly what he was saying. Once back in uniform again the gulf between them would widen. A relationship between a colonel and a corporal was not acceptable in the army. 'And I quite understand.'

'I know you do, but we're friends, Rebecca, and don't you forget that. If I want to see you and talk to you, I shall do so, but I'll try not to make things too difficult for you.' He cast her a stern look. 'And just because I'm home I don't want you to stop visiting my family. They have become very fond of you.'

'And I of them.'

He paid the bill and they left the café, both silent now, and as Becky drove back to the house she knew this brief interlude of relaxed friendship between them was over. After worrying about him for months, she must now remember that he is an officer, and treat him that way. But perhaps it was for the best, for she had become far too fond of him.

But he was alive, and well enough to return to duty, and she was grateful for that.

It would have to be enough.

Eighteen

There were half a dozen letters in front of him and Will wasn't sure he should read those from his family. They were all regular cinema-goers and were bound to have seen the film by now. It was being shown everywhere, and the response had been excellent. A copy had been sent to the bomber crews and they had praised it highly. That meant more to him than anything else.

With a wry twist of his mouth he slit open the first letter and began to read. He was smiling with relief by the time he had finished it. There was only praise for his work; not one word about taking stupid risks. He'd had their love and support ever since he'd been born, and it was something he treasured. He went on to the one from his sister next, and what she told him had him fired up with enthusiasm. She had sent him the colonel's address with an invitation to meet him, and that was something he would dearly love to do. The memory of that man wading back to the beach was etched clearly in his mind. What a story that would make!

Will was already writing a reply saying he would call in three days' time. If he could have the colonel's permission to write his story, he could contact some of the other survivors of Dunkirk, and see how they were now. And he was curious about this man of whom his little sister was so fond.

Three days later Will was knocking on the door of the imposing house, and when a maid showed him into a side room and asked him to wait, he began to have concern for his sister. This was way out of their class, and she could be in for a lot of hurt.

After no more than a couple of minutes, Colonel Hammond strode into the room, in full uniform, and shook his hand.

The smile Will received was genuine. 'I'm very pleased to meet you again. We'll go into my study; we can talk there. But you'd better meet my parents first, or I'll never be forgiven if I whisk you away without introducing you to them.'

A dog jumped on Will as soon as he stepped in the room, and a little girl rushed to grab it. 'Stop it, Becky!' she scolded. 'You know we've told you to behave. This is Rebecca's brother, and you must be kind to him.'

That was too much for Will – he burst out laughing. So this was the animal they had named after his sister. 'I can see why you've given her that name. We were always telling my sister that when she was little.'

'Hard to manage, was she?' Mr Hammond asked, shaking Will's hand with enthusiasm.

'Very, but she's grown out of it – almost. She's still very good at speaking her mind, but my father says she was born with an abundance of common sense.'

'That is obvious.' David glared at the still boisterous animal, and said, 'Sit!'

When the dog instantly obeyed, Will wasn't surprised it recognized the voice of authority. This wasn't someone man or beast disobeyed.

Mrs Hammond was laughing as she greeted Will. 'And our son was born giving orders, so the army was the best place for him. We are delighted to meet you. Rebecca speaks of you often.'

'Indeed she does, and thank you for the excellent letter Rebecca gave us. It was a comfort to know someone had seen David during the evacuation.'

'Your delightful sister has been a tower of strength to us, William.'

'My sister has a kind heart, Mrs Hammond. Even as a little girl she was always the first one there if one of us hurt ourselves. She cares, but too deeply I think sometimes. It's easy for her to be hurt, but she hides it well.'

Sara tugged at his jacket to gain his attention. 'Look what Rebecca gave me. Isn't it lovely?'

Will bent down and looked at the bracelet he knew so well, and reached out with his left arm to stop the dog from pushing him over. Becky must indeed think a lot of these people to have given away one of her treasured possessions. 'It looks lovely on you.'

The little girl smiled shyly. 'I wear it all the time. What's the matter with your arm?'

'Sara!'

'It's all right, Colonel,' Will said, holding out both of his arms so the girl could see the difference. 'One is shorter and weaker than the other. I was born like that.'

'Oh. My daddy was hurt in the war and I thought you had been too.' She cast her father a worried glance. 'Shouldn't I have asked? William's Rebecca's brother so he must be nice, like her.'

'William didn't mind, sweetheart, but it isn't polite to ask such questions of someone you've only just met.'

'Oh, I'll try to remember that, Daddy.' She leant towards Will and whispered, 'Sorry if I was rude. I didn't mean to be.'

'That's all right. I didn't mind at all,' he whispered back, and then stood up, still smiling at Sara.

'We'll be in my study for a while,' David told them.

'Would you like tea sent in?' his mother asked.

'Tea or something stronger?' David raised an eyebrow to Will in query.

'Whatever you have will be fine.'

'Right. Don't bother with the tea, Mother.'

'Don't keep William all to yourself,' Mr Hammond said. 'We'd like to talk to him as well.'

'Give us a couple of hours and we'll be with you.'

Once settled in the study with a small glass of whisky in his hand, Will waited for the colonel to speak first. There were many questions he wanted to ask, but knew from experience not to rush in.

'I want to thank you for getting some of my men to safety.'

'I wish we could have taken you with us, sir. Did you manage to save the rest of your men?'

'Most of them.' David took a swallow of his drink. 'Tell me about yourself, William.'

'Call me Will, please.' It only took him a few minutes to give a brief outline of his life, and explain that he had become a War Correspondent in the hope of playing a useful role in the war.

'I would say you're already doing that.' David refilled their glasses.

Will placed his on the desk, hoping he could leave it there. He wasn't used to drinking whisky. 'I'd like to do a follow-up story on some of the men who were rescued. Would you be willing to tell me what happened to you?'

'I wasn't rescued.'

'No, you weren't, but you eventually made it home. I've contacted several of the men who were in our boat, and they've been given permission to speak to me. It will be a written piece for the newspapers, but names will not be mentioned, and no photographs.' Will paused briefly. From the expression on the colonel's face he doubted he was going to learn this man's story. He was disappointed, but kept on trying. 'No one will know it was you, sir. But, hopefully, it will be an encouraging story for the people to read.'

He stopped then. It was now up to the man sitting with him to agree or refuse.

David gazed into space for a while as he considered Will's proposal. He stood up and paced to the window, looking out on the garden for a moment. Then he turned. 'There will be things I can't tell you. I must protect the people who helped me move across France. They put themselves in grave danger by helping me, and I'm not the only one.'

'Understood. No names or details. We could simply say you made your way across France to safety.' Will's hopes rose. 'I'll show you a copy before it goes to press, and if there's anything you don't agree with, you can cross it out. You have my word that only what you, and your men, approve, will be published.'

David nodded. 'On those terms I'll tell you what I can.'

The notebook was already in Will's hand, and for the next hour he listened to the most incredible story of one man's determination not to be taken prisoner. How he wished he could print it all, but he'd given his promise, and wouldn't dream of going back on that.

When David stopped talking, Will was almost breathless with excitement, and full of admiration for everyone who had been involved. He put the pad in his pocket, determined to keep this account in a safe place because one day, when the war was over, this could be told in full.

The colonel sat back. 'When will you have the copy for me to read?'

'I've got more interviews to do, but it will be ready in a week. I'll bring it myself and we can go through it together.'

'I shall expect you a week from today, then.'

'I'll be here.' Will had warmed to this man now and felt he could speak freely. 'My sister's a nice girl, Colonel.'

He frowned. 'I'm aware of that.'

'What I'm trying to say is that I wouldn't like her to be hurt.'

'I'm sure you wouldn't, and neither would I. She is not a fool.'

Will felt contrite and gave a wry smile. 'Sorry, sir, but I've always had the habit of looking out for her.'

'Your sister is a sensible and determined girl, and is quite capable of looking after herself.' David stood up, effectively ending this particular subject. 'Time we joined the others.'

Resigned, Will followed him back into the lounge. The colonel was obviously not prepared to discuss his sister any further, and he was quite right. Will had no right to question this man's motives in befriending Becky. She'd always had her head screwed on the right way, and would make her own decisions in life. And right or wrong, she would live with her choices, as they all had to.

The next week was hectic for Will. He had interviewed three men who had been in his boat, and two more who had had different experiences. He'd also spent an enjoyable day with Doug, the owner of the *Lucky Lara*, and was delighted to see it fully repaired. Determined to keep his promise, he worked long into the night to prepare the draft for the colonel to see.

Finally satisfied with it, he kept his appointment on time, and found David waiting for him. They went straight to his study.

It was an anxious wait as the article was read, then read again. Will watched the pen in the colonel's hand as it hovered over the pages, but he only used it twice.

Finally, the pages were handed back. 'You've done an excellent job. I've only had to make a couple of minor changes.'

Much to Will's pleasure he spoke the truth. One sentence had been crossed out completely, and one word had been changed. It made no difference to the flow of the piece. 'Would you be happy for this to be published as it now stands, sir?'

'Yes, go ahead.'

Will was on his feet, smiling with satisfaction as he shook hands with the colonel. 'Thanks for your cooperation, sir. I'm grateful to have had the chance to meet you.'

'My pleasure, Will. You take care, whatever you're doing.'

'I will,' he said laughing. 'My sister will never forgive me if I get careless. Now, I must get back to London. I'm on a tight deadline for this story.'

Once this assignment was finished, Will was eager to start the next one. He knew he would have to go where he was sent, but he could always make suggestions. Perhaps he could sail on a merchant ship, or one of the navy vessels. And he was very intrigued to know what Jim was up to. There was so much going on . . .

* * *

'Thank God the winter's over.' Bob turned his face to the sea, feeling the breeze ruffle his hair. That was the coldest I've ever felt.

Reg nodded and lit another cigarette, feet apart to steady himself against the motion of the ship. 'Those winter convoys will stay in my memory forever. Bloody dangerous, and with no chance of surviving long in freezing water.'

'No.' Bob patted his pocket. 'I've left my fags below. Have you got a spare one on you?'

'Here, take the packet.' Reg flicked his cigarette end into the sea. 'I'm back on duty in five minutes.'

'Thanks.' Bob lit one and gazed out at the sea, thinking how pleasant this would be if it weren't for the constant threat from U-boats.

He was enjoying a quiet few moments when he became aware of excited voices, and Reg tearing up to him.

'We've just received some staggering news. Guess what that bloody fool Hitler has done now?'

'Surrendered?'

'No, you fool! Two days ago – the twenty-second of June – he invaded Russia!'

'You're not serious?'

Reg nodded vigorously. 'It's true. Let's hope he's had to take forces from Europe and given us a breather.'

'I can't believe he would do such a thing. He's supposed to have had a treaty with them.'

'Not worth the paper it was written on, evidently. That man has got to be stopped, Bob.'

'He will be.' Bob leant on the rail. 'If only America would come into the war, but that's unlikely. Public opinion there is against it, and truthfully, it must seem as if it's all a long way away from them.'

Reg shrugged. 'We'll just have to carry on alone. We haven't done too badly up to now. At least he wasn't able to mount an invasion against us.'

'I've just had a terrible thought. We could end up on convoys to Russia. Now that would be really cold, but they're going to need aid.'

'I wish you wouldn't get thoughts like that.' Reg groaned, and rushed back to his duty.

And Bob was left with a lot to think about. This was another turn of the tide.

In advance of publication, Becky received a bulky letter from her brother. It was a copy of his follow-up on Dunkirk. The only remark he made was that no names had been mentioned, but he thought she would be interested in the article.

She knew immediately it was about David and some of his men who had been rescued by her brother and the owner of a little boat.

She was enthralled as she read. It was a wonderful piece of journalism, and she was more than impressed with Will's growing talent. He seemed to get better with every report he made. It was hard to understand where his mastery of words had come from because no one else in the family had this ability.

Although she would have liked more details of David's flight to freedom in France, she knew for security reasons that would not have been allowed. Nevertheless, she now had a much better idea of what he had gone through.

Carefully folding the article she put it safely in her locker, not intending to show it to anyone. When the article appeared in the newspapers it would be in with all the other war stories, and it was doubtful if anyone would associate the account with David.

She knew who it was about, though, and it was something she would treasure.

Nineteen

'I don't know where the summer's gone, Alice.' Becky shivered in the cold wind. 'It doesn't seem long ago we were looking forward to Christmas, and it will soon be here again.'

'I know. I've only got three days' leave this year, so I'll make a quick visit to Anthony's parents and then go to see my parents. What are you doing?'

'I'm staying on camp this year. My family's disappointed, but I can't expect to have every Christmas at home. If I can get out for a couple of hours I'll see Mr and Mrs Hammond, just to wish them a happy Christmas and take a couple of small presents I've bought them.'

'Hmm. Have you heard from David lately?'

'I write regularly because he said he wants to know how I'm getting on, but I've only had a couple of short notes from him.'

'Pity. I thought at one time there might be something between you two, but it seems not.'

'There never was a chance of that.' Becky shook her head. 'An officer doesn't associate with a girl in the ranks. Think of the raised eyebrows that would cause. He's a career soldier and wouldn't risk it.'

'No, I suppose not. Try not to get too fond of him then.'

'Too late for that piece of advice, but don't worry, Alice, I'm well aware of the situation. And I accept it.'

Alice nodded, and changed the subject. 'Have you heard from the boys?'

'Not for some weeks. I expect a pile of letters will all arrive at the same time.'

'Adams!' the sergeant called. 'Report to the office at once.'

'Yes, sir!' Becky grinned at her friend. 'Another officer stranded somewhere, I expect.'

'You're getting a lot of driving jobs these days. They must be impressed with you.'

'Maybe.' She shrugged. 'I do enjoy it, and I'd better not keep them waiting. See you.'

The captain in charge of transport looked up when she walked in. 'London this time again. There are two officers at HQ who need to come here for a meeting. I see from your record you've been there several times before.'

'Yes, sir. I know where it is. Who do I ask for?'

'Major General Villiers. The car is outside and ready to go, so don't dawdle. This is important.'

'Sir!' Becky took her paperwork, saluted smartly and went out to the car, wondering what had made the captain so animated. He was usually a rather dour person, with a bored expression as a permanent feature of his face, but there was no sign of that today.

She made good time and went up to the soldier on duty. 'Transport for Major General Villiers,' she told him.

After making a quick phone call, he said, 'He'll be down in around ten minutes. Wait over there.'

'Will you give me a nod when he's coming? I haven't seen him before.'

'Right.'

Twenty minutes passed and Becky amused herself by watching the various people coming and going – civilians and military. It didn't take her long to notice that the officers were all high ranking, and there was more than usual activity. Something was going on.

Unable to contain her curiosity, she wandered over to the soldier at the desk. 'He's late. I haven't missed him, have I?'

'No, I'll let you know when you're needed.'

'There's an awful lot of top brass around. What's going on?'

'A war,' he said sarcastically. 'Hasn't anyone told you?'

'Very funny.' She didn't laugh. 'You know very well what I mean. I've been here several times over the last few months, but today is different. The atmosphere in here is fairly buzzing.'

He opened his mouth to say something when the phone rang. 'Yes, sir, your driver's here.' Then he said to her, 'Two minutes.'

She looked pointedly at her watch.

'That's him coming down the stairs now.'

'Gosh, that was only a minute.' She looked up and stared at the two officers walking towards her, unable to move.

'Jump to it,' the soldier said under his breath.

She did just that, stepping forward and saluting. 'The car is right outside the door, sir.' Then she saluted the other officer and walked out to the car, holding the rear door open for them.

Without so much as a flicker of recognition she got in the car, started it smoothly, and pulled away from the HQ. He looked exactly as he had when she had first met him, and she was sure he'd given a slight wink as he'd climbed into the car.

She took a deep breath and tried to keep her expression serious, but in truth she wanted to smile. It was good to see David again, and looking so fit. She had visited his parents several times, but this was the first time she'd seen him in months.

'Can you get us to Aldershot by two o'clock, driver?' the Major General asked. 'We're running a touch late.'

'Yes, sir.' She pressed on the accelerator. They were in a hurry, and if David had been on his own she would have asked him what the rush was all about, but with the other officer in the car she had to speak only when spoken to.

They were talking quietly in the back, but so softly she couldn't hear what was being said. However, part of her job was to be discreet and not repeat anything she might overhear while driving officers around, so she concentrated on getting them to their destination as quickly as possible. If anything important had happened, she would eventually hear about it on the news.

They arrived ten minutes before the appointed time, and she jumped out quickly to open the door. The Major General was the first out, and after telling her to wait, headed straight for the building in front of him.

When David got out she held her military pose, but did allow a slight smile to touch her lips.

He reached back in the car for his case, and said softly in her ear, 'Japan has attacked the American Fleet at Pearl Harbor.' Then he was gone.

Stunned by the news, she took her polishing cloth out of the boot and began removing any marks she could find on the car. Not that it needed this kind of attention, for it was pristine already, but it gave her something to do while she waited and pondered this momentous news. It was a terrible thing to have happened, and what would America do now? The world seemed to have gone mad, with almost every country wanting to fight someone. She longed to dash off and seek more information, but didn't dare leave her post. She had been told to wait, and that's exactly what she would do.

It was a good job she had resisted the temptation to dash off for a few minutes because they were back in just under half an hour.

'Take Colonel Hammond to his home,' the Major General instructed. 'He'll give you directions, and then drive me back to HQ.'

'Yes, sir.' She stood to attention as she held open the car door for them, wondering how David was going to handle this.

As she drove through the camp gates she decided to give David an opening. 'Where to, Colonel Hammond?'

He played along by giving her detailed directions.

'Thank you, sir. I know the road.'

She drove right up to the front door, and was out of the car in an instant, making sure she faced away from the house. The last thing she wanted was for Sara to spot her and come running out calling her name.

'Thank you,' he said as he got out. 'You are to come for me at eight hundred hours tomorrow. I shall be returning to London.'

'Eight hundred hours, sir.' She closed the door, struggling not to break into a huge smile. They might get a chance to talk if he was the only one travelling with her to London.

After dropping off the Major General, Becky headed back as fast as she could, and found the camp buzzing with speculation.

The news of the attack was now coming through, and the loss of ships and men was devastating. It had been an attack carried out without warning, and the American fleet had been caught unprepared. Everyone agree that it was a cowardly thing to do. Becky had been kept too busy and was hearing the details for the first time from Pete and Alice.

'Dear Lord.' Becky shook her head in disbelief. 'What a terrible thing for the Japanese to do, and without a declaration of war.'

'There will be now,' Pete said. 'Drink up, Becky, we're two beers ahead of you. Where have you been all day? As soon as the news broke I came looking for you.'

'I've been driving a Major General Villiers back and forth to London. And David was with him,' Becky told Alice. 'I have to take him back to London in the morning.'

'Oh, how is he?'

'He looks good, and there's no trace of a limp. We had to pretend we didn't know each other, of course. The Major General wouldn't have been amused if I'd greeted David like a friend, but it was good to see he'd recovered so completely. The next drinks are on me.'

The next morning, right on time, she pulled up outside the Hammond house, and waited by the car, as she was supposed to do.

The door opened almost immediately and David strode out, followed by Sara, the dog, and his parents. Becky held her military bearing as she saluted him and held open the car door for him.

When it looked as if his family were going to leap on Becky to say hello, he stopped them, but couldn't stop a smile turning up the corners of his mouth. 'You and the dog will have to behave yourselves, because if my driver's uniform is messed up, I'll have to put her on a charge.'

Sara shrieked with laughter. 'Oh, Daddy, you wouldn't!'

'Perhaps I'd make an exception in her case.' He swung his daughter up and hugged her, then handed her over to her grandfather. 'I don't know when I'll be home again.'

'We understand, David,' his mother said.

He turned his attention to Becky. 'Same place as yesterday, and you will be on duty all day.'

'Yes, sir.' She waited for him to settle in the back of the car, and then closed the door. Before getting in the driver's seat she gave Sara and Mr and Mrs Hammond a quick little wave, making them all laugh. She winked at the dog, sending him into ecstasy, as he tried to get at her, but Mr Hammond had a firm hold on the animal. Without wasting any time they were driving out to the road and heading for London.

She glanced in her rear-view mirror and saw that he was engrossed in some paperwork, so she remained quiet. After about half an hour she heard him sigh and toss the papers on the seat beside him.

'Do you enjoy driving us around?' he asked, breaking the silence.

'Yes, very much, Colonel. Do you enjoy working in London?'

'No, I damned well don't. I'm a soldier, not a diplomat or politician. And we're the only ones in the car, so you can stop being so formal for a while.'

She nodded. He was not in a good mood, and no matter what

he said, she wasn't going to get careless. If she started to be too informal with him, she might slip up when others were around, and that would never do. She intended to keep her record clean.

'Will we be in London for long . . . ?' She left off the 'sir' with difficulty.

'You will probably be needed all day. The Major General will give you your orders when we arrive.'

'Very good, sir.' Blast!

'What did I just tell you?'

Now she was getting cross. 'Well what am I supposed to do? You're an officer and I'm on official duty. I can't treat you informally in this situation. I just can't, sir!'

'I'm sorry, you're quite right. That was thoughtless of me.'

She was so hurt. It was very clear that a relationship between them – even friendship – was fraught with difficulties. She was beginning to be sorry she had visited his family after they'd seen Will's letter. She should have stayed away, but what could she have done? They had asked to see her, and she hadn't seen any harm in it at the time. Of course, it was always easy to be wise in hindsight, and becoming so friendly with his family had been a mistake. She was a naive fool to have allowed herself to fall for him – and that's what she had done.

'You can talk to me,' he said gently.

'The Japanese attack on the American fleet took everyone by surprise,' she said, choosing a safe subject.

'It was, and that's why the casualties were so high. Your brother's on his way there now.'

'What? How do you know that?'

'I know a great many things since they tied me to a desk job.'

'If you dislike it so much, can't you get a transfer?'

'I've been trying, and now the tide of war has taken a dramatic turn, I'll have more chance of getting back to active duty. By the way, I bought Sara two more charms to go on the bracelet you gave her. We have a job to get her to take it off even when she goes to bed.' He laughed quietly.

'I'm glad she likes it.'

'What are you doing for Christmas?'

'I'm on duty.'

'Your parents will be disappointed. Would you like me to see—?'

'No, sir!' She stopped him quickly. There was no way she was going to allow him to try and get her a pass for the holidays. His recommendation that she be sent to a transport division was in order because he had interviewed her at the recruitment office, but this was different. 'I'm quite happy to stay in camp this year. Some of us have to stay behind and I did have last Christmas at home. Will you be able to spend time with your family?'

'For a couple of days, as long as another part of the world doesn't erupt into war.'

Becky was relieved when she pulled up outside the HQ. She had been looking forward to the journey this morning and seeing David on his own for a while, but it had been awkward, to say the least. She got out and opened the door for him.

'You'd better come in and find out what your orders are for the day. They will have been left with the reception.'

She watched him take the stairs two at a time, and then turned to the man on duty. 'I believe orders have been left with you for me. I'm Major General Villiers' driver.'

He handed her the written instructions, then nodded towards the stairs. 'Your last passenger's a brave man, from all I've heard.'

She didn't comment, but studied her duties. 'I'm going to be needed all day, so is there anywhere I can wait?'

'There's a room set aside for drivers.' He pointed to his left. 'Wait in there and I'll call you when you're needed. There's sandwiches and tea provided.'

'Thanks.'

She didn't get much chance to enjoy the facilities, and it was a very busy day as she drove various officers, and even civilians, from one meeting to another. By six o'clock she was tired and hungry as she brought the Major General back to the HQ.

'You won't be needed again today,' he told her. 'You can return to Aldershot.'

'Yes, sir. Will Colonel Hammond be returning with me?'

'No, he's staying the night.' He started to walk away, then turned back to her. 'You have performed your duties well today. You know your way around London.'

'Thank you, sir. I was born and bred here.'

He studied her intently for a moment, and with a slight nod of his head, he walked away.

'You've impressed him,' the soldier on duty told her. 'And he isn't easily pleased. He got rid of two drivers because they didn't come up to his expectations.'

She rotated her stiff shoulders. 'It's nice to know he's happy with the way I do the job. Can I get a cup of tea and something to eat before I head back to camp?'

'Just go and help yourself. You know where it is.'

With her hunger satisfied and feeling more relaxed she headed out of London. She hadn't seen David at all during the long day, and it seemed lonely to have an empty car. She'd certainly had an assortment of interesting passengers, but as much as she'd enjoyed the day, it was good to be going back to camp. She was looking forward to having a beer and a laugh with her friends.

Twenty

After the attack on Pearl Harbor on 7th December, events moved with speed. On 8th December President Roosevelt made a speech, calling the attack 'a day of infamy'. Britain, Canada and the Allies declared war on Japan, and on 11th December Hitler declared war on the United States, which, in response, declared war on Germany and Italy. In just a few days the whole picture of the war had changed.

During this time Becky had been called upon to drive Major General Villiers twice, but there had been no sign of David. She hoped he had been able to return to his regiment. It was what he wanted.

The mess was filled with chatter and laughter as she arrived to enjoy a festive meal on Christmas Day.

'Over here, Becky.' Pete was waving and holding out a seat he'd saved for her.

'Oh thanks.' She grimaced. 'What a racket.'

'Everyone's in high spirits. We've had a hard fight to stop Germany adding Britain to its list of conquests, but we held out, and now we're no longer alone, Becky. The tide has at last turned in our favour.'

'You sound as if you think the war is as good as over,' she laughed.

'Far from it. We still have a long battle ahead of us, with defeats as well as victories, but with our combined efforts we'll have a greater chance of defeating the Nazis.'

'I'll drink to that.' She raised her glass in salute, and everyone around her did the same.

At the end of the meal the camp commander called for quiet. 'I'm sorry to put a damper on the festivities, but we have just received news that Hong Kong has surrendered to the Japanese.'

There were groans all round and Becky nudged Pete's arm. 'It didn't take long for a defeat to happen, did it? What next, I wonder?'

'Well, brace yourself because I hear that the Americans will start arriving here at the end of January. Boatloads of them.'

She couldn't help bursting into laughter when she saw the differing expressions around the table. 'That's good, isn't it?'

'Good for you girls, but how on earth are we going to compete with them? I'm told they're better paid and better dressed. We're not going to stand a chance.'

'Pete! You're a happily married man.'

'I know.' He gave a comical leer at her. 'But I can look, can't I?'

That broke the gloom of the bad news about Hong Kong, and had everyone laughing again. It was Christmas and they were all determined to enjoy it.

Once the tables were cleared, one of the men played the piano and they all sang at the tops of their voices, determined to make the most of this festive season in camp. Many of them not on duty that night had a little too much to drink, but Becky kept her intake modest. Only once she'd had too much and hadn't liked the feeling at all. It wasn't something she was going to repeat.

It was around midnight when she finally made it to bed. She missed her family, but it wouldn't have been right to allow David to wangle her a pass.

She drifted off to sleep, thinking of all those she loved, and hoping they were safe and had been able to celebrate Christmas in some way, wherever they were.

The next day Becky was given a driving assignment. She wasn't surprised, for with so much going on it was doubtful if many of those in charge had time to enjoy the festive season.

'You've made quite an impression with your driving,' the duty officer told her. 'Colonel Hammond has asked for you. You are to collect him from his home and take him wherever he needs to go. It will be a long day, and you will be his driver until he dismisses you.'

'Yes, sir. Will Major General Villiers be there as well?'

'It's only the Colonel this time. He has requested a driver because he is still recovering from injuries he received in France.'

Becky nearly burst out laughing, but managed to control herself. 'Really, sir?'

'Don't keep him waiting.'

She took her instructions, tucked them in her pocket and marched out to collect the car, wondering what David was up to.

He was stretching the truth more than a little, for as far as she had seen he was fully recovered.

Within half an hour she was there, and when the maid answered her knock, she said, 'Would you tell Colonel Hammond his car's here, please?'

Mrs Hammond immediately appeared. 'Come in, Rebecca, and say hello to everyone.'

'I'm on duty, Mrs Hammond, and ought to stay with the car.'

'David said you were to come in and wait.'

'Oh, in that case . . .' Becky followed Mrs Hammond into the lounge and was greeted by the family. There was no sign of David.

Mr Hammond gestured her to a chair. 'We're so glad you could make it, Rebecca.'

'Er . . .' She was confused. They were acting as if this was a social visit. 'I was told to report to the colonel as his driver for the day.'

They were all smiling, highly amused about something, when David strolled into the room wearing civilian clothes and an expression of innocence.

It dawned on her what everyone was finding so amusing. 'Oh dear, I've got a nasty feeling I could get into trouble. If you don't need a driver, then I must return to camp at once.' He was up to his tricks again, and she wasn't going to have this. She turned to leave.

'Stay where you are.'

She spun back. 'Look, it's lovely to see you all, but this isn't right. I like the army and love what I'm doing, and when this war's over I might even consider staying in, so I will not do anything to put a blot on my record.'

'Stop worrying and sit down.' David stepped up and led her to a chair. 'I am returning to my regiment, but my plans have changed and I'm not leaving until after lunch.'

She stood up again, relieved. 'Oh. In that case I'd better come back this afternoon. What time will you need me?'

'You will stay here until I need you – and that's an order.' He was every inch the officer now.

'Daddy, don't tell Rebecca off,' Sara protested, taking hold of Becky's hand. 'Please stay. I want to show you my presents, and I've painted another picture for you. I told Daddy I wanted to see you.' She turned to her father, her little face worried. 'This is my fault, isn't it, Daddy? We mustn't upset Rebecca, because it's Christmas.'

David stooped down in front of his daughter. 'No, sweetheart, it isn't your fault. We all wanted to see Rebecca, but she's on duty over Christmas, and this was the only way I could think to get her here.'

'Oh.' Her face cleared and she smiled at Becky. 'Please stay. Daddy will see it's all right.'

What could she do? It was silly being so paranoid about not breaking the rules, but if a full-blown colonel said she had to wait here for him, then that's what she had to do. But she didn't like him bending the rules to get her here. She unbuttoned her jacket, cleared the indignant expression from her face, and smiled at the little girl. 'Where are these lovely presents you've had?'

'You stay there and I'll bring them to you.' Excited now, Sara bounced out of the room.

'Don't forget the painting,' she called. She sat down then and had to fend off the dog as it tried to sit on her lap.'

'Stop that, Becky!' Mr Hammond hauled the animal away. 'You're far too big to go clambering over people now.'

The dog gave a disgruntled huff and sat by the fire, never taking his eyes off her. 'Now that's settled I think we'll all have tea and a piece of Christmas cake,' Mrs Hammond said.

Sara came back with her arms laden with parcels and a painting sticking out of her teeth. Becky took the painting from her and was rather disconcerted to see the little girl had attempted a painting of her father, in full uniform. 'Oh, that's lovely,' she said, not daring to look at David. 'Thank you so much, Sara.'

'I thought you could put it with the other one,' Sara suggested. 'I'll do Grandma and Grandpa next for you.'

'And one of yourself,' Becky suggested, 'then I'll have everyone.'

'All right.' Sara beamed at the idea, and then began to show her gifts one by one, and they were all duly admired. It was while she was chatting to Sara that the tea trolley came in, and Becky could hardly believe her eyes. 'Is that real icing on the Christmas cake?'

'Yes.' Mrs Hammond cut a generous slice and handed it to Becky. 'I had the ingredients in my store cupboard.'

The cake was delicious and she relaxed, telling everyone what Christmas had been like at the camp. David said nothing, and from the expression on his face she suspected that he was feeling smug that his ploy had worked.

Finally, she just had to make him say something. 'You must be pleased to be returning to duty. It's what you said you wanted.'

'I am, and it is. I'm considering having you transferred to Bordon as my permanent driver.'

She choked on a mouthful of cake, and when she'd recovered, she glared at him. His eyes were shining with amusement. Damn him! 'Don't you dare. I like it where I am.'

While he chuckled quietly, she turned to his parents, shaking her head. 'I'll bet you had trouble with him when he was growing up.'

'Oh, my dear, the tales we could tell you.' Mrs Hammond sighed in mock horror. 'There was that time—'

'Mother!'

They all dissolved into laughter as he stopped his mother, and Becky knew then that he had been, and still was, a handful.

'Tell me what Daddy did.' Sara giggled, enjoying the fun.

'I'm afraid you'll have to wait until you're older. Some of the tales are not fit for little girls' ears.'

Sara pulled a face at Becky. 'I'm always being told that.'

David stood up. 'I'll take Rebecca out of harm's way before my life history is aired. We'll be in my study for a while. Call us when lunch is ready.'

He waited for her to stand, and she couldn't resist saying, 'Are you ordering me?'

'Of course.'

She followed him and fell in love with the study as soon as she saw it. The room was lined with bookshelves and crammed with volumes she would have loved to browse through. There was a large oak desk with a dark green leather top, and matching leather chairs around the room. There was also a wood fire burning in the grate. As soon as the door was closed she faced him, determined to make her position clear. 'I'm finding it difficult to tell if you're the officer I must obey, or a friend who's intent on teasing me. You're not being fair, David. I'm quite prepared to keep the two separate, but you must help me here. If I'm on duty then you are the officer, but otherwise I am a friend. Is that so?'

'I would like to be more than a friend, Rebecca, but I agree that the blasted uniform keeps getting in the way. My parents, Sara, and even the dog love you . . .'

She drew in a deep breath. 'What are you saying?'

'I'm not going to lie to you, but getting trapped in France made me see quite clearly that I might not survive this war. I was worried about my daughter growing up without a mother or father. I need a wife who will be a good mother to my daughter. I've been attracted to you since the moment you walked into the recruitment office. I know I'm older than you, but I can give you all the good things in life, and a ready-made family. It would ease my mind to know Sara had someone to love and care for her should the worse happen.'

'You're asking me to marry you?' When he nodded she didn't think she could hurt so much. Not a word of love or affection. Attraction, yes, but that wasn't enough. 'David,' she said, her voice husky with emotion, 'I appreciate you being honest about this, so I'm going to do the same. You are offering me material things, and the care of your lovely daughter. I agree that Sara needs a mother, but marriage without a true and abiding love on both sides wouldn't do for me. I'm sorry, but I'm going to refuse.'

He studied her expression carefully, and then took a deep breath. 'I do care very much for you, but I loved too deeply the first time, and that ended in sadness. I'm not sure I want that intensity again, but we could be happy together. Does it worry you that I'm older than you?'

'That doesn't even come into it, David. But what does concern me is that I'm just an ordinary girl from Stepney with an elementary education. You need a wife who can stand by your side at important functions – one who has been brought up to mix and be at ease in the company you keep as an officer. I'd be terrified all the time that I was letting you down.'

'Rebecca, you're a caring, loving, bright girl, and I don't give a damn about your background.'

'You tell yourself that now, because your main concern is to have a mother for your daughter, but the day would come when you'd look at me and wonder how I was going to handle certain people who might be important to you. I care too much for you to do that to either of us.'

'That doesn't say much for me, does it?' He was clearly hurt by her words. 'I know you would never let me down, or Sara. I wouldn't be asking you to marry me if I wasn't sure it was the right thing to do.'

'I know, and you must have had a lot of time to think about it while you were trying to get home again.' She was desperate to make him understand why she was refusing. 'David, I am who I am, and not ashamed of it, but a girl who likes nothing better than to take engines apart and get covered in grease is not the right person for you. You need a sophisticated, cultured woman who will help your career by entertaining the upper classes when necessary. I do love you, but I'd be like a fish out of water.'

She took a deep, shuddering breath. 'Please understand, for both our sakes, that I am not the woman for you, no matter how much I might wish to be. It just wouldn't work. You must see that.'

He was absolutely still for a moment, then stepped towards her, running his fingers gently down her cheek. 'You think too much, and I wish you weren't so sensible.'

'Perhaps it was growing up with the boys that made me aware of life from a male point of view. Or maybe I'm just a fool and throwing away the greatest chance of happiness I'll ever have.'

'The last thing you are is a fool, Rebecca.' He dipped his head and kissed her lingeringly, folding her in his arms. When he reluctantly broke the embrace, he said, 'Is there the faintest chance that will change your mind?'

She shook her head, unable to speak.

'I didn't think it would, but I've wanted to do that from the moment I saw you.'

Becky's head was reeling. She had never been kissed like that before, but David was a full-grown man – and she was a fool! But deep inside she knew she had made the right decision. What he felt for her was physical attraction, and he saw a suitable mother for his daughter. She could understand his motives, but a marriage like that would tear her apart, and ultimately bring unhappiness to his family. He was offering her a marriage of convenience, but this wasn't the 1800s. At least he wasn't trying to deceive her into thinking it would be a love match.

He stood back, 'You won't marry me, so where does that leave us?'

'That leaves us with friendship,' she said sadly.

David grimaced. 'Not enough – but it will have to do – for the moment. I want you to keep visiting Sara and my parents, please.'

'Of course.' She wondered what he meant by 'for the moment'.

He held out his hand. 'Friends?'

She nodded and smiled as they shook hands. 'One day you'll thank me for turning you down.'

'I doubt that very much, my little mechanical genius. But I want you to know that I understand everything you've said, even though I don't agree, and my respect for you has deepened even more. You're a special girl, Rebecca, and I warn you now that I haven't taken your refusal as final. I'm not a man to give up this easily.'

'Oh, one day an elegant woman will come into your life and you'll soon forget about me.'

'Never! You will always be a part of our lives now. Your caring heart has touched us all.' He smiled down at her. 'Now, we must join the others for lunch.'

Twenty-One

'Is it all right if I wish you a belated happy New Year?' Alice tipped her head to one side, examining Becky carefully.

'Of course, and a happy 1942 to you as well. Did you have a good Christmas with your family?'

'Lovely, but what's happened, Becky? You're troubled. Are the boys all right?'

'As far as I know.' Becky glanced around the mess to see if they would be overheard if she spoke freely, but they were sitting at a table away from everyone else. Whatever was said between them would not be heard.

When Becky still hesitated, Alice prompted, 'It sometimes helps to talk things through, and whatever you tell me won't go any further. If it isn't the boys, then it must be the colonel. What's he been up to now?'

Becky couldn't help laughing. 'There you go again, Alice. Are you sure you can't read minds?'

'Positive. Though I am good at reading expressions. Talk, my friend, and you'll feel better. It was something I should have done after Anthony was killed, but I kept it all inside me. I knew that had been a big mistake as soon as I saw Jim at the funeral of his parents. Tell me, Becky,' she urged gently.

'On Boxing Day, in the morning, I was given a driving job. I had to go and collect David, and be his driver for the day. When I arrived I found he wouldn't be going anywhere until the afternoon . . .'

Alice settled as comfortably as she could in the hard chairs, and listened as the story poured out.

'Am I a fool, Alice? Did I do the right thing?'

'That isn't for me to say. You did what you thought was right, and that's all any of us can do. Don't hold on to regrets or doubts, or you will be hurting yourself unnecessarily. I know you adore the man, and I think you've been brave and sensible. My opinion, for what it's worth, is that you've probably saved both of you a lot of future pain.'

Becky nodded. 'That's how I feel. He didn't try to fool me into thinking it was a great passion on his part. He wants a mother for his daughter, and as I get on so well with Sara and his parents . . . Well.' She took a deep breath. 'He finds me attractive and amusing, and that might be enough for him but it isn't for me. My mum and dad love each other through the good and the bad times, and that's the kind of marriage I want.'

'Then you must wait for it.' Alice reached across and patted her arm. 'Don't accept second best, and as far as I can see, that's what he's offering you. You would have had to leave the army, and I know you don't want to do that. If anyone was made for this kind of life, it's you, and I expect he knows you would make an understanding wife for a career soldier. He's also very concerned for his little daughter and his family; after all, it isn't fair to expect grandparents to bring up a child. They should be thinking of retirement now and some time to themselves. But he's asking too much of you, Becky.'

'I'd have been prepared to do all of that if I'd been sure he really loved me, but he's never once used that word. He's choosing with his head and not his heart, and that makes me doubtful about marrying him.'

'Then you've done the right thing. Remain his friend and write to him, and keep visiting his family. And be happy, Becky. You had enough sense not to fall into a golden trap, and in time, you'll both be grateful it's turned out this way.'

'You're right.' Becky sat up straight and smiled at her friend. 'Thank you for listening; I feel better now.'

'Good.' Alice glanced at the clock on the wall. 'What say we go to the dance in the Town Hall tonight? Music and lively company will do us both good. You know, we are all living unnatural lives at the moment, and with the danger, uncertainty, and never knowing if someone you love is going to die suddenly, it's easy to become confused. Many hasty marriages are taking place which could end in unhappiness.'

'You're right again. Decisions are being made that wouldn't have been considered in peace time.' Becky was on her feet, smiling now. 'Let's go and see if we can cadge a lift to the dance.'

'I've already arranged it in the hope I could persuade you to come dancing,' Alice told her as they walked out of the mess. 'Where is the colonel stationed now?'

'I drove him to Bordon after lunch, and after he'd checked in I took him and another officer to Headley Down, and left them there. They were getting a lift back to Bordon later in the day.'

'Isn't that where the Canadians are based?'

'Yes, Headley Down is quite close to Bordon. I met some of the Canadians and they seemed a nice bunch.' Becky grinned. 'They insisted I have coffee and something to eat before driving back. Anyone would have thought I'd had a long journey instead of only a few miles.'

'We'll have to see if we can get an invite there some time. When you write to the colonel ask him if they hold dances at the camp, and if so, could we come, please. Don't forget to add the "please".'

'Alice, you're incorrigible.'

'Don't look so shocked. Nearly all the girls here would jump at the chance to go. It's no good having contacts in high places if you don't ask the occasional favour And you've been learning some long words lately, haven't you?'

'I do know a few,' she joked. 'Anyway, I'll do what you suggest, but if David is able to arrange something, then you'll have to organize the girls.'

'Perhaps we could take a lorry or two full of girls.' Alice was enthusiastic about the idea. 'I'm quite happy to make the arrangements here. Write to him tonight.'

Becky glanced at her friend. 'I'm pleased to see you're beginning to socialize again.'

'I made Anthony a promise that I would get on with my life if he was killed. He knew his chances of surviving were not good, and he didn't want me to waste my life grieving for too long. I intend to keep my promise, hard though it is.' Her smile was tinged with deep sadness. 'When I've had a bad day and tears come too easily, I feel as if he's standing beside me saying, "Come on, my girl, that's enough of that!"'

'So he might be for all we know.'

'True, and if that's the case then he'll be glad we're going dancing tonight.'

There was quite a crowd waiting to get on the lorry to take them to the dance, and when Pete saw Becky, he called her over.

'I'm glad you're coming. You don't drink much, do you?'

Laughing, she said, 'In other words, will I stay sober and drive back?'

'Oh, thanks for offering. I can relax and enjoy myself now.'

'I didn't offer, but if I think you've had too much I will take over.'

'You're a pal. You're the most sensible girl on the camp.'

She pulled a face, remembering what David had said. 'I've been called that before.'

'Right, everyone in,' Pete shouted, 'and you'll all be pleased to know we've got a relief driver. If the top brass are safe with her, then we certainly are.'

A cheer went up and a voice called, 'Good on ya, Becky. Save the first dance for me.'

She looked straight at Aussie, as everyone called him. He was English really, but had lived in Australia for some years, and as soon as war had been declared he'd come straight back and volunteered. He was also another survivor of Dunkirk. 'Can they dance down under?'

'Sure, I'll show you some real fancy footwork.'

A lot of teasing and rude remarks were flying around as everyone climbed in the back of the lorry.

Pete beckoned to Becky and Alice. 'You two are in the front with me. You don't want to cram in with that rough crowd.'

The Town Hall was packed when they arrived, and Aussie immediately whisked Becky on to the dance floor. As it turned out he hadn't been boasting and was an excellent dancer. So was she; her father had taught her, and had even shown her how to do the Charleston. They'd had such fun dancing around the kitchen table to jazz music.

The girls were never without partners for the entire evening. They might be living in uncertain times, but everyone loved to forget the war for a while and dance. It was a favourite way to spend an evening. Alice and Becky smiled at each other with understanding as they let off steam, pushing the heartaches, doubts and fears to the background for a few hours.

As expected, Pete had had far too much to drink, so Becky drove the lorry back to camp at the end of the evening. She had been careful to only have soft drinks. It didn't worry her because most of the time she would rather have a cup of tea, never having acquired much of a taste for alcohol.

When they all tumbled out of the lorry at camp and made their way to the various billets, Alice caught Becky's arm.

'Don't forget to write to your colonel before you turn in.'

'Not tonight,' she groaned. 'I'm too tired.'

'All right, but do it in the morning before you go on duty.'

'You're a slave driver, Alice. Is this how you treat your Major?'

'Of course; it's the only way to get things done, so you be sure to do the letter.'

'I promise, but he probably won't even answer.'

'I'll bet you five shillings he does, and right away. It's a good idea.'

'You're on!' she said before they went their separate ways, with smiles on their faces, each one confident they were going to win the bet.

Four days later a letter arrived from David saying that he liked the idea of a dance for the Canadians, and if they could manage to fill a lorry with girls, he'd see what he could do about setting it up. The Canadians would love a chance to meet some of the ATS, and he'd let her know the date as soon as possible.

Becky paid a smug-looking Alice her winnings.

Twenty-Two

The notice about the dance to be held at Headley Down came through official channels. All women who would like to attend were instructed to give their names to Major Brent. It was no surprise to Becky that David had enlisted the help of the Major, because she knew the two men were good friends. The arrangements were left to Alice, as expected.

'My goodness,' Alice said as she counted the names on the list. 'Well over half the women at this camp want to come.'

Becky leant across to study the list. 'Hmm. Three lorries might do it.'

'Will you drive one?'

'I don't mind, but it's not up to me. You must see the officer in charge. He'll allocate the lorries and choose the drivers.'

'Right.' Alice stood up. 'I'll do that now. You coming with me?'

After glancing at her watch, Becky shook her head. 'Sorry, I've got to take your Major to London in half an hour.'

'Oh, I didn't know you were to be his driver.'

'Word seems to have got out that I know my way around London, and I'm getting most of those runs. I don't know what time I'll be back.'

'Make him get a move on and I'll meet you in the NAAFI this evening.'

Becky laughed. 'You might talk to him like that, but I'll be on a charge if I do.'

'No you won't. He's a sweetie really. You tell him I've got a drink lined up for you.'

'I won't do anything of the kind.' Becky studied her friend and pursed her lips. 'You know, when I first met you at the recruitment office, I thought you were posh. Someone without a hair out of place and determined to get on in life. But you're nothing like that, are you? The person you present in your job is quite different from your true nature. You're like the boys – the same devilish sense of humour and likely to get me into trouble quite easily.'

Alice laughed out loud. 'Darn it, you've worked it out at last. I'll tell your commander that you've volunteered to drive one lorry, shall I?'

Raising her hands in surrender, Becky shook her head. 'You'll do whatever you want, no matter what I say. I don't know how your Major puts up with you.'

'Ask him.' Alice winked at Becky, then marched away, heading for the transport section.

Having a few minutes to spare, Becky went to check that the car was in order, a thoughtful expression on her face. Since Anthony had been killed her friend had changed. It was as if she was determined to enjoy every day, and in that way honour her promise to him. All news, good or bad, was taken calmly. When it was bad she would say that the tide would change – it always did. The loss of the man she loved had made her more resilient, stronger. Perhaps the danger and uncertainty they were living through now was doing the same to all of them. Who knows, she thought, giving the windscreen of the car an extra buff. It was easier to see the changes in other people than in yourself.

She was always very careful to be punctual, and Major Brent appeared as soon as she drove up to the door.

They had been driving for about fifteen minutes when he said, 'Are you looking forward to the dance?'

'Yes, sir. Thank you for arranging it.'

'No trouble. Fortunately I have a very efficient assistant.'

Becky hid her smile, knowing full well that Alice was doing all the work. 'Will you be coming, sir?'

'I'll be there, but the officers will be keeping well out of the way. I shall be dining with Colonel Hammond and the Canadian officers.'

That answered the question lingering in her mind. It was unlikely she would see David. 'Will you be needing a driver, sir?'

'No, I shall be taking my own car. I will only be in London for about two hours today, and would like to be back by seven at the latest.'

'Yes, sir.' The subject of the dance had been closed, so she settled to enjoy the next few hours. Driving was her passion, and she was grateful to the army for giving her such excellent, wide-ranging training. She secretly hoped to be given her own officer one day. It would be a permanent assignment she would love, and that was why she was careful to see that her passengers had a comfortable and trouble-free ride so they arrived at their destination relaxed.

The girls had all decided to wear their best frocks for the dance, and ditch the uniforms for a change, but this posed a problem for Becky. The only frock she had was a summer one – the same she'd worn when David had taken her out for dinner. After their house had been bombed she should have bought some new clothes, but she hadn't bothered. She did have the decent coat she'd been given for Christmas, and the cardigan from Mrs Hammond. She should have brought more of her clothes with her, but she hadn't known the damned Luftwaffe was going to drop a bomb right on their house. The old frock would have to do because she couldn't be the only one to turn up in uniform.

'What are you wearing?' Alice asked, as they snatched an afternoon cup of tea together.

'I've only got one frock. It's a bit old, but it'll look all right after a press.'

Alice shook her head in disapproval. 'The first chance we get I'm taking you shopping. You don't care much about clothes, do you?'

'I was always with the boys, messing about with the old motorbike, so it didn't seem to matter what I wore.'

'I'll have to cure you of that,' Alice told her. 'You're such a pretty girl, and ought to wear nice things. I wonder . . . Come with me.'

They went to Alice's billet and she pulled a case out from under her bunk. It was full of clothes.

'Your things won't fit me,' Becky protested. 'You're at least three inches shorter, and I'm a larger build.'

'I know that, but I'm handy with a needle.' She rummaged in the box and pulled out a dark green skirt. 'This is too long for me. Now, what can we put with it? Ah, this, I think.'

'Oh that's lovely, but I'll never get in that.' Her friend was holding up a cream blouse covered in self-coloured embroidery.

'Hmm.' Alice examined the garment. 'It's got short sleeves, so that won't be a problem. I could move the buttons over and let out a couple of darts. We've got a few minutes to try the skirt and blouse on so I can see what needs to be done.'

Becky was sure this was a waste of time, but her friend was insistent, so she did as ordered. The skirt wouldn't fasten, and neither would the blouse. She was disappointed because they were nice. 'I told you they wouldn't fit.'

Alice ignored her, tugging and measuring. 'Don't fuss. The skirt's long enough, and as it's full, the hips are no problem; I just need to alter the waist. There's two darts back and front of the blouse, and that should make it big enough for you.' She stood back to take a good look. 'It suits you. Take it off, and I'll have it ready by tonight. What about shoes? There's no way mine will fit you.'

'I've got a pair of black shoes with a small heel.'

'They'll have to do.'

Becky hurriedly dressed again in her army trousers and shirt. 'I've got to get back.'

'Come here an hour before we leave for the dance, and that will give me enough time to make any last-minute alterations.'

'I'll bring my frock with me – just in case.'

'There's no need; I know what I'm doing. Now go, or you'll be late.' Alice waved her away, already picking at stitches.

There was great excitement in the camp as the girls anticipated the evening ahead, and as instructed Becky went to Alice early. Her friend was a picture in lilac, with her blonde hair loose for a change. Her frock had short sleeves, fitted to the waist, and then fell away to flare around the hem. The only jewellery she wore was the gold chain with Anthony's ring hanging from it. It brought a lump to Becky's throat. 'Just wait until those Canadians get a look at you,' she teased. 'I'll get crushed in the stampede.'

Her friend waved away the compliment. 'Come on, try these now.'

Much to her amazement the skirt and blouse fitted perfectly, and when she looked at herself in the mirror she could hardly believe it. She looked smart and elegant, which was unusual for her, she thought wryly.

Alice did a final check and then stood back, viewing her friend critically. 'It's a treat to get you out of shirt and trousers. You've got a lovely shape, and no wonder the colonel finds you attractive enough to want to marry you. With a bit of care and decent clothes you're stunning, and he knows that. He's not daft, is he?'

'He might believe he could make me look the part, but the illusion would end the moment I opened my mouth. But don't let us talk about things that can never be, and just enjoy ourselves tonight.'

'Good idea. Subject closed.' Alice picked up her bag. 'You're driving by the way.'

'I already know that.'

There was a lot of laughter and excited chatter from the girls as they climbed into the lorries. Men weren't allowed on this trip and quite a few were standing around complaining bitterly about being left out. Even the drivers were women.

When they arrived at the camp a Canadian soldier jumped in beside Alice, looked across at Becky and said, 'I'll show you where to park.'

'Thanks.'

'Straight on, past the first huts, turn right and you'll see a crowd of eager men waiting to escort you to the mess. We've made it look real good.' Then he swivelled around to look at the girl in the back. 'Evening, ladies, we're going to have a great night.'

Becky parked and the other lorries followed, stopping in a neat row. So many girls had wanted to come, but they had just managed to get them all on three lorries. As soon as the engines were turned off, men swarmed around to help the girls down.

The men had certainly worked hard to transform the room into a suitable dance hall. The place was decorated with streamers, and Canadian and British flags were everywhere. As soon as they stepped inside and were divested of their coats, the Canadian band struck up a lively quick step, and the evening was under way.

They were such a good crowd, and as there were more men than women, all the girls were swung on to the dance floor without a chance to rest.

'My feet are killing me,' Becky gasped, trying to catch her breath after a particularly energetic dance.

'Well, they're playing the last waltz . . .'

That was all Alice had time to say as they were both pounced upon for the dance.

After both the national anthems were played, they were formally thanked for coming, and were given a round of applause for making it such an enjoyable evening.

'I'd better round up the girls,' Alice said.

'And the best of luck,' Becky remarked. 'I have a feeling some might be missing.'

'I'll sort them out.' Alice did a good impression of a sergeant major as she set about gathering up all the girls.

Becky began walking towards the lorries parked a short distance away, and because of the strict blackout it was quite dark.

'Did you enjoy the evening?' a quiet male voice asked as he fell into step beside her.

Startled, she spun round and was looking up at David. 'Oh yes, very much, and the men seemed to have a good time as well.'

'So they should with three lorry loads of attractive girls to dance with.'

Everyone was now streaming over to the vehicles. 'Thank you for arranging this for us. I must go, but I'll write and tell you all about it.'

'You're driving?'

She nodded.

'I'll walk with you.' When he saw her doubtful expression, he said, 'Don't worry, Rebecca. You're not in uniform, and you were the one who asked me to set up this entertainment, so it's only natural I should want to know how it went.'

'Yes, Colonel,' she said in a clear voice in case anyone wondered what she was doing with an officer.

'You look lovely in that outfit. Did you buy it for this evening?'

'No, it belongs to Alice, and she altered it to fit me. Er . . . how did you know what I was wearing?'

'I slipped in, unseen, a couple of times, just to make sure the men were behaving.'

'You needn't have worried on that score. They're the politest bunch of soldiers I've come across.'

'I also wanted to see you as well.' He caught hold of her arm and stopped her walking. 'Will you marry me, Rebecca?'

'Pardon?' She was more than surprised by his proposal. 'I thought we'd agreed to be friends after I refused last time?'

'I did tell you that I wasn't about to give up yet. I've decided to ask you six times, and then I will accept your refusal, but not until then. So, what is your answer?'

Taking a deep breath she said, 'My answer is the same, and you already know the reasons. I can't marry you; it wouldn't work, David.'

'I disagree. However, I still have four more chances. Drive carefully, Rebecca.' Then he spun on his heel and disappeared into the shadows.

'He's not going to give up, is he?'

Becky jumped. 'Oh, Alice, you gave me a start. Have you rounded up the girls?'

'All present and correct. And stop changing the subject. Your colonel isn't giving up, is he?'

'He won't take no for an answer.'

'Ah, he's determined to wear you down. I do like him.'

'So do I, and that's the trouble.'

They reached the lorries and Alice did a quick count just to make sure all the girls were there, and with the help of the soldiers they were soon in the lorries. The soldier who had joined them at the gate as they came in jumped into the cab again. His name was Rob, and he was evidently doing the same job as Alice.

'Great evening.' He cast Becky a curious look. 'I saw you talking with the British Colonel. Do you know him?'

'I've been his driver a few times.' Becky looked out of the window, waiting for the signal to tell her everyone was ready to go.

As they pulled away and headed for the gate, Rob turned his attention back to Becky. 'We've heard some stories about that colonel. We were told that he could have saved himself at Dunkirk, but wouldn't leave his men. No wonder his men respect him so much. I also heard he's up for a medal; you know anything about that?'

'No.' Becky shook her head. At least she could answer that honestly.

Rob jumped out at the gates. 'You gals are welcome here any time. Great of you to come.'

Alice waved as they swept out of the camp. 'Phew, what a night.'

'You can say that again,' Becky laughed. 'I'll bet some of the girls will be coming here again.'

'Bound to. It's good to see the different nationalities mixing like this.'

'Yes, it was a good idea.' Becky fell silent, concentrating on her driving; she had a lot to think about.

Twenty-Three

'Sorry, sir,' Becky gasped as she slammed her foot on the brakes, making the car come to a shuddering halt. 'They just stepped off the pavement without looking. Are you all right?' She turned round, anxious to check that her passenger was unharmed.

Major General Villiers gave a wry smile as he gathered up his scattered papers. 'It wasn't your fault. They drive on the other side of the road in America.'

'Of course. That's why they were looking the wrong way.'

There was a tap on the window, and she opened it. Two faces peered in. 'Hey honey, you all right? We ain't got used to the traffic here yet.'

'We're fine, thank you, but you must be more careful. I nearly ran into you.'

One of the soldiers was nudging his friend. 'High rank in the back, Ed.'

The one called Ed leant further into the car to get a good look at the Major General, and then he grinned. 'Sorry, sir.'

'Apology accepted. Now, kindly step away from the car; you are making us late for an appointment.'

'OK.' Ed's head disappeared smartly and the two soldiers stood to attention as Becky drove away, still with wide grins on their faces. They had gathered quite a crowd and she could hear them laughing.

She continued with caution, not trusting the new arrivals to stay on the pavements. 'Good Lord,' she murmured, 'they're everywhere.'

'And intent on enjoying themselves,' the officer remarked. 'Nice driving, by the way. You have excellent reflexes.'

'Thank you, sir.' The Major General was asking for her quite often now, and she was more at ease with him, but it was quite something to be given a compliment by him.

'When we reach the War Office we are to collect Admiral Jamison. You will take us both to the Houses of Parliament for a meeting with the Prime Minister.'

'Yes, sir.'

They were only five minutes late but Becky saw the Admiral glancing irritably at his watch. She jumped out and marched up to him. 'I apologize for keeping you waiting, Admiral, but we had an incident on the way and it delayed us. Major General Williams is waiting for you in the car.'

'What was the incident?' he asked, striding ahead of her.

She had to move sharply to reach the car before him so she could open the door. 'Two Americans stepped off the kerb without looking, sir. I nearly hit them.'

His only reply sounded like a grunt, and she wasted no time in getting under way again. The Admiral didn't seem too happy.

Normally she blocked out any conversation going on in the back of the car, but something about shipping caught her attention.

'The losses for March have been the most we've sustained so far. We're losing ships at an alarming rate.'

Becky went cold. Bob was out there somewhere.

'Come on, mate!'

Bob was so cold he couldn't feel the hands reaching out to haul him into the lifeboat. He sprawled in the bottom of the small boat and managed to gasp, 'Thanks.'

'Sit up,' someone ordered. 'And start moving. You've got to get the blood circulating.'

'Sod off!' He just wanted to be left alone and go to sleep.

'You sleep now and you're a dead man, and I'm not gonna let you do that. So move yourself, and flap your arms around. I'll rub your legs to get the life back in them for you.'

Bob was dragged to a sitting position and someone was pummelling him until he hurt. He wasn't sure it was a good idea to get the feeling back in his body. When the second torpedo had struck he'd been thrown across the deck, crashing with force against something. When he'd regained consciousness the ship was going down fast and he'd just had to jump into the sea and swim away from the stricken ship. The rubbing and pulling carried on, and he managed to open one eye to peer at his tormentor. When he saw it was his friend he could have cried with relief. 'Thank God you made it, Reg. I was looking for you when the second hit came.'

'And nearly got yourself killed. Now, come on, mate, make an effort to move. That water's still bloody cold.'

It took a tremendous effort, but Bob began to move his legs and flap his arms, groaning all the time.

'Are you injured?' Reg was trying to pull his clothes away so he could inspect him. 'You've got some vicious marks across your body.'

'They're only bruises.' He clasped Reg's arm. 'You all right?'

His friend nodded, then spun round when a cry for help was heard. There were eight already in the boat, and each one was now anxiously searching the sea.

'Over there,' Bob gasped. 'I think there's someone in that direction.'

Men grabbed at the oars and moved as fast as they could in the direction of the faint cries.

They found two men in the water, but one was dead, and the other not far off. They pulled him into the boat and began to try and warm him up.

'There's another lifeboat over there!' someone called.

When they reached it there were twelve men in it; some were all right, but a couple were in a bad way. They lashed the two boats together, and then set about searching for any other survivors. They found no one else alive.

'Oh, look at that.' It was the Petty Officer who spoke, his gaze fixed on the burning ship. 'She's going down.'

They all watched with sadness as the bow of the ship rose out of the water, shuddered, and then slipped beneath the waves. There was an eerie silence after that and no one spoke, still unable to take their eyes off the empty spot where their ship had once been.

Bob finally tore his gaze away and looked around, but all there was to be seen was miles and miles of empty sea. They had been on their way to meet up with a convoy coming from America when the U-boat had attacked. Like everyone else in the boat he continued to scan the sea in the hope of finding survivors, but there was nothing moving, or cries for help.

'Dear God, Bob, is this all that's left?' Reg's voice was thick with emotion.

'Looks like it.'

Unable to admit that everyone else was lost, they continued to search the sea but didn't find anyone alive. Exhausted, they eventually gave up. The men in the two boats were all that was left of the crew.

A petty officer was the highest-ranking sailor amongst the survivors, and although in a bad way, he took charge. 'We don't know how long it will be before we're found, so we've got to do everything we can to stay alive. Try and rest during the night because we'll have more chance of being seen in daylight. I'll keep watch for the first part of the night, and then in the morning I want to see you all exercising. Make it a regular routine and no slacking, no matter how tired you are.'

Bob and Reg took charge of the exercise periods the next day, encouraging and even swearing at the men who didn't want to move. Every movement was agony for Bob, and he knew he'd been hurt more than he'd first realized, but that didn't stop him from joining Reg in the effort to keep the other men alive.

'You all right, mate?' Reg asked, after one session.

'I bloody well hurt all over, but I don't think anything's broken, just badly bruised.' Bob sincerely hoped that was true, but he really wasn't sure. 'I'm all right, and like everyone else, must keep moving.'

'Well, you let me know if the pain gets worse.' Reg studied his friend with concern.

'I will, don't you worry about me. I'll take a little rest now. Wake me up if I sleep too long.'

One day merged into another until Bob had to fight not to drift into indifference. As the men became weaker the exercise periods dwindled, and the few supplies they had were almost gone. One man had already died and the petty officer was in a very bad way. If they were not rescued soon many more wouldn't make it.

'How long have we been in this bloody boat?' Reg asked, unable to raise his voice above a croak.

'A week – two weeks? I've lost track.' Suddenly fury raced through Bob. 'Where's that damned convoy? It should have reached us by now!'

'We're just a tiny dot on the ocean, and they might have sailed past us during the night.'

'That's not good enough, Reg.' The anger running through him had sparked some life back into Bob. 'They must know we've gone down. I'm not going to die out here! I'm not!' He shook his fist at the empty ocean. 'Come on, you buggers. We're here! Use your eyes.'

Bob's defiant shouting roused the others from their stupor, and those still able to joined him in his fury. They were going to fight to the last breath.

'Corporal Adams, there's a phone call for you in the Commander's office.'

'A phone call?' Becky wiped her hands on a rag.

'That's right. It's your brother, so don't keep him waiting.'

She went cold with dread right down to her toes and took off, scattering tools in her haste. Something bad must have happened. They never received phone calls, unless . . .

The phone was held out to her as she burst through the door. 'What's happened, Will?' She was gasping from her mad dash.

'I've got some bad news. Bob's ship has been sunk . . . and they haven't found any survivors yet.'

She gripped the edge of the desk to steady herself. The news came like a physical blow. 'Oh, not Bob.'

'I'm afraid so, Becky. I'll let you know the moment I hear anything, but I thought you ought to know what's happened.'

'Oh, Will, this is terrible. Bob's parents will be devastated. Have you seen them?'

'Yes, and they're with Mum and Dad, so they will help them through this. All we can do is hope and pray that he's still alive. Sorry to phone with such terrible news.'

She had never heard her brother this upset, and she tried to stem her own tears. Dear, gentle Bob. 'We mustn't give up hope. We thought David had died, but he turned up.'

'That was on dry land, Becky. The sea is a very hostile place, and the last message received from them was over a week ago.'

'Why didn't you let me know sooner?'

'I was hoping he would be found before I had to make this phone call. Sorry. I'll phone again when there's some news.'

'I understand, and thank you for letting me know now.' That was all she had time to say before he put the phone down.

Standing motionless with the phone still in her hand, Becky fought an inner battle to retain her composure, when all she wanted to do was give in to her grief. All around her people were coping with the loss of family and friends, but they carried on with what had to be done, and that's what she must do. Bob would expect it of her.

She replaced the phone and took a deep breath. It hurt so much.

Bob had always been her favourite. He was the one who had included her in whatever the boys were doing. Sometimes, Will and Jim would try to sneak off without her, but Bob wouldn't let them. They gave up trying to dodge her in the end, and by the time she was nine they had become a permanent foursome. She'd always known that eventually the boys would find girlfriends and they'd split up, but she would have been happy to see them settled with families of their own. She bowed her head in sorrow. To lose any of them like this was too cruel.

Someone touched her arm and she started out of her reverie.

'Sit down for a moment,' one of the girls from the office said kindly. 'I'll get you a cup of tea.'

Becky straightened up. 'Thank you, but I must get back to the car I'm working on. It's needed for an officer in an hour.'

'Someone else will finish it. You've obviously had some bad news. You're as white as a sheet.'

'I'm all right, really.' She gave the girl a tight smile, and hurried out of the office, glad to breathe in the fresh air.

For the rest of the day she was kept busy and that was a blessing. Numbness had settled over her, but not for a moment did she allow it to interfere with her work. If she stopped and allowed herself to think, her fear for Bob would overwhelm her.

Alice was on leave, so Becky spent the evening on her own, writing letters to Bob's parents and her own. When a couple of the girls tried to get her to join them in the NAAFI she refused. She had got through the day quite well, but the thought of being with others and trying to make polite conversation was asking too much at the moment. Perhaps she would feel more sociable tomorrow when, hopefully, the pain and shock wouldn't be quite so severe. And there might be news. As with David, the not knowing was agony.

Twenty-Four

Another week passed without news of Bob, but Becky carried on, never saying a word to anyone about it. Alice was due back from leave soon, and it would be a comfort to have her friend around.

She was giving the car a vigorous polish prior to collecting an officer, when she looked up and saw Major Brent coming towards her with a civilian. It took her a moment to realize who it was, but she didn't forget to salute the Major first, even though she was filled with dread.

'I met your father at the gate.' Major Brent shook hands with Bill Adams. 'It's a pleasure to have met you, Mr Adams. Your daughter will escort you back to the gate. Don't stay too long.'

'I won't, and thank you, Major.'

As the officer left them Becky caught hold of her father's hand. 'There must be news for you to have come here, Dad.'

'I came as soon as we heard. Bob's safe, darling. We haven't any details, but we have been told he's been picked up by an American merchant ship.'

'Thank God! That's wonderful news. Is he all right?'

'We don't know that, Becky; those poor devils have been in open boats for two weeks, but Will's on the story, so he'll get all the details.'

'What an ordeal that must have been.' Becky drew in a shuddering breath of relief. 'But he's alive, and that's the main thing.'

'Yes, that's very good news, and soon as we know where he's being taken, we'll let you know. Now, you'd better see me off the camp. The Major very kindly allowed me to see you, but I don't think I should really be here.'

'You all right, Reg?' Bob leant on the bunk to see his friend.

'Just about.' He reached out with a shaking hand to take the glass Bob handed him and drank thirstily. 'That was a close call. Who picked us up?'

'An American merchant ship on his way back to New York. Only twenty of us got to the lifeboats, and one died, as you know.

Now the petty officer's in a very bad way.' Bob bowed his head, lines of distress etched on his face. 'Everyone else – gone . . .'

'You shouldn't be up yet, sailor.' The ship's medic steadied Bob as he swayed. 'You're too weak.'

'Is it right we're heading for New York?' Reg asked, hoisting himself up to a sitting position.

'Yes, we'll dock tomorrow evening. Messages have been sent and your folks will all have been told you're safe. Ambulances will be waiting to take you to hospital as soon as we arrive.'

'Thanks, mate.' Reg flopped back, exhausted. 'How long have we been on board?'

'We spotted you three days ago, and to be honest we thought you were all dead.' The medic's mouth turned up at the corners. 'Until we heard an English voice call, "Where the bloody hell have you been?"'

'Come on, chum.' Firm hands gripped Bob as he began to shake. 'We'd sure like to get you all there alive.'

'What are the chances of that?'

'Hard to say at this point, but we'll do our best. Now, back to bed with you, and don't get up again. We don't know if you've sustained any internal injuries, so I'd like you to stay as still as possible until the doctors get a good look at you.'

Bob allowed himself to be led back to his bunk, and sighed with relief when he was lifted in. 'God, but I feel terrible.'

'That isn't surprising; you've had a hell of a time. You all have injuries – some more severe than others – and your immediate need is for food, drink and rest.' The medic smiled. 'Just wait until you get to the hospital. The nurses are going to make a great fuss of you.'

'Are they pretty?' the man in the next bunk croaked.

'Just like Betty Grable.'

'What luck!' Reg called. 'And not one of us with as much strength as a new-born baby.'

A ripple of laughter went around the sick bay, and it was a welcome sound from a group of men who had been so close to death.

Bob closed his eyes, a slight smile on his face, and immediately fell asleep.

It was the noise that woke him; the sick bay was alive with activity as men were being lifted out of bunks and put on stretchers.

Doctors were quickly checking each of the survivors before allowing them to be moved, giving quiet orders as they worked.

'These two first. Get them to the hospital fast. Stay put, sailor. No, you can't walk . . .'

He listened to this. They must have docked, but he'd been completely unaware of time passing.

'I tell you I'm walking off this ship!' Reg complained. 'I am quite all right.'

'OK, let's see you stand up.'

There was much puffing and grunting, then an American voice saying, 'I've got you, chum.'

'Do as you're told, Reg,' Bob called, when he saw how shaky his friend was.

'I ain't got no choice, mate,' he answered. 'My legs won't hold me.'

A doctor reached Bob then and began to examine him. 'Hmm, we'll have to see if anything's broken. Your body's taken a pounding. How did you come by these injuries?'

Bob looked at the man in amazement. 'Some silly devil blew up our ship.'

'I know that, sailor.' The doctor gave a wry smile. 'What I meant was did something hit you?'

'Ah, I see. Well, I got thrown across the deck when the second torpedo hit, and I crashed into something. Don't remember much after that until I was in the lifeboat.'

'This one next,' the doctor ordered, 'and be careful with him.'

'He's not hurt bad, is he, Doc?' Reg's worried face appeared next to Bob as he was being carried out. 'He's been the life and soul of the party in the lifeboat.'

'I'm all right.' Bob gave his friend a reassuring smile. 'I'd have known if I'd been badly hurt. They're just being careful. See you at the hospital.'

'Hey, mate.' Reg called over an orderly. 'Are we all going to the same place?'

'Yeah, you'll all be together.'

'That's all right then. We sort of got used to each other's company,' Reg quipped.

The scene on the dockside was unbelievable. Although it was dusk, the place was ablaze with lights, and crowded with people. Encouragement was shouted to each of the survivors as they were carried to the waiting ambulances. After the strict blackout at home it was fascinating.

Bob was loaded into an ambulance with the petty officer. A doctor was already dealing with him, and a nurse sat with Bob, wiping his brow with something sweet smelling. He hadn't realized he was sweating. 'Oh, that feels good,' he murmured, and then closed his eyes when the sirens began to scream. The vehicle was going at breakneck speed and he wished they would slow down a bit. The nurse said something he couldn't quite hear, her voice seemed to be coming from a great distance, but he could feel her warm hand in his, and he held on tight. He felt bad.

He thought she called the doctor, and then a man was bending over him. 'The other one's gone. We got to him too late, but after all these poor devils have gone through, we've got to save this one.'

What's he talking about? Bob thought. *I'm all right, and I don't hurt any more. I'm just tired – so very tired.* But they wouldn't let him sleep. Why wouldn't they let him sleep? Everything was such a rush. They were wheeling him along . . . running . . . why were they running?

Gradually Bob became aware of being in a comfortable bed that wasn't moving around, clean sheets and a disinfectant smell . . .

'Bob! Wake up, mate. Please wake up.'

'Hmm?' A straw was put in his mouth and he sucked at it. Orange juice? It was lovely.

'My goodness, you did enjoy that,' said a female voice. 'Open your eyes now, Bob, your friend wants to talk to you.'

It was such an effort, and as consciousness returned so did the pain, and he gasped.

'We've given you something for the pain and it will ease soon,' the voice told him.

Fully conscious now, he opened his eyes and looked straight at Reg, who was leaning over him.

'Thank God! We thought you were going to die, like the petty officer.'

'What the hell happened? I was all right.' The doctor arrived then. 'What happened to me, Doc?'

'When you were thrown across the deck two ribs were cracked, and you had received a severe blow across your abdomen. The merchant ship that picked you up sailed into a storm and you were all tossed about. A weakened blood vessel began to leak, but we got to you just in time. If it had burst completely you would have been dead in minutes. You'll make a full recovery now.'

He listened in disbelief. 'Why didn't I realize I'd been hurt that bad?'

'Because you had been in cold water and then in an open boat. It had numbed you, and it was only once you were warm the trouble began to be felt.' The man smiled and patted his shoulder. 'You rest now. We've repaired the damage and you'll be as good as new in a few days.'

'Thanks. Did the petty officer die in the ambulance?'

'I'm sorry to say he did.'

'Oh, hell, he was a brave man.'

'You all are.' The doctor took hold of Reg's arm. 'And it's time you were back in bed. Your friend's going to be fine, and you're right next to him, so you can keep an eye on him.'

Reg nodded, smiled with relief at Bob, then climbed into the next bed, propping himself up on his arm so he could still talk to his friend. 'When you feel better we'll all go out on the town,' he said. 'They don't know the meaning of the word blackout here, and it's a real pretty sight.'

'You're on. Do you think we can persuade some of the nurses to come with us?'

'Of course we can. We're gonna need looking after, aren't we? Go to sleep now, Bob, we've all got to get our strength back.'

For a week they were content to rest, eat good food, and enjoy the fuss being made of them. But that was enough, and the survivors, to a man, began to ask the question uppermost in their minds.

'How are we going to get back home?' Bob was the first one to bring up the question. 'We're grateful for the care you've given us, Doc, but we need to get back now.'

'Sure you do, but leave it another couple of days and someone will be coming to see you soon.' The doctor looked at the men gathered around him. 'It won't hurt you to have a couple more days of rest.'

'That's all very well, Doc,' Reg told him, 'but I want to get my own back on that bloody U-boat. And we're not going to get a chance to do that sitting here.'

'We're all that's left of our crew. All our mates went down with her,' Harry, one of the other men explained. 'Those devils under the sea aren't going to get away with it. That ship had been our home since the start of the war, and the crew were our mates. This is very personal now.'

The doctor was thoughtful for a moment, then said, 'You know when France fell the opinion of some here was that Britain couldn't survive on her own, but after meeting all of you I can see why she's held out against all the odds.'

Reg shrugged. 'Ah, we heard that tale, but we're stubborn enough not to believe it. Tell me, Doc, what would you have done if you'd been faced with the same situation?'

'Fought to my last breath to stop being invaded.'

'Exactly! There really isn't any choice, is there?'

'None at all.' The doctor began to examine Bob. 'You guys nearly died out there, but you've all made a good recovery, and I can see you're wanting to give up this idle life now you've recovered from your ordeal.'

'I'm not sure we'll ever completely recover,' Bob told him seriously. 'We'll carry the memory of those who died for the rest of our lives.'

'That hurt I can't heal, I'm afraid.' Then he hurried off to answer an emergency call.

'Who's this?' Reg nudged Bob. 'He's British army.'

Bob blinked, unable to believe his eyes. Then he swung his legs out of bed and stood upright, grinning in delight. 'Will, what on earth are you doing here?'

The friends greeted each other with great pleasure. 'Am I glad to see you! We thought we'd lost you. Becky sends her love.'

'How's my mum and dad?'

'Fine since they were told you're all right.'

'Well, aren't you going to introduce us?' Reg interrupted.

'Sorry, this is my friend Will I've told you so much about.'

Reg beamed. 'You're the War Correspondent. Great to meet you, Will.'

Bob introduced the men who had gathered around and waited while they shook hands, then chairs were dragged from everywhere so they could all sit down together. Will was known to many of the men through his reports and newsreels, and they were eager to talk to him.

'You guys having a party?' one of the nurses asked.

'We would if you could rustle us up some tea,' Reg teased.

'You English and your tea. I'll see what I can do, but keep the noise down.'

'Yes, Nurse,' they all said in mock obedience, and she hurried away, laughing.

'It's wonderful to see you, Will, but what brings you here?' Bob couldn't get over his surprise.

'I'm here to do a story on how the ordinary Americans feel about going to war – a war they didn't want or ask for.' Will studied the faces around him. 'Then I want your story, if you don't mind talking about it?'

'We'll tell you what happened, won't we?' Reg asked the others, and then turned back to Will when they all nodded in agreement.

'Thanks. And lastly, I'm here to take you all home. The *Queen Mary*'s been turned into a troop ship, and we're sailing on her in three days.'

A cheer went up and two nurses appeared.

'Quiet! There are a lot of sick people here.'

'Sorry, Nurse.' Bob lowered his voice. 'But we'll soon be out of your way. We're going home!'

Twenty-Five

There was a stream of American soldiers boarding the *Queen Mary*. Will, Bob, Reg and the rest of the British sailors watched the scene from an upper deck.

'What a good job you got us on early,' Bob told Will. 'This ship is going to be packed, and I suppose you'll be gathering stories during the crossing.'

'That's why I'm here. I'm hoping to get quite a few reports from this.' He grinned at his friend. 'And to bring you back, of course.'

'Hmm. How did you wangle it?'

Will laughed. 'When I found out where you were I put in a request to report on the Americans coming over.'

'And they fell for it.'

'I can be persuasive when necessary – and I had Becky hounding me for information about you. She only stopped pestering me when I told her I was coming to get you.'

'Ah well, you didn't have a choice then. When Becky decides something needs doing there's no arguing with her.' Bob turned his attention back to the dock again and leant on the rail. 'How's that colonel of hers?'

Will frowned. 'I've no idea if there's something between them. He won't talk about it, and she insists they are just friends.'

Bob nodded. 'A relationship between them would be fraught with difficulties, and Becky's not daft. Every aspect of getting involved with an officer will be weighed up and thought through with the utmost care. What's your opinion of him?'

'He's a career soldier, and at a guess, around ten years older than Becky. He's at least six feet with sandy-coloured hair. I'd class him as handsome in a tough kind of way, although this is tempered by a sense of humour and a ready smile. He's a brave man, as I saw at Dunkirk, and is greatly respected by his men.' Will took a deep breath. 'But I am concerned for Becky; she can declare all she likes that there is nothing romantic between them, but I'm not sure. She could get hurt.'

'I'm sure you don't need to worry about that, Will.' Bob slapped his friend on the back. 'Our girl's got a good head on her shoulders, and can take care of herself. We've brought her up well,' he said with a laugh.

'That's more or less what the colonel told me.'

'Blimey, Will, you didn't ask him about his intentions towards your sister, did you?'

A smile touched Will's mouth as he remembered the encounter. 'I did hint at it, and he more or less told me to mind my own business. In a very gentlemanly way, of course.'

'I can imagine.' They were both smiling now. 'Don't ever tell Becky this, or she'll have your hide.'

'I'm not daft either. Anyway, she's mellowed a bit now she's all grown up. She's turned into a damned good driver, and spends most of her time driving the top brass around.'

Reg, who had been listening to the conversation, said, 'Hey Will, when we get back I'd like to meet your sister. She sounds smashing.'

'If we ever get home the same time as her, I'll see what I can do, but if you fancy her then you'll have some serious competition.'

'I gathered that. Ah, it looks like they're finally all aboard. Now perhaps we can get under way.'

Two days later it was pouring with rain and they were all below decks passing the time by playing cards.

'Have you seen this?' Will came and sat with them, holding out a small booklet.

'Hmm.' Bob threw down his hand of cards. 'You win again, Reg.'

'We've all got one.' Harry fished it out of his pocket.

'Any of you read it?'

'Why would we want to read it? It's telling the Americans about Britain. They've just handed them out to everyone on board.' Bob began to shuffle the cards.

'Read it, I'd like to know what you think of it.' Will watched the expressions of amusement on their faces as they read the booklet.

Well?' he asked, when they'd all turned the last page.

Bob smirked. 'This should be a help to our American friends – as long as they don't take it too seriously. It makes some valid points though. It's right to mention the differences in our language or they could shock some of the locals. We've been to New York several times, and we know how easy it is to say the wrong thing. Bob tucked the booklet back in his pocket. 'I must show this to Becky when I get a chance.'

'I've got her a copy, Bob.'

They continued to discuss the differences in their culture when a group of American soldiers approached them. 'Mind if we join you?' one of them asked.

'Not at all; grab some chairs.' Will was already pulling his notebook out of his jacket pocket.

There was much moving around to make room for the six men. Names were exchanged, and one called Hal asked, 'What are you guys doing on a troop ship? You're not part of the crew.'

'We were picked up by one of your merchant ships after our destroyer was sunk by a U-boat,' Reg explained. 'We're going home after spending just over a week in hospital.'

'Gee, that's tough.'

'More than that, mate.' Harry's mouth set in a grim line. 'We were the only ones to survive.'

The soldiers cast worried glances at each other, and one by the name of Greg had lost all colour in his face. 'Um . . . how long before you were picked up?'

'A couple of weeks.' Bob felt sorry for the boy, for that was all he was. He supposed they'd all seemed like that at first, but they'd had to grow up quickly, and felt more mature than these fresh-faced youngsters.

'Getting on for three weeks,' Reg corrected. 'You were in a bad way and didn't know what was going on most of the time.'

'Listen to who's talking,' Harry chided. 'I remember you threatening to walk back to England, saying you'd had enough of looking at bloody sea. We had to hold you back.'

'What makes you think I couldn't have done?' Reg joked. 'My feet are big enough.'

The sailors all burst into laughter. It might have seemed strange to others that they could joke about their ordeal, but it was their way of coping with it.

Greg didn't see the funny side and began handing around cigarettes with a slightly shaking hand.

Bob took one and smiled at the American as he dragged his chair closer to Bob. 'Where are you from?'

'Boston – and you?'

'London.'

'What's it like there?' Greg drew deeply on his cigarette. 'We've heard such terrible stories.'

'Well, everything's in short supply, and the bombing has been bad, but you'll find everyone's getting on with things. There are dances, concerts and cinemas you can go to, and the pubs, of course. Your big bands like Glenn Miller are very popular.'

'Really? Hey, that's great. Do you hear that? They like swing music over there.' Greg turned his attention back to Bob. 'Do you think the U-boats are out there now?'

'They'll be there, but the ocean is a big place, and the *Queen Mary*'s a fast ship, so the chances of them spotting us are slim.' Bob was pleased to see the boy relax a little.

'Ah, well, you should know about these things.' He actually smiled. 'Would you tell me what to expect when we land?'

'Of course.' Bob glanced at Will, but he was too busy making notes of the conversations between the different groups.

They had attracted a large gathering around them, and there was much laughter as the British sailors explained the differences the Americans were likely to encounter once they were ashore. Bottles of beer arrived, along with packets and packets of cigarettes.

By the end of the evening the worry had cleared from Greg's face, but he still stuck close to Bob. 'If everyone's as great as you guys then it won't be so bad. This is the first time I've ever been away from home, and my folks are real worried because I'm going to a country under attack.'

'You'll be all right, mate.' Reg slapped him on the back. 'Where are you being stationed?'

'Um . . .' Greg fished a paper out of his pocket. 'A place called Medstead, in Hampshire.'

'Ah, you'll like it there. They've got some good pubs, as long as you don't mind warm beer. You'll get used to it though.'

'Hey, I've heard about the English pubs,' Hal said. 'A neighbour's son was one of the first to land in England at the end of January, and he told them the pubs are great.'

This started another long discussion as the rest of the soldiers wanted to know about these places.

By eleven o'clock, Bob was so tired he could hardly keep his eyes open. He got to his feet. 'Sorry to leave you, but I've got to get some sleep.'

'Me too.' Reg stubbed out his cigarette. 'What about you, Will?'

'I'll stay a while longer, but the rest of you should call it a night. You've only just come out of hospital.'

The worry returned to Greg's face. 'Oh, hell, we should have thought of that. You mustn't overdo it. Can we talk some more tomorrow, Bob?'

'Of course. I'll see you on the promenade deck after breakfast, shall I?'

'That'll be just fine. Don't rush though. I'll wait around for you.' He smiled. 'You sleep well.'

'And you. There's nothing to worry about, Greg; you'll be fine in England.'

'Yeah, I think I will.'

All the sailors were weary now and walked to their bunks together. 'Looks like you've made a friend,' Harry said.

Bob nodded. 'The poor devil has been taken from home and family for the first time in his life, put on a ship sailing through hostile waters to a country he's heard terrible tales about. It's enough to worry anyone.'

'Some of them are taking it as a great adventure,' Reg remarked, stifling a yawn. 'We should be able to sleep tonight. I'm tired out with all that talking.'

They had the luxury of a section all to themselves as they had just come out of hospital, which was a good thing. They laughed and joked during the day, but at night it wasn't unusual for one or two to have nightmares. Their nights were often restless and disturbed. The doctors had told them they would gradually fade, and Bob hoped this was so as he climbed into his bunk.

The next morning Bob was up early, and enjoying a quiet smoke while most of the others were still asleep. He liked to lean on the rail and watch the sea, picking out the many different colours. After all those days in the lifeboat he had wondered if he would ever enjoy the sea again, but he did. It could be incredibly cruel, but also very beautiful.

'Hey, I didn't expect to see you around so early.' Greg came and stood beside him. 'Didn't you sleep well?'

'I had a few hours.' He offered the American a cigarette.

'No offence, Bob, but your cigarettes are terrible. Have one of mine.'

'Thanks. Couldn't you sleep?'

'I've always been an early riser. I like to watch the dawn coming up.' Greg leant on the rail beside Bob. 'You know, I've never been to sea before, but I like it, and if it wasn't for the thought of U-boats lurking beneath the waves, I would find it quite fascinating. You got a girl back home?'

'Not really. There's Will's sister, Becky.' Bob then told him about the way the four of them had grown up together, and how the war had split them up for the first time in their lives.

'You sound like a fine family, and I hope I'll be able to meet folks like yours. My mom told me to mix as much as I can and not stay with a bunch of soldiers all the time. She said we all need to be kind to each other in this war.'

'Your mother sounds like a nice woman.'

Greg nodded. 'She's great, and so is my Pa. I miss them already.'

'Tell you what.' Bob wrote on an empty cigarette packet and handed it to the American. 'That's our address. We've moved to the outskirts of London now, so if you feel like it any time, go and visit my parents. I'll tell them you might turn up one day.'

Greg looked quite overcome as he took the packet from Bob. 'Gee, thanks, I'd like that. You sure they wouldn't mind?'

'They'd be pleased to see you. You'd be able to meet Will and Becky's parents as well because we all share the same house.'

He placed the packet carefully in his pocket, beaming with pleasure. 'Just wait till I write home about this. Did you move to get away from the bombing?'

'We didn't have any choice. Our three houses were flattened one bad night, and two of our friends – Jim's parents – were killed in the raid.' Bob drew deeply on his cigarette. 'Becky was in London helping with the rescue work, and was horrified when she saw a bloody great crater where our houses had once been. When I arrived home for the funeral I couldn't go and look. I didn't want to see the place we'd called home in ruins.'

'That's terrible; I'm so sorry. It's hard to imagine what it would be like to find your home wasn't there any more.'

'It's a shock, but you just have to get over it.'

'Yeah, I guess so. Thanks for telling me that. We've been told not to ask what people have been through, in case they don't want to talk about it. My Ma said we mustn't be nosy; people will talk if they want to.' Greg studied Bob for a while, then said, 'You tell me to shut up if I start asking questions you don't want to answer, but I'd sure like to know as much as possible before we land in your country. I've read every newspaper, listened to radio reports, and seen picture newsreels, but they don't tell the whole story. That rescue from France was an unbelievable operation. Were you there, Bob?'

'Dunkirk?' Bob shook his head. 'You need to talk to Will about that. He was in one of the little boats.'

'What?' Greg gasped. 'He never said anything about that last night.'

'No one asked him.' The more Bob talked with this young American, the more he liked him. There was no secret about Will's exploits, they had been widely reported on, so he grinned and said, 'I'll tell you something else my crazy friend has done, shall I?'

Greg was nodding enthusiastically.

'He hitched a ride in a Wellington Bomber and went with them on a raid over Berlin.'

'Ow hell, Bob, you guys are amazing.' Greg was waving his arms in excitement. 'I gotta talk to Will. Is he up yet?'

'He was awake when I came up here, and knowing Will, he's probably at breakfast by now.'

'Let's go and find him. Can we find him, Bob? Will he tell me about this? Will he mind talking to me?'

'Of course he won't mind. It's his job as a War Correspondent to write and talk about the war.'

Catching hold of Bob's arm and towing him along, they hurried towards the dining room.

'Where are you two off to in such a darned hurry?' Hal stopped them.

'We've got to find Will.' Greg was bursting with excitement. 'I've just found out he was in one of the little boats at Dunkirk, and he went on a bombing raid over Berlin. And Bob's home was completely destroyed by bombs, and Will's sister was in London helping with the rescue services. She's in the army . . .'

'Whoa!' Bob laughed as Greg's words tumbled out. 'Don't forget to breathe.'

The American gave a sheepish smile. 'I do get excited. My Pa's always telling me to calm down.' Greg caught hold of Hal's arm. 'Bob said I can visit his folks,' he said proudly.

'Hey, that's great.' Hal peered around Greg so he could see Bob. 'Could I tag along as well? We won't be no trouble.'

'Of course you can. I'll tell my parents to expect two of you.'

'Thanks. Now, let's find Will.'

He was tucking into a huge breakfast, and grinned as Bob sat next to him. 'Did you ever see so much food? There's enough on my plate to feed one person for a week at home.'

'Don't get used to it,' Bob reminded him. 'Once we arrive home it will be back to normal rations.'

'We'd better make the most of it then. Go and get your breakfast. The ham just melts in your mouth.'

Bob leant over to whisper to his friend. 'I'm afraid I've dropped you in it. Greg and Hal want to know all about Dunkirk and your bombing raid. Here they come with their food. Best of luck.'

After an uneventful voyage, much to the relief of many on board, the big ship edged her way into Southampton, and the Americans were crowding the rails to get their first glimpse of England. The British sailors were silent, each with their own thoughts. They were alive, and they were home. It was an emotional moment for them, but even after everything they had gone through, not one of them allowed the emotions to show.

The dock was bustling with activity as preparations were made to deal with the large contingent of soldiers arriving. It would be quite an operation to disembark and get them all transferred to their bases.

They had said their goodbyes to those they had become friendly with on the trip. Greg and Hal were going to write to Bob, and Will had taken a list of names, as he wanted to follow their progress as they settled in a country they knew little about.

As soon as the gangplanks were in place, a couple of British medics made their way on board, spoke to a member of the crew, and then headed for the sailors.

'Looks like they're coming for us,' Reg said.

'They are,' Will told them. 'You're all going to hospital first. They've got to see what shape you're in, and you'll each have to give a report of exactly what happened.'

'I can tell them that in one sentence.' Bob scowled. 'Two torpedoes from a U-boat hit us.'

'How long will all this take?' Harry sighed. 'I want to go home.'

'A day or so, I expect.' Will gave them a sympathetic look. 'Then you'll get leave until they can assign you to another ship.'

This was something Bob had tried not to think about, as it was quite likely they would be split up. They had been together from the beginning, and the time spent in the lifeboat had created a bond between them. He would particularly miss Reg if he was put on a different ship. But he knew, as did everyone else, that personal feelings had no part in what they had to do.

The medics reached them. 'Welcome home, men. We've got ambulances waiting. Are you all able to walk without aid?'

'We're all right,' Bob told them.

'Good, let's get you off before the Americans begin to disembark.'

When they reached the dock, all of them stopped and turned to look up at the sea of faces on the ship, searching for Greg and Hal, and the others they had come to know.

Suddenly a great cheer went up and a group on the upper deck started waving frantically. They smiled and waved back.

Bob cupped his hand around his mouth and shouted, 'Good luck!'

They answered, but the words were snatched away by a stiff breeze.

The sailors turned and walked towards the waiting ambulances. Their interlude of relaxation was over. Now they were back on duty.

Twenty-Six

It had been an agonizing wait but Becky had just heard that Bob was safely home, and she had put in a request for leave so she could go and see him. Will's letter had told her that Bob had been in a bad way when rescued, but the doctors in New York had saved his life. She wouldn't be completely happy until she saw him for herself.

'You under there, Becky?' Alice called, bending down to peer at the person whose legs were sticking out from under a car.

Becky pushed herself out and gazed up at her friend. 'It isn't lunch time, is it?'

'Not quite, but I've got some news for you. You've been given the pass you requested, but it's only for forty-eight hours.'

'That's better than nothing.' She scrambled to her feet.

'I've got one as well.'

'Wonderful! Come home with me, Alice. Everyone would love to see you again.'

'I'd like that. My family are too far away for a short pass. Perhaps we can take Bob for a night out in London.'

'What a good idea.' Becky smiled with pleasure. 'We could take him dancing at the Hammersmith Palais, providing he's fit enough, of course. He's a lovely dancer and has always enjoyed it.'

Alice's face lost its smile. 'We'll have to see how he is before we suggest it. I'll see you tomorrow morning then. Do you think there's any chance of cadging a lift? It will save time.'

'I'll see what I can do.' Becky winked.

'What are you two planning?' Pete appeared from behind a lorry.

'We were just wondering if we could get a lift to East Sheen in the morning.' Becky looked pointedly at the vehicle Pete had been working on. 'That will need a good test run now you've changed the gearbox, won't it?'

'Absolutely. I've already arranged to take her out at six o'clock tomorrow morning. Of course, if I see two ATS girls walking towards the station at that time, it would only be polite to pick them up.' He walked away whistling.

'See you at five-thirty, Becky.'

'You're making an early start,' the guard on the gate said. 'Trains might not be running yet.'

'We've only got forty-eight hours, and we're going to make the most of it.' Alice smiled sweetly. 'We're going dancing in London.'

'Ah, well, you watch those Yanks. London's full of them. They're good at dancing though, I've been told, and have a lot more money than us poor devils.'

They heard a truck coming towards them, so they hurried through the gate and up the road.

Pete soon stopped beside them. 'Hop in.'

'Thanks, you're a real friend.'

In no time at all they were at the house, and as soon as Pete had dropped them, he turned and headed back to camp. He'd told them that the lorry was needed by ten o'clock.

'Hope he makes it in time.'

'Don't worry, Alice, if he's late he'll tell them he broke down again, but he's got plenty of time to get back.'

While they were talking the front door opened. 'Are you going to stand there all day?'

'Will!' Becky rushed to greet her brother. 'I didn't know you'd be here as well. 'Where's Bob? Is he still in bed? Is he all right?'

'He's fine,' said the tall sailor standing right behind her brother.

She held out her arms. 'There you are! I thought you might still be asleep.'

'Fat chance,' he snorted. 'What did you arrive in – a tank?'

Delighted to see he was still the same as always, she grinned. 'It was a bit noisy, wasn't it?'

'Come in, Alice.' Will smiled. 'It's good to see you again. I hope you're staying with us?'

'I'd love to, but we've only got forty-eight-hour passes.'

'That's fine. Mum!' Will called. 'We've got visitors, so put the kettle on.'

Then everyone was there, and they were soon sitting around the kitchen table, talking and laughing, happy to be together again. Becky took this opportunity to study Bob. He'd always been slim, but now he was quite thin, and his ordeal showed in the blue smudges around his eyes. He was no longer a boy, but a man who had seen his shipmates die. Her heart went out to him, and she couldn't help feeling a sense of loss for the boy she had grown up with. This war was changing all of them, and it was something that had to be accepted.

She put the smile back on her face. 'I'm glad you're here, Will, because we thought we'd take you and Bob dancing tonight.'

'And we're paying,' Alice told them.

'What an invitation.' Bob smiled at Will. 'That's an offer we can't refuse, isn't it?'

'I'll say. Where are we going?'

'How about the Hammersmith Palais?'

'That will do nicely.' Bob moved his arms out of the way as his mother began to clear the table of cups.

'Why don't you all go in the other room while I make us some breakfast?'

The girls immediately dived into their bags and began pulling out packets of tea, sugar, biscuits, and even a little butter.

'Oh, that's a big help,' Becky's mother said. 'Will and Bob brought us some tins of American food they got on the boat, so we'll have enough.'

'I haven't finished yet.' Alice was still looking in her bag. When she put two tins of salmon on the table everyone stared in amazement.

'Where did you get those?' Becky gasped.

'Those nice Canadians gave them to me for arranging the dance. I've been saving them for a special occasion, and this is it.'

'But we can't take both tins.' Becky's mother pushed one back to Alice. 'You keep one for your family.'

'No need. They've already had their share.'

'How many did they give you?'

'Four.' Alice smiled broadly at her. 'Well worth all the hassle of getting the girls to and from the dance, don't you think?'

Becky was shaking her head in disbelief. 'Just look at her. You wouldn't think their was a devious thought in her head.'

The boys were laughing and studying the lovely girl with interest.

Mavis didn't argue and put the tins in the kitchen cupboard. 'I'll make some salmon fishcakes for lunch, and then there will be enough for all of us.'

The morning was spent catching up with each other's news.

The girls listened intently to Bob and Will's account of the voyage on the *Queen Mary*, but not one word was said about the sinking of Bob's ship, or what had happened to them. Becky and Alice had enough sense not to bring up the subject. Bob would, hopefully, talk about it when he was ready.

In the evening when they were getting ready to go out, Becky was able to catch her brother alone for a moment. 'Is Bob all right?' she asked anxiously. 'Would he rather stay home instead of going dancing?'

'He's looking forward to it, Becky. You know how much he's always liked dancing.'

She nodded, relieved. 'I was afraid in case we were forcing him to do something he wasn't ready for.'

'Stop worrying about him. He's had a bad time, but he's coping well. The soldiers we became friendly with on the ship thought he was terrific – and he is. I've always thought Bob was a special kind of person, and now I know that for sure.'

'You're right, and I'm worrying too much again.' She reached up and gave her brother a peck on the cheek. 'And you're a very special man as well, so don't you ever forget that.'

Her brother laughed. 'You're not too bad, either. You've always put others before yourself, but you matter as well, Becky. Don't you ever forget that!'

'I'll try, and you be careful, Will Adams. You're getting yourself into some dangerous places.'

At that moment Bob came down the stairs holding out his arms. 'Sisters shouldn't ration their hugs to brothers.'

Seeing the glimpse of the boy again in his eyes, Becky hurled herself towards him. His arms tightened around her and he rocked her gently, kissed the top of her head, and then stepped back. 'That's better. Now I'm ready for an evening of dancing with two beautiful girls.'

'And so am I.' Will held his hand out to Alice and helped her down the last few stairs.

Alice raised her eyebrows to Becky. 'You forgot to tell me what a couple of charmers these boys are!'

'Hmm, they do seem to have learnt some manners just lately,' she teased, and when they laughed she felt the evening had started on a happy note. Bob was hiding the effects of his ordeal well, but she could see a lingering sadness in his eyes, and that worried her. This evening out was a good idea.

Both sets of parents came into the hallway, and Becky's mother said, 'My goodness, what a smart looking foursome you make.'

'That's because you pressed our uniforms, Mrs Adams, 'Alice said. 'And Mrs Walker has polished our shoes until we can see our faces in them.'

'It was a pleasure.' Bob's mother smiled. 'Now, off you go and enjoy yourselves.'

The dance hall was packed with servicemen and women of all branches of the armed services, and quite a few different nationalities. The noise was deafening when they walked in, and they all stood watching for a moment, fascinated.

Becky couldn't take her eyes off a group of Americans. 'What are they doing?' she asked Bob.

'They call it the Jitterbug, or Jiving. It's all the rage in America.'

'Gosh, it looks fun.' She looked up at him. 'Can you do it?'

'As a matter of fact I can. We were once delayed in New York waiting for a convoy to assemble, and some US sailors gave us lessons. Want to try?'

Alice and Will were doubled over with laughter as they watched Becky try to master the steps.

An American Airman tapped Bob on the shoulder. 'Hey, you take my partner and I'll show your girl how to do it. I was a dance teacher before the war. Come on, honey,' he said, swinging her away from Bob. 'Just relax and follow my lead.'

He was an excellent teacher, and in only a short time Becky was making a good attempt at the dance, and thoroughly enjoying herself.

'Ah, you'll soon pick that up.' The American beamed at her when the band stopped playing. 'You've got rhythm, honey.'

When she looked round she saw that Alice was with another American, and his partner was teaching Will. Bob came back to them, flushed and laughing. It did Becky's heart good to see him relaxed and happy.

'That was fun,' she told them. 'Thank you very much.'

He waved away their thanks. 'It's my mission to teach as many of you as possible how to dance to the swing music. It's a great way to have fun.'

'Can we buy you a drink?' Bob asked.

'Sure, that would be great.'

After exchanging names, they all headed for the bar. The Americans would only allow them to buy one round between them, and insisted that the rest of the evening was on them.

By the time the dancing started again they had gathered quite a crowd around them. They were an assortment of English, American, Canadian, Polish and even a couple of Frenchmen, and it turned out to be a hilarious evening. By the time they left the dance hall they ached from so much laughing and vigorous dancing. But it had been such fun – and now they could all Jive!

The next morning was Sunday, and Becky was the only one in the kitchen at seven o'clock. Everyone else was still in bed, but she had never been one to linger once she was awake.

'Is the tea in the pot still hot?'

She jumped at the sound of Bob's voice and turned her head to look at him. 'Yes, I've only just made the tea. I didn't expect to see you before midday.'

'They have the habit of dragging us out of our bunks at all sorts of unearthly hours, and it disturbs our sleep patterns.' He sat opposite her and took the cup she gave him.

'So I see. Want some breakfast?' she asked, checking the larder. 'I can do scrambled eggs on toast – made with powered egg, of course.'

'That'll do.' He watched her while she worked. 'How's your colonel?'

'All right. He's back with his regiment now.' She glanced over her shoulder. 'And he isn't *my* colonel. He did ask me to marry him, but I refused.'

There was a moment of silence, then Bob asked, 'Why did you do that? I know you're fond of him.'

She put the plate in front of him and sat down again. 'You're right; I am very fond of him – too fond really – but there are many reasons I won't let our friendship go any further. After his narrow escape from France I believe he's attempting to put his life in order in case he doesn't make it through the war. He wants a mother for his daughter, and as I get on well with Sara, it must seem like a good idea to him. He likes me, is even attracted to me, but that isn't enough to build a lasting relationship on. I'm not going to rush into anything and find out when it's too late that I've made a terrible mistake. Because people are unsure whether they are going to live or die, some are rushing into things they wouldn't normally do. It doesn't matter to me how uncertain life is at the moment, I'm not going to make a stupid mistake that could ruin the rest of my life.'

She had always been able to talk to Bob, and it felt good to unburden herself like this.

'I understand how you feel.' He smiled and reached out to squeeze her hand. 'You've always had a sensible head on your shoulders, Becky.'

She sighed. 'Sometimes I think I'm too sensible and that might hold me back from doing the right thing, but there's so much against us. He's from a different class, and I'm afraid I wouldn't fit into his lifestyle and be the kind of wife he needs. Can you imagine me entertaining a bunch of officers and their wives?'

'As a matter of fact I can. You're being too hard on yourself, Becky. You're as good as anyone else, and I suspect he knows that. This war is changing people's perception of the class divide. We're all fighting together no matter where we come from. He wouldn't have asked you if he hadn't believed you would be a perfect wife for him, no matter how worried he is about his daughter.'

'I thank you for that, Bob, but I still have grave doubts. He's an officer, and that throws a barrier between us, though I have to admit that I seem to be the only one it bothers. But he's a kind man, has a sense of humour and a gentle side to him. He's also a brave man and loyal to those he cares about.'

'I can't argue with that as I've never met him, but I'm glad you're being cautious because I wouldn't like to see you unhappy.'

'What's this about being unhappy?' Will joined them and felt the teapot. 'This is cold.'

'I'll make a fresh pot,' Becky offered, and put the kettle on to boil.

'That sounded like a very serious discussion you two were having. What was it about?'

'Don't be nosy,' she teased.

'Brothers are allowed to be nosy.'

'We were discussing the colonel,' Bob told him.

'Ah, that accounts for the serious faces. Is he giving you trouble, Becky?'

'I'm quite capable of looking after myself. Now sit down and I'll make you some breakfast.'

'Quite right.' Alice walked into the kitchen. 'You tell them, Becky.'

She smiled at her friend. 'Did you sleep well?'

'Lovely; I don't even remember getting into bed.' Alice sat down and took the cup of tea Will had poured for her. 'What were you talking about, anyway?'

'A certain imposing officer,' Will told her.

'I see. He's hard to resist, but Becky's managing him quite well.' Alice began to talk to the boys as if Becky wasn't there. 'He's a determined man, though, so we'll have to keep an eye on things.'

When Bob and Will began to nod in agreement, it was too much for Becky, and she was sorry she'd ever brought up the subject. She was so used to pouring out her troubles to the boys, especially Bob, and it had always helped in the past, but she now realized that the problem was hers, and hers alone. In this case she was the only one who could make a decision. 'Not another word, or I'll leave you all to get your own breakfast. Mind your own business.'

Three pairs of eyes studied her for a moment, then Will said, 'The weather's good today, so what are we going to do?'

'That's better,' Becky muttered to herself as she set about measuring out the powdered egg, and ignoring their grinning faces.

Twenty-Seven

It had been a frustrating wait for a new ship, and in spite of everything that had happened, Bob was longing to get back to sea. He stood on the dock at Liverpool and drank in the sight of the new destroyer. From the information he had been given, she was faster than his last ship, and bristling with armaments. He was going to enjoy inspecting her. His only concern about the new posting was what the crew would be like. He was going to miss those he'd sailed with before, and the sadness for the many who hadn't survived tugged at him, but he pushed it away. The past was done and nothing could change it. It was time to move on.

Sailors were arriving and going on board, but Bob stayed where he was, wondering where Reg had been posted. They kept in touch, of course, but neither of them had known where they were to be sent until the very last moment.

'Impressive beast, isn't she?'

Bob spun round at the sound of the familiar voice, a broad smile lighting his face. 'Reg! Are you on this ship as well?'

'He is, and so are we.'

Suddenly Bob was surrounded by the survivors from his last ship, and they greeted each other, laughing with amazement.

'They're putting us all together again,' Harry told Bob. 'We've only just found out. I think this must be a fairly new crew, and they've gathered together as many experienced sailors as they can.'

'Bloody marvellous, isn't it!' Reg was obviously thrilled about the whole thing. 'Let's get on board, lads, and have a good look at this elegant lady.'

'And we've got to check out the crew, as well.' Harry hoisted up his kitbag. 'I expect quite a few are raw recruits.'

'I feel this is a good omen,' Bob said to Reg as they walked on to the ship.

His friend nodded. 'They won't get us a second time, mate.'

They reported to the First Officer, and saw at once that he was an experienced man. When he'd checked them all in he stood up, regarding them with interest. 'You're all from the *Stranraer*.'

'That's right,' Reg answered for them all. 'She was a fine ship – not as pretty as this one though. Still, we were kind of attached to her.'

'I know how you feel. 'I'm from *Ark Royal*, which was sunk last November. You will find quite a few others who have lost ships to U-boats, and some who have never sailed before. We're pleased to have you on board. Go with the Petty Officer, stow your gear, and then come back here.'

The bunks they had been allocated were close to each other, and Bob couldn't be more pleased. After their experiences it was almost as if they were family, and would look out for each other. It was comforting and he was glad he hadn't been put on a ship where he knew no one. Everything so far had a good feel about it. He wasn't normally a superstitious person, but he couldn't help thinking that the omens were right.

When the entire crew had reported in, they assembled on deck to meet Captain Sutton. He told them that as this was a new ship they would spend a week on sea trials to iron out any faults they might find. After that they would be told where they were going.

The experienced men soon fell in to the routine of the ship as they prepared to get under way.

Later that evening, when Bob was off duty, he went out on deck. He loved gazing up at the heavens: the stars always seemed brighter when they were at sea. Although it was early September there was a fresh wind whipping around him, and Bob took a deep breath of sea air. It had a special smell to it, and it was something he'd loved from his very first voyage.

'Good to be back at sea,' Reg said as he joined him. 'It was what we all needed to do. The waiting was hard.'

Bob nodded, knowing exactly what his friend was saying. No matter how hard he'd tried, the lingering doubt had been there that they might find it difficult to put the sinking and loss of friends behind them. How would they handle the memories? Would it make it difficult for them to function efficiently?

'Everyone's all right.' Reg handed Bob a cigarette, already lit. 'And relieved.'

Bob took the cigarette. 'It's helped to find ourselves together again, and once the sea trials are over we will have settled in to our new ship.'

Reg drew deeply and blew the smoke out, watching it scud away on the stiff breeze. 'They seem like a good crew.'

Bob nodded. 'Of course they are; they've got us with them.'

'True,' his friend said laughing, then because serious. 'I'd love to get that U-boat.'

'Me too, but they won't always have the upper hand. Our day will come.'

'That's a good thought. Let's go and see how good this cook is. I'm starving, which is more than can be said for a couple of the new recruits. They're not interested in food.'

'Poor devils.' Bob stubbed out his fag. 'Do you remember the first time we set sail?'

'Yes. We both wondered if we would be seasick, but fortunately we never have been. Not even in that lifeboat.'

'No, thank goodness. Hope this cook knows his business.'

'Time for us to find out.'

Sleep wouldn't come that night, but Bob tried to stay still and relax. He wasn't on duty until five hundred hours, so he could at least rest. The motion of the ship as she surged through the water was soothing. They weren't under full power yet, but when they were the speed would be quite a lot faster than his other ship. His mind began to drift and settle on his family and friends. It was hard on the people at home waiting for news. The relief on his parents' faces when he'd walked through the door was something he would never forget. And it had also been a worry for Becky; he could imagine how frustrated she must feel not knowing what was going on, and not being able to do anything about it. She had always been a girl of action. Will had told him all about the colonel she was involved with, and there was no doubt he had a lot of courage. Funny, but he'd never thought that one day their Becky would grow up, find a husband, and not always be with them. The war had changed all that, of course, and now they were all going their separate ways. Those days would never return, but they had been good.

He sighed, trying to get comfortable. He was tall and the bunks on a ship were never quite long enough for him. There was no point worrying about Becky; she would do what she wanted to. Will was doing well, and he was pleased his friend had found some way to become involved in the war, because he had been very upset when they'd rejected him for active service. Then there was Jim – the tough daredevil one of the group. He'd changed almost beyond recognition during the course of the war – but then they were all changing. It was an inevitable result of war . . .

The sea trials went smoothly, with no great problems arising, and this period had given the men a chance to meld into an efficient crew. As they made their way back to Liverpool there was one thing on their minds – where would they be deployed? There was much speculation, but Bob felt sure it would not be convoy duty. This was a fast, well-equipped ship, and would be sent where she could be the most effective.

'What's your opinion?' Harry asked Bob after they'd docked.

'I think we could be going after some of the German battleships.'

'Me too. But whatever it is, this is going to be playing a very different role from our old ship.'

The men were not given leave or any shore time. Instead the ship was made ready to sail within twenty-four hours. Nothing was said about their destination, but this wasn't unusual. They would not be told until they had been at sea for a couple of days.

'Phew!' Reg exclaimed as he joined Bob below for a quick cup of tea. 'We've taken on enough armaments to sink a battleship.'

'Suits me.' Harry came and sat with them. 'I want to get back at those sods, and I don't care if they're on the sea or under it.'

Bob understood Harry's anger. He had lost a close friend on their last ship, and it still hurt.

'I'll drink to that.' Reg clinked cups with them.

Suddenly the order came and they all scrambled to their positions. They were on their way.

'Ah, there you are.' Becky finally found Alice in the mess, drinking tea and reading letters. She was smiling. 'Something funny?'

She looked up. 'Hello, Becky. Are you off duty now?'

She nodded. 'Unless I get called on. I can't leave the camp this evening. Are you going anywhere?'

'No.' Alice folded the letter and put it back in the envelope. 'When we were on leave Will asked me if I'd write to him. I hope you don't mind?'

'Why would I mind? Letters are very important and I'm pleased you're keeping in touch with my brother. You did appear to get on well with him.'

'You can wipe that hopeful gleam from your eyes. Will knows we can only be friends.'

Becky laughed mirthlessly. 'Oh, that sounds familiar.'

'How is the colonel, by the way?'

'Friendly.' Becky shook her head as they grinned at each other. 'I think he's enlisted his family to his campaign. Not only am I receiving regular letters from him, but also from Sara and his parents.'

'Ah, he's consolidating his attack. Are you about to surrender?'

'No,' she said firmly, and then pulled a face. 'When I refused him it was so clear to me that marriage between us wouldn't work, but I do have far too many moments of doubt. You have much more experience than me, so how do you know if someone is right for you, or you for them? After all, we're talking about a lifelong commitment.'

Alice looked at her friend's worried expression. 'That's just about impossible to explain, and all I can say is that if you have any doubts, don't commit yourself to anyone.'

'The trouble is I really am in love with him, and that seems to cloud my judgement.'

'How many times has he asked you to marry him now?'

'Three. Twice in person and once by letter. He said he's going to ask six times before he even considers giving up.'

'He's a man with a strong personality; don't allow him to persuade you to do something against your will, Becky. I don't suppose you've met anyone like him before.'

'No, I haven't. I've always been with the boys, and even as we grew up, there was never anything but a comfortable friendship between us.' Becky pulled a face. 'They sheltered me, didn't they?'

'It sounds as if they did, but you're managing just fine. Though you've picked a tough test for your first real romantic encounter. Come on, I'll buy you a drink.' Alice stood up.

'It will have to be lemonade as I'm on call.'

As they walked to the bar, Alice asked, 'Have you had many boyfriends? I don't mean Bob and Jim. Have you gone out on dates with other boys?'

'A couple, but I never went out more than twice with them. I was happy with my brother and the boys.' Becky bit her lip. 'What you're saying is that I'm very inexperienced where men are concerned.'

'Yes I am,' Alice said gently. 'And I think you've shown extremely good sense in not allowing the colonel to railroad you into marriage.'

'He did say he wished I wasn't so sensible.'

'Of course he does.' Alice smiled and changed the subject. 'Have you heard from Bob lately?'

Twenty-Eight

The convoy of lorries arrived back at Aldershot and Becky jumped out as soon as they had parked. They had just taken a large contingent of soldiers to Portsmouth and it had been an early start. She was ready for breakfast.

Pete joined her. 'Wonder where that lot are going?'

Becky was about to speak when a jeep came tearing towards them at breakneck speed.

'What the—?' Pete exclaimed. 'Those Yanks drive like lunatics.'

'That's a British Officer,' another driver said, as a tall man got out of the vehicle and strode towards them. 'And he's in a damned hurry.'

Hardly able to believe her eyes, Becky just gathered herself together in time to salute like everyone else.

'Come with me,' David ordered, looking straight at her, then spun on his heel and walked back to the jeep.

Pete nudged her, speaking out of the side of his mouth. 'Better hurry; he doesn't look too happy.'

Finally springing to life, she managed to catch him up.

'I've only got twelve hours, Rebecca. Will you marry me?'

She gasped and without answering his question, asked one of her own. 'What's going on?'

'My regiment is being shipped out, and you haven't answered my question.'

She was so staggered that she forgot he was in uniform. 'No, David. And anyway, it would be impossible in just a few hours.'

'I agree it would be hasty, but I could arrange it. It would be legal and we could arrange a proper church wedding when I return.'

'No, no, no!' She shook her head. 'I won't agree to this. My answer is still the same as the first time you asked me. Where are you going?'

'You know I can't tell you that.' He took a deep breath. 'Damn it, Rebecca, this isn't the way I want to do it either, but I had to try. Will you do something for me?'

'Of course, if I can.'

'Go and see Sara as often as you can. She loves being with you, and takes great comfort from your company.'

'I promise,' she said, hiding the bitter disappointment she felt. He was worrying about leaving his daughter again, and this suggestion of a hasty marriage was so that Sara would have a mother with her while he was away. It hurt, but she understood his concern that this time he might not come back. She wanted to reach out and assure him that everything would be all right, but there were too many curious pairs of eyes watching them. 'I'll be a lifelong friend to Sara, but that's the only promise I can make you, David.'

'Thank you, Rebecca, that's some comfort.' He tipped his head to one side. 'I keep putting you in a difficult situation, and I apologize for that.'

'You'll be coming back from wherever they're sending you, David.'

He smiled then. 'I've got to, because I still have two more chances to persuade you to marry me, and I'll make sure I have the time to do it properly next time.'

'You really ought to give up this crazy idea, you know.'

'Not a chance. I haven't been able to convince you we could have a good marriage together, but I wouldn't keep asking if I wasn't absolutely sure.' He gazed around and cursed quietly under his breath. 'Last time we had an enjoyable meal together. I should dump you in the jeep and tear off with you.'

'And what a scandal that would cause!' She couldn't help laughing, knowing he wasn't serious because the amused gleam was back in his eyes. Being careful not to let anyone see, she touched his hand gently and felt his long fingers curl around hers. 'You take care, and don't worry about Sara. She's quite happy with her grandparents, but if it will make you feel any better, I'll also watch over her for you.'

He squeezed her hand, and then without another word he climbed back in the jeep, started the engine, and roared off.

Watching him disappear she became aware of someone coming to stand beside her.

'Shipping out, is he?'

'Yes.' Knowing Pete was a proud father, she said, 'Colonel Hammond has a little daughter, and he's asked me to visit her as often as I can while he's away. I became friendly with his family when he was missing in France.'

'Ah, that's right. I remember you said your brother had been there as well.' Pete smiled at her. 'Do you know, Becky, if I didn't love my wife and kids so much, I could fall for you. You're one hell of a nice girl, and I bet the colonel thinks so, too.'

'You can stop that,' she laughed, keeping her tone light as she lied. 'He came to ask a favour, that's all. Now let's gets some breakfast. I'm starving.'

They walked towards the mess together. 'Your brother's making quite a name for himself. I've seen him on newsreels and listened to his broadcasts. You must be proud of him.'

'I am.' She smiled; relieved Pete had changed the subject. 'I've always been proud of him.'

There were two ships in dock, and both were packed with soldiers and equipment. Will remembered the trip he'd made on the *Queen Mary* with Bob. That ship had been full of Americans; these were crowded with British troops. He'd been told they would have a naval escort, and wouldn't it make an interesting story if his friend were on the escort ship! He knew their destination, but the troops would not be told until they were out of sight of land – though being issued with tropical gear rather gave the game away. A victory in North Africa would be a tremendous boost to morale at home, and Montgomery was determined to defeat Rommel.

He leant on the rail watching the last of the troops come on board, excited and apprehensive about what was in front of him. He was pretty sure Jim was out there and he hoped he'd get a chance to see him. The letters they received from him were brief, infrequent, and heavily censored, so apart from being told he was all right, they had no idea what he was doing. Knowing his friend as he did, Will would bet his last shilling that it was something dangerous.

A figure making his way up the gangplank of the other ship caught his attention. He was too far away to be absolutely sure so he quickly brought his binoculars up to his eyes. 'Damn!' he muttered as the gangplanks were taken away. It was Colonel Hammond, and there was no way he could get to him now. How he would love to talk to him again, but he would have curb his impatience until they reached Alexandria.

The ship began to edge its way slowly out to sea, and he scanned the ocean until he found what he was looking for. Waiting for them was a navy destroyer, one of the latest. He wished he knew the name of Bob's ship, but it was too much to hope it was his.

During the voyage Will found plenty to keep him occupied. With so many soldiers on board he wasn't short of stories for his notebook. It looked as if a big push was being planned, and he couldn't wait to get to North Africa.

The heat, smells and noise as the ships began to unload assaulted his senses, and Will was fascinated. He had never seen anything like it. The war was certainly giving him a chance to visit countries he would never otherwise be able to see. His first thought was to catch Becky's colonel, but it had taken him so long to disembark that Hammond and his men had already left when Will finally set foot on land. Disappointed, he climbed in a lorry with some of the soldiers, to be taken to his appointed destination. As soon as they reached the camp, Will sought out the officer in charge, and introduced himself.

Major Dalston had a ready smile, immediately making Will welcome. 'Glad to have you here. How was the journey?'

'The voyage was uneventful, sir. Colonel Hammond was on the other ship and I'd like to catch him if I can. Do you know where he will be stationed?'

'No idea at the moment. Join us for dinner tonight and perhaps we'll have more news for you.'

'Thank you. There's another man I would like to find. I'm a friend of his, but I'm not sure if he's here. His name is Jim Prentiss.'

'My goodness, you're pitching into your work already, aren't you?' There was a pause before the officer said briskly, 'I can't help you with that, I'm afraid. Dinner will be at eight.' He called a sergeant over. 'Show Mr Adams where to stow his gear. We have orders to cooperate with the press, so give him a tour of the camp. See you later,' he said to Will, and then marched away.

Not prepared to give up easily on finding out if Jim was here, he tried the sergeant. 'I expect you know everyone, Sergeant. I'm looking for a friend of mine, Jim Prentiss. Do you by any chance know if he's here?'

'Prentiss, you say?'

Will nodded, and waited while the sergeant thought this over.

'Hmm. I do know a Prentiss.' He gave Will a studied sideways glance. 'This one's with that crazy lot of Special Forces.'

'That's him.'

'Ah, well, he'll be in those tents on the edge of the desert. They keep to themselves. A friend of yours, you say?'

'We grew up together. Can you show me where he is?'

'Ah, well, I'd better come with you.' The sergeant smirked. 'A word of warning: don't go near their tents in the dark; it could be dangerous. They're a tough bunch and don't like people creeping up on them. But if you want hair-raising stories, they're your men.'

'Knowing Jim, I'm not surprised at that,' Will joked. 'Let's go there now. It's still light.'

The sergeant chuckled. 'I've heard you war correspondents like to get in amongst the action. Come with me, and whistle a happy tune so they know we're friendly.'

'I do believe you're exaggerating, Sergeant.' Will was highly amused.

The sergeant said nothing, and began whistling 'The White Cliffs of Dover'.

Men were sprawled out in any bit of shade they could find. 'They're all asleep,' Will said, taking in every detail of the scene.

'Nah, they're just conserving their energy.'

'What do you want, Ed?' one asked without opening his eyes. 'We haven't got a card game going.'

Will snorted back a laugh. So much for the sergeant being afraid of this group.

'I've brought you a visitor. Says he's a friend of Jim's.'

That caught their attention and they began to sit up and study Will through narrowed eyes, reading the badges on his uniform.

'War Correspondent.' One stood up and came forward. 'You must be Will Adams. Jim's told us about you.'

'That's right. Is he around?'

'His group are out at the moment.'

'What!' the sergeant exclaimed in mock horror. 'It's broad daylight.'

'Don't take any notice of him. He tells everyone we're vampires and hide when the sun shines.' The soldier shook hands. 'Pleased to meet you, Will. My name's Dan. We're expecting them back at any minute. Why don't you wait?'

'Thanks.' Will was introduced to the rest of the men, although no surnames were given.

'I'll leave you to it then, mate.' The sergeant turned to go and looked back over his shoulder. 'Don't forget you're dining with the officers tonight.'

'I'll be there – and thank you, Sergeant.' Will watched him walk away, whistling another Vera Lynn song.

A mug of tea was handed to Will and he sat down with the men, wondering if he could get a story about this strange group of men, but that hope was instantly dashed.

'You'll have to forget you're a reporter when you're with us. We don't exist.'

'That's a shame.'

One of the men surged to his feet, looking out across the desert, shading his eyes against the glare of the sun. 'Here they come, Dan.'

They were all on their feet now and Will joined them, but he couldn't see a thing. 'There's nothing there.'

'Look slightly to your right,' Dan pointed. 'See that cloud of dust?'

'Ah, I see them now. Your eyesight must be exceptional.'

'You just have to know what you're looking for.'

The tiny specks grew larger, and in no time at all two jeeps skidded to a halt by the tents. In them were eight dirty, weary men, and it was impossible to pick out Jim. The others surged around the vehicles, and Will thought it wise to keep out of the way as they talked quietly.

After a while one man jumped out of the first jeep and walked towards Will, a huge smile on his face. There was no longer any mistaking who he was.

'Will, what the hell are you doing out here?' Jim slapped him on the back, clearly delighted to see him.

'I've come to report on the North Africa campaign.' Will couldn't believe his eyes. The grin on his friend's face was almost boyish – almost like old times.

The rest of the group joined them, and by the time the introductions were made, Will's head was reeling. He had an excellent memory but the names had been rattled off, and the men seemed to blend together, until he couldn't distinguish one from the other. He was never going to remember their names, and he suspected that was intentional on their part.

'We have to report in, Will. Are you going to be around here for a while?'

'I'm not sure, but I'm having dinner with those in charge this evening, so I'll probably find out what story they want me to cover.'

'Well, I hope to catch you later, and you can tell me all the news from home.'

Will never did get the chance to see Jim again, because on 23rd October, Montgomery's plan to capture El Alamein began with a huge barrage on the German positions. The flashes and deafening noise of around one thousand guns was awesome to behold, and the colonel's Artillery Regiment was bound to be a part of it. Troops began to move forward and Will was right behind them. He stayed with the advancing force, recording as much of the action as he could with the camera. Any time they stopped he wrote frantically, but even for him it was hard to put the intensity, courage and determination of the men into words.

He never complained about the danger or harsh conditions, he just kept moving to keep up with the action. The armoured division had offered him a lift, but he'd refused. It was the soldiers slogging their way forward on foot that he wanted to record. That had earned him respect, and they'd begun to call him Press. He was proud of that.

On 4th November they broke through, and the prize of El Alamein was theirs. Rommel and his troops were in full retreat, and it was only when they'd stopped that Will realized just how tired he was. Sitting on the ground and leaning on what was left of a ruined wall, he closed his eyes, yearning for a cold beer.

'You do like to get yourself into dangerous situations, don't you?'

Will's eyes shot open, a slow smile crossing his face as he took the bottle being held out to him. 'That's rich coming from you. How are you, Colonel?'

'Tired, like everyone else.' He held out his hand to pull Will to his feet. 'I'll find you somewhere more comfortable to rest.'

'You haven't by any chance got a nice communications centre set up yet, have you? My portable has packed up.' Will gathered up his equipment, and began walking beside Colonel Hammond.

David studied the boy beside him and was impressed. 'Have you carried that lot all the way?'

'I needed it.'

'I know the armoured division offered you a lift, so why didn't you take it?'

'I wanted to be with the foot soldiers,' he said simply.

'Hmm, I can see where your sister gets her determination from. I saw her briefly before I left.'

'Did you? How was she?'

'Too sensible for my good,' David said wryly.

Will gave him a puzzled glance. 'Don't you mean too sensible for her own good?'

'I know what I mean. Here you are, this is the communications centre you asked for. When you've finished what you have to do come to that house across the road and I'll find you somewhere to sleep.'

'Thanks, Colonel.' Will watched the tall man walk away, still trying to work out what he'd meant. It sounded as if he was having trouble with Becky, and that didn't surprise him too much. Once she made up her mind about something it was hard work making her change it. He'd love to know what was going on between them though.

An hour later Will stepped out of the communications post and saw Jim striding towards him.

'Ah, I thought I'd find you here. If you've finished all your business I think it's time for a couple of drinks.'

'Good idea. I'm as dry as a bone. I've been offered a place to sleep over there, so let me dump my gear and you can lead me to the beer.'

Twenty-Nine

Churchill had ordered the church bells to be rung in London to celebrate the victory at El Alamein. Fortunately Becky had been in town that day, and to hear the chimes that had remained silent since the start of the war brought a smile to her face. Rommel had been defeated in North Africa and was in full retreat.

She sang happily to herself as she packed her bag for seven days' leave. Although the triumph at El Alamein had been two weeks ago, they would still celebrate because her brother had just arrived home. She knew from the news reports that he had been there, and she could not wait to hear all about it from him, first-hand. He would be able to tell them things that he couldn't put in the official reports.

'You off then?' Alice looked in the door. 'Have you got a lift?'

'No, I'm going by train. I'm sorry you can't come as well. Will would love to have seen you.'

'You tell him well done from me, and we'll try to meet up sometime soon.'

'I will.' Becky glanced at her watch, grabbed her bag and headed for the door. 'I'll have to hurry or I'll miss the train. See you when I get back.'

'Bye then, have a good time!'

The station had been packed with service men and women, and when they all crammed into the train, it had been a job to shut the doors. Becky had had to stand all the way, but that wasn't unusual. The trains could be few and far between, so when one came along you had to get on it no matter how crowded, in case there was a long wait for another one.

As she walked up her road she saw two soldiers studying a map. They kept looking at her house and talking animatedly.

'Can I help you?' she asked when she reached them. 'Are you lost?'

They spun round to face her. 'Ah, no, we think we're in the

right place.' One of them held out a piece of paper for her to see. 'Is this the right address?'

She recognized Bob's writing and smiled at the two Americans. 'Are you Greg and Hal by any chance?'

'We sure are.' They stared at her for a moment, then Hal exclaimed, 'Gee, you must be Becky, Will's sister. You look just like him.'

'I'm pleased to meet you.'

Greg beamed in delight. 'Bob told us we could call on your folks, but we ain't sure about going in. Is it all right?'

'Of course it is, and you're in luck because my brother's at home right now.'

'Oh, wow, we sure picked the right day.' Hal relieved her of her kitbag, and they started to walk up the path just as the front door swung open.

'Hey, Will!' The two Americans rushed to greet him, talking excitedly.

'Come in! Mum's got the kettle on already.'

Becky followed, and as soon as she could get near her brother she hugged him. He looked thinner, but tanned and clearly healthy. 'Alice is sorry she couldn't come as well, but she said to tell you well done, and that goes for me as well. I'm so proud to have a famous brother.'

He kissed her cheek, laughing. 'You do exaggerate at times, Becky. I'm only one of many War Correspondents.'

'I know, but you're the one I notice.'

With his arm around her shoulder they walked into the kitchen where the Americans were already sitting at the table with her parents and Bob's. They were looking a bit doubtful about the steaming cups of tea in front of them.

'Haven't you got used to our national drink yet?' Will asked.

'It's taking time.' Greg reached for the sugar, but Becky stopped him. 'Try drinking it without sugar and see if you like it better.'

'Can you do that?' When Becky nodded Greg took a doubtful sip, then another. 'Hey, that's better. You try it, Hal.'

Becky and her family watched with amusement as the Americans tried to decide if tea tasted better with or without sugar. Finally, it was decided that Greg preferred it without, but Hal needed the sweetness to make it palatable. It was obvious they still didn't like it much, but were too polite to refuse. After giving their heartfelt thanks to everyone for allowing them to visit, they turned their attention to Will.

'How's Bob, Will? I've had a couple of letters from him, and would sure like to see him again.' Greg took another sip of tea and managed not to grimace.

'He's fine, as far as I know. When I went out to North Africa we had an escort, and I wondered if it was Bob's ship, but I didn't know the name of the one he's on now, and they were gone as soon as we arrived.'

'We've been following the desert action,' Hal told him, concern written all over his face. 'And you were in the thick of it. Man, you do like to frighten everyone, don't you?'

'I was all right, Hal.' Will smiled. 'And it was the only way to get the story I wanted.'

'Well, we hope you're going to be with us when we go into Germany, because you've got a charmed life, pal.'

'I'll have to go where they send me, but I'll keep an eye open for you both. How are you settling down in this country?'

'We're OK. The people in the village were wary of us at first, but they're friendly when you get to know them.' Greg pulled a face. 'Some of the guys can get a bit loud at times, but they don't mean no harm. Me and Hal get on fine though, and some of the local kids are teaching us how to play your football.'

Hal laughed. 'When I picked up the ball and ran with it they said I was playing rugby. We've thrown a couple of parties for them, and you ought to see their little faces when they see so much food. It's good to give them a treat.'

'That's kind of you.' Becky's mother refilled their cups. 'I'm sorry we haven't got coffee for you, but have a biscuit with that, it might help – and you must stay for lunch. I'm sure you'd like to have a long chat with Will.'

'Oh, thanks, ma'am, but we can't eat your food. You don't have enough for yourselves.' Greg reached for a bag he'd put on the floor and tipped it out on the table. 'We brought you this.'

Hal began riffling through his many pockets and brought out several packets, putting them on the now large heap in the middle of the table.

'My goodness!' Bob's mother exclaimed. 'We can't take all that. It's far too much.'

'Sure you can, ma'am.' Greg looked around at everyone. 'Some of us were real scared about coming over here. We'd heard such tales about the war. We expected to find a country in ruins with the people demoralized, and it was only when we met Will and Bob on the *Queen Mary* we realized we were wrong. Sure, London and other cities have taken a terrible pounding, but everyone still knows how to smile. And we don't know how you manage on the small rations you're given, but you do. When we write home we tell them exactly what it's like here, and how nothing is wasted because it costs lives to get the shipments through. We also tell them about the funny things that happen to us, and what a beautiful country this is.'

'That's right.' Hal nodded in agreement. 'I told my folks that when this war's over they've got to come and see England for themselves, and meet some of the fine people we've come to know. Bob and Will were real good to us. They took the time to talk and explain how things really were. But do you know what impressed us the most?'

They all shook their heads, fascinated by the American accent.

'Bob and his pals had been torpedoed, left adrift in an open boat for a long time, but they couldn't wait to get their hands on the bastards – pardon the language,' he apologized. 'They were on a boat again, and they weren't afraid! That sure as hell made us think.'

'Yeah,' Greg said. 'We really appreciated them taking the trouble to put us at ease. And to you for welcoming us into your home, so you take the food, OK? We don't expect you to feed two hungry Americans without a contribution from us.'

'Well, thank you.' Becky's father smiled. 'And we're delighted to meet you at last. You're welcome to come here any time you feel like it.'

'Thanks, sir. We'd like to visit when we can.' Greg watched the women begin to gather up the food and gave a satisfied nod, then he turned his attention to Will. 'So what was it like in the desert?'

'Hot.' Will grinned at his sister. 'I met Jim out there.'

'Oh, how is he?' Becky spoke for the first time after letting the Americans talk as much as they wanted to. They were obviously so happy to see her brother again that she had resisted the urge to interrupt.

'He's fine, but you ought to see the group he's with. They have a fierce reputation.' Will had them all roaring with laughter as he told them what the sergeant had said about approaching them with caution. 'He was exaggerating, of course, but try as I might, I couldn't get Jim or any of the others to talk. After El Alamein had been taken, Jim and his mates invited me to join them for a drink, and what a night that was. Then when your colonel came in with the Special Forces commander, the drink really began to flow.'

'David was there?' Becky rounded on her brother. 'Why didn't you tell me that before?'

'I was saving that piece of information.' A wide grin spread across Will's face. 'Boy, can he hold his drink, and that man is just as tough as Jim and his group.'

Becky slumped in the chair. 'Well it sounds as if he's all right then. You must write to his parents and let them know you saw him out there. It will make Sara happy to know her father's all right.'

'I've already written a letter, but I only posted it yesterday.'

'Thanks, Will. I'll go and see them as soon as I can.'

Bill Adams glanced at the clock. 'The pub's open now, so why don't we go and have a drink while the women see about lunch?'

The men all began to stand up, nodding in agreement, and Becky was about to do the same when her mother touched her arm, shaking her head.

'Let them go on their own,' her mother said softly.'

'Oh, of course.' Becky sat down again quickly. 'I'm so used to going everywhere with the boys that I forget I'm a girl sometimes.'

'We'll be back in a couple of hours,' Bill told his wife.

They all filed out of the room with the Americans smiling, delighted to be going with the men to the local pub.

When they'd gone, Becky's mother said, 'It isn't that they wouldn't want you with them, dear, but with all men together they can talk freely.'

'I understand, Mum. What do you think of the Americans?'

'They're nice boys, and so polite. It must be hard for them so far away from home.'

'They're bound to miss their families, just as we miss our boys. Perhaps we could ask them to join us for Christmas. They might enjoy being with a family,' Bob's mother suggested.

'That's a good idea, Sal. Now, let's get on with the meal. They'll be starving when they get back.'

Greg and Hal stayed until early evening, reluctant to leave the family atmosphere. Just before they left, Becky's mother invited them for Christmas if they could make it. They accepted with enthusiasm, shaking hands with everyone and thanking them all for a lovely day.

The men went with them to make sure they caught the right train, and Becky was able to relax with a nice cup of tea as she waited for her brother. She had so many questions to ask him about Jim and David.

'Those boys seem to really like Will and Bob, don't they?' Bob's mother said as she sat down with a sigh of relief after a busy day.

'I expect it's because our boys took the trouble to be friendly when they were coming over. They must have wondered what on earth they were going to find when they arrived.' Mavis Adams sat down with them, her eyes showing sadness. 'When I watched the youngsters laughing and joking today I couldn't help wondering what horrors they were going to face when the push to defeat Germany begins.'

'I don't think it will be for a while yet,' Becky said. 'We're nowhere near ready.'

The men walked in as they were talking and Will immediately picked up on the conversation. 'Becky's right. A move won't be made until they're sure of success. It will have to be decisive because they won't want another Dunkirk.'

'And it will be a long and bloody battle,' Bob's father said grimly. 'When it does begin I'll be quite relieved that Bob's at sea and not fighting over land. Hitler won't give in easily, and the Allies want total surrender.'

Becky waited patiently as they all discussed the war, and when everyone except Will had retired for the night, she turned eagerly to him. 'Now you can tell me all about North Africa – and Jim and David.'

For the next hour she listened, entranced, to Will's detailed account of the attack for El Alamein, and his meeting with their friend and the colonel, as he always called him.

It had been a lovely week, and twice Will and Becky had persuaded the parents to come dancing. It had been wonderful to dance with her father again, and she was the teacher this time as she showed him how to Jive. He quickly picked it up, and soon Bob's parents were also having a go. They laughed until their sides ached, and they decided to bring Greg and Hal if they managed to visit for Christmas.

Becky left early on her last day because she wanted to call in on the Hammonds before reporting back after her leave.

Sara and the dog came running out to meet her before she had even reached the top of the driveway. The little girl was growing fast and attending a junior school now. She braced herself for the enthusiastic welcome she knew was coming.

'Rebecca!' The girl threw herself at Becky, and the dog wasn't going to be left out. 'We've had a letter from your brother. There was a note inside just for me, and I could read it without any help.'

'Well done. He told me he'd written to you.' She finally freed herself, laughing at the dog's determination to play with her. There was a pang of sadness as she took hold of Sara's hand. She loved the little girl, but it would be wrong to enter into a marriage just because of that. In fact it could turn out to be disastrous. A one-sided love was not a strong enough foundation, and without love on both sides the marriage would eventually crumble.

Mr Hammond was waiting at the door for them. He called off the dog, and smiled. 'How lovely to see you, Rebecca. Come in and join us; we're about to have lunch.'

'We've had a letter from Will,' Mrs Hammond told her after kissing her cheek.

Becky was taken aback. David' parents always seemed pleased to see her, but they'd never shown this kind of affection before. 'I've been home for a few days and he was there. He told me all about it.'

'Splendid news about North Africa.' David's father relieved her of her coat. 'How long can you stay?'

'Until four o'clock.'

'Good.' Mrs Hammond turned to leave the room. 'I'll set another place for you.'

'Are you sure it's all right, Mrs Hammond? 'You weren't expecting me and I can't eat your rations.'

'I made a large pan of vegetable soup and there's a fresh crusty loaf. It's a simple meal, but there's plenty. We grow our own vegetables, like everyone else.'

'In that case I'd love to stay.' Becky wondered where the maid was as Mrs Hammond was doing everything herself.

As if reading her mind, Mrs Hammond smiled. 'We've lost Doris. She's gone into a factory, but we were lucky to keep her for as long as we did. I'm quite enjoying being kept busy.'

Over lunch Becky told them all Will had seen and done in North Africa, and about the two Americans. Sara listened with great interest, taking in every word.

'We met some Americans,' the girl informed Becky, her eyes shining. 'They were nice and they gave me some chocolate! I shared it with two more children in the park. It was lovely.'

'What a treat.'

Sara nodded, serious now. 'I expect they get lonely a long way from home, just like my daddy does.'

'Yes, they do, and it's hard for those waiting at home as well.'

'I worry about my daddy.'

'I know you do, sweetheart, but he's quite all right.' Becky smiled reassuringly at Sara. 'My brother's keeping an eye on him for you.'

'I like your brother.' The concern cleared from her face. 'I like getting letters from him, so would you ask him to write again, please?'

'I'll ask him next time I write to him.'

'Thank you, Rebecca.'

Becky helped Mrs Hammond clear the table and wash up after lunch, and while they were alone, David's mother said quietly, 'We've had a letter from David today, and he told us he'd asked you to marry him, but you'd refused.'

Sure that they would not approve of a marriage between them, Becky answered firmly. 'I had to. It wouldn't do.'

'Why?'

'Pardon?' She sent Mrs Hammond a startled look, as she'd expected her to agree that a marriage between them wouldn't be the done thing.

'Why do you think it wouldn't do?'

Now she was flustered, but as with David, she spoke plainly, giving the same reasons for her refusal.

By the time she'd finished, Mrs Hammond was shaking her head. 'You're a lovely, well brought up girl, Rebecca, as well as intelligent and kind. You understand army life and would make David an excellent wife. Class doesn't come into it, but a sound character does, and that's what you have. You would fit in anywhere, and I must say we were both disappointed to hear you had refused. Don't you love him?'

'Very much, but he doesn't love me.'

'Nonsense! We know our son, and he adores you. His wife wasn't right for him. She hated army life, but he was besotted with her. What he feels for you is a different kind of love – the lasting kind. But he hasn't recognized that yet.'

Becky stared at her, thoroughly confused now.

'You have to be patient with men, my dear. Don't give up on him, please.'

Thirty

Because her leave had been in November, Becky wasn't able to get home that Christmas, but she received a long letter from her parents. None of the boys had made it home either, but Greg and Hal had turned up, and by the sound of it they had had a lively time. Becky's father seemed particularly fond of the two Americans, and was writing to both of them regularly now.

The new year, 1943, had arrived on a bitter cold wind, and on 17th January London had suffered a night-time raid, the first for quite a while. But over the last few months there had been heartening news. The German forces at Stalingrad had surrendered, and just last week, on 13th May, the German and Italian troops had also surrendered in North Africa.

It would be lovely if Jim and David could now come home. Since her talk with Mrs Hammond all those months ago, Becky had begun to think over her reasons for refusing David's proposal, but she needed to see him, spend time with him. How could anyone come to important decisions like this when so much time was spent apart? However, his letters were very regular and made her laugh. She did love his sense of humour . . .

'What's he been up to now?' Alice asked as she sat down opposite her friend. 'I know from that expression that you're reading a letter from the colonel.'

She grinned. 'I've also had one from Will. Have you?'

'Three arrived at once this morning. Do you know where he is?'

'No idea. He might be in North Africa again, but David hasn't mentioned him. I do have a piece of good news though. Bob arrived home two weeks ago with a pretty Wren on his arm. Helen, her name is.'

'Oh, do you mind?'

Becky stared at her friend, puzzled. 'Why should I mind? Of course I'll have to look her over to make sure she's suitable.'

'Of course.' Alice shook her head. 'I thought you were fond of Bob?'

'I am, but he's like a brother to me, and like Will, I want him to be happy.'

'And I'm sure they both will be, once this blasted war's over.' Alice pursed her lips. 'As for us, we've got problems to resolve, haven't we?'

'We certainly have. 'You have to come to terms with losing Anthony, and I've got to decide what to do about David. I thought I was clear in my mind, but since talking to Mrs Hammond I don't know where I am. I was really shocked to discover that they would approve of me as a wife for their son.'

'It shows they're genuinely fond of you.' Alice smiled. 'But don't worry, we'll eventually sort ourselves out, and I still think you've done the right thing.'

'Wish I did.' Becky glanced at her watch. 'I've got to go. See you tonight?'

Alice nodded. 'I'll check if there's a dance somewhere, shall I?'

'Good idea.' Becky hurried back after her break.

'Hey, Becky!' someone called. 'Come and have a look at this. The darned thing keeps stalling on me.'

Her face lit up with pleasure as she rushed over to the vehicle, and was soon completely absorbed in what she was doing. When the sergeant shouted, 'Officer present,' she jumped and hit her head as she scrambled out. Sliding off the vehicle she hit the ground with a thump, straightening and saluting smartly. When she looked into the officer's face he was having a terrible job not to laugh.

'A tank?' he said.

'Yes, sir. They're having trouble with it and asked me to have a look.' She wanted to smile, but didn't dare. If she started she wouldn't be able to stop herself laughing. The men always roped her in like this, knowing how much she loved to get her hands on any kind of engine. Sometimes there wasn't much wrong, but they let her probe around to her heart's content, waiting to see if she could discover the fault. She took a deep breath. He looked so good, tanned and leaner.

'And have you discovered what the problem is?'

'Not yet, sir.' Then she murmured under her breath, 'No one's removed any vital parts though.'

He laughed out loud then. 'When you've sorted it out I want to see you. I'll be with Major Brent.'

'Yes, sir!' He walked away still laughing. She had never seen him so relaxed.

'He keeps turning up,' Pete remarked dryly. 'Where's he been this time?'

'North Africa.'

'Thought so. He'll be in for a promotion soon, I expect. He'll be a general in time for the invasion,' Pete teased.

Becky cast Pete a horrified look. 'Very funny. Just imagine the strange looks that would cause when he comes looking for me. This encounter has set a few minds working overtime – just look at their faces. He didn't even pretend he needed me for a driving job.'

'He doesn't care, Becky. He's considered a hero after what he's accomplished, and no one's going to criticize him for being with a lovely girl. You're a friend of his family, so why shouldn't he talk to you? That's what I tell anyone who asks me.'

'You get asked?'

'I have been, but you haven't got anything to worry about. You act in a proper military way when you meet him in camp, and what you do off duty is none of their business.'

'We don't do anything when we're off duty!' she said tartly. 'But you're quite right, I worry too much.'

'You do,' Pete agreed. 'He's a well-respected man, Becky, and a damned fine soldier. Any chatter coming from some of the other girls is only because they're jealous. Take no notice of it.'

'That's what Alice keeps telling me.' She started to clamber back on the tank. 'Let's see if we can sort this beast out.'

An hour later she looked into Alice's office. 'I've been ordered to come here.'

'They've been waiting for you.' Alice looked her up and down. 'Couldn't you have changed first?'

'I've washed off the grease and put on a clean shirt.'

'But you're still wearing those blasted trousers. You've got a pair of legs I'd give anything for, and you've always got them covered up.'

'I'm going straight back to work after this, and I can't climb over a tank in a skirt, Alice.'

'Tank!' Alice groaned. 'What are we going to do with you?'

'They are having trouble with it so Pete and I have been fixing it.' Becky's grin spread. 'There's another one—'

'Don't tell me any more.' Alice was shaking her head in dismay. 'Your brother and the boys have a lot to answer for.'

They both looked up sharply when they heard quiet laughter. The two officers were standing in the doorway, highly amused.

'I take it the tank is in good working order now?' David asked.

'Of course.'

The major walked past Becky, chuckling quietly to himself. 'Use my office, David. I'll take Alice for a walk.'

Becky watched them leave. This was all very informal . . .

'Come in, and don't you dare salute.'

She followed him into the office, wondering if this was going to be another proposal.

'Sit down, Rebecca.'

After dusting off her trousers, just in case they marked the posh chair, she sat and waited.

'I've arranged for you to have a day's leave tomorrow. We're all going on a picnic to celebrate my homecoming. Sara's looking forward to it.'

She stared at him, speechless.

'We'll pick you up from the gate at ten in the morning.' His mouth quirked at the corners. 'Nothing to say, Rebecca?'

Her pent-up breath came out in a whoosh. 'What is there to say? It seems I'm going on a picnic, and you needn't come to the camp for me. I'll meet you at the house.'

'No!'

'But it will cause talk, and you've got a position to maintain.'

'To hell with that,' he said sharply, standing up and towering over her. 'Since this war started I've been bombed, shot at, trapped behind enemy lines, dug holes in the sand like a rat, while someone has been doing his best to kill me. People can think what they like. I no longer care. If anyone tries to make things difficult for you, I'll deal with them.'

She was astonished. 'You've changed.'

He stooped down in front of her and took hold of her hands. 'And about bloody time, too. But we've all changed, my dear. Now, will you come on the picnic with us?'

'I'd love to.'

'Thank you.' He squeezed her hands and then stood up again. 'So we'll meet you at the gate.'

'I'll be there.' She certainly wasn't going to argue again. If this was how he wanted it, then she'd go along. If the gossip around the camp didn't bother him, then she would try to ignore it as well. He was flouting the rules where she was concerned, and that wasn't a comfortable feeling, knowing the army was his life. She would be upset if his prospects were harmed because he was consorting with a girl from the ranks. Of course it went on, she wasn't that daft, but it was usually a discreet relationship. David was making no attempt to hide her friendship with him and his family. It was unsettling, but her respect and admiration for this complex man just grew and grew.

'We'll look forward to a pleasant day. Now, walk me to my car.'

She did that and watched him drive away. At that moment Alice returned.

'Was that another proposal?'

'No.' Becky shook her head. 'I've been invited to a picnic tomorrow.'

'Lovely. Hope the weather holds for you.'

It was a beautiful day and Becky decided to wear the skirt Alice had insisted she keep, a plain white blouse, and a pair of flat sandals. In case it turned chilly she draped the cardigan Mrs Hammond had made her around her shoulders. With a bag of biscuits as a contribution to the picnic she walked to the gate, showed her pass and waited outside.

She had only been there about five minutes when the Rolls Royce purred into view with Mr Hammond driving, and Sara waving frantically from the back seat.

'My goodness,' she exclaimed as they pulled up beside her. 'Where did you get the petrol to run this, Mr Hammond?'

'I've been saving my ration and thought this was a good time to use it.' He gave a wry smile. 'We can't go far though.'

'I should think not. Hello, Mrs Hammond, it looks like we have a lovely day for it.' She greeted the family first, not forgetting the excited dog, before turning her attention to David who was now standing beside her. He looked happy and relaxed in civvies.

Before opening the rear door for her he kissed her gently on the cheek. 'You look lovely, Rebecca.'

'Thanks.' She smiled up at him. 'You don't look too bad yourself.'

Laughing, he opened the door for her. 'In you get.'

'We're so pleased you could get a pass for today,' Mrs Hammond said, clearly delighted with the prospect of a day out together.

'That was your son's doing. I was just told I had a pass and would be coming on a picnic today.'

David's mother smothered a laugh. 'Still giving orders, is he?'

'He's very good at it.'

'The trouble is, Mother, she doesn't always obey me.' David glanced back at them.

'Oh, Daddy, you mustn't tell Rebecca off today. We're going to have a lovely picnic.'

'I wouldn't dream of it, sweetheart.' He smiled and winked at his daughter. 'I only do that when we're in uniform. Have you shown Rebecca your new charm?'

'Not yet.' Sara searched through the charms on the bracelet until she found the new one, then she held it out. 'Look, it's a camel.'

'How lovely.' Becky spent a while admiring the charm, pleased she had thought of giving Sara the bracelet. It was giving her so much pleasure. 'Where are we going?' she asked Mrs Hammond.

'Virginia Water. It's a lovely place and we have just enough petrol for the trip. Have you ever been there?'

'No, I haven't.'

'You'll like it, my dear.'

'I managed to get hold of these to add to the picnic.' She held out the small bag of biscuits. 'It isn't much, but it was the best I could do at short notice.'

'Shortbread!' Mrs Hammond exclaimed. 'I haven't seen those for a while. Thank you, Rebecca.'

Pleased she had been able to contribute something to the day out, Becky sat back to enjoy the ride in the luxurious car. At least, as much as she could with the dog trying to lick her face and sit on her lap.

Hearing the tussle going on in the back, David turned round and caught hold of the animal's collar. 'On the floor!'

Giving a disgruntled huff, the dog did as she was told.

Sara grinned. 'Daddy's the only one she will obey.'

'I'm not surprised. You ought to see the soldiers at camp spring to attention when he walks by, and that includes me. No one disobeys a colonel.'

'Brigadier now,' Mrs Hammond told her proudly. 'His promotion has just come through. That's another reason for the celebration.'

Becky tapped David on the shoulder, making him turn round. 'Congratulations. You didn't tell me that.'

'Didn't I? I must have forgotten. By the way, your friend Alice is now working for a colonel. Steve Brent has also been promoted.'

'She'll like that,' Becky laughed. 'When the war started she told me she was aiming to be working for a general by the end of the war.'

'Ah, well, she's got a way to go yet.'

'A couple of the men were speculating that you'd be a general by the end as well.'

'That's most unlikely. The war will be over in a year to eighteen months. Plans are well under way for the invasion, and it's going to be a busy year.' His eyes shone with devilment. 'I could need a permanent driver. I'll have to put in the request.'

'I'm sure Pete Markham would like the job, and he's the best.'

'Major General Villiers says you're the best driver he's ever had.'

'That's kind of him.' She was well aware David was suggesting he ask for her, but as much as she would relish the job, she wasn't sure it would be a good idea. Fortunately they had reached their destination and that put an end to the conversation.

They parked, and as soon as the door was open, the dog took off, with Sara tearing after her. 'She's in the water! Help! She'll drown.'

Becky broke into a run and caught up with the distraught girl. 'It's all right, Sara. She can swim. See?'

'How can she do that? She's never been in water before.' Sara was jumping up and down. 'Come back, Becky! You're in the middle and it's deep there!'

David had joined them and let out a piercing whistle, causing the animal to turn and paddle back towards them.

'There, she's all right,' Becky soothed as the dog climbed out of the water and made for them, her tail wagging frantically as she shook herself. Everyone scattered to avoid a soaking from the spray.

The sun was shining and the war seemed miles away as they explored the area, then settled down to eat the sandwiches, biscuits and home-made cake. Sara and the dog were tired out from all the running around, and they both went to sleep on the blanket.

David stood up and held out his hand. 'Let's walk, Rebecca.'

He continued to hold her hand as they strolled along. 'I really am going to need a driver, so would you object if I asked for you to be assigned to me?'

'I'd love to do it, David, but it's awkward.'

'Explain.'

'A couple of the girls have made remarks, loud enough for me to overhear, about girls who run after officers. Alice told me to ignore them, but I don't like to think there's talk about our friendship. That's why I'm so careful to respond to you in a military way.'

He swore under his breath. 'I'm sorry, Rebecca. I'll deal with it.'

'How can you? You can hardly post a notice on the board for everyone to read, explaining that there's nothing improper in our friendship.'

'No, but I can start another rumour. I knew you before you joined the army, and as your family are friends of mine, I have naturally taken an interest in your progress. How does that sound?'

She nodded. 'That might stop some of the speculation, but how will you do it?'

'You leave that to me, but on reflection, it might be wiser not to ask for you as my permanent driver. It might only make things more uncomfortable for you. What did you say Pete's surname was?'

'Markham.'

'I'll use him for a while.'

'You won't be disappointed; he's very good.'

'I will be disappointed.' He smiled down at her. 'The last thing in this world I want to do is hurt you, my dear. If the nasty remarks continue, I want you to let me know.'

'I will, but Alice is right, and I'll just ignore them from now on.' She'd been rather upset when she'd found out some nasty things were being said, but felt better now he knew about it. She gave him an impish smile. 'It's stretching the truth a bit to say your family and mine are friends, isn't it?'

'Not at all. We know your brother, and I have no doubt we would like your parents very much. They have brought up two fine children.'

She began to laugh. 'Will told me about that night after El Alamein had been taken.'

'Ah, was he sober enough to record it in his notebook?'

'Of course.'

They turned and walked back to the others, smiling and completely happy in each other's company.

Thirty-One

'I know where Will is.' Alice slid a newspaper over to Becky. 'He's in Sicily. It looks as if the Allies have got their sights on Italy first.'

Becky was silent while she read her brother's report, then she looked up. 'Wonder if he's on the newsreels?'

'Shall we go to the pictures tonight and see?'

'I'd like to, but I'm on duty.'

'Shame, but never mind. I'll probably go on my own. I haven't seen much of you over the last few weeks.'

'I know, I'm sorry, but they've kept me very busy. I've been out on the road nearly every day, and I don't know what happened to June and July.'

'Mind if I join you?'

'Not at all, Pete.' Becky gave him a suspicious look. 'I hope you haven't come to collect me? This is the first break I've managed in over four hours.'

He put his mug of tea on the table and sat down. 'I've just heard something interesting and thought you might like to know.'

Becky sighed. 'Not more rumours about me and a certain officer.'

'Hmm.' He grinned at her exasperation. 'The story going round now is that you knew the Brigadier before you joined up. Is that true?'

'Yes.' David was certainly doing his best to stop some of the speculation about them, but she wasn't sure it was working. This was really becoming quite a nuisance.

'If I'd known that, Becky, I would have put those two girls in their place before now.'

'Would it have made any difference?' She pulled a face. Her parents had brought her up with the rule that if you couldn't say something nice about a person, then don't say anything. She did try to abide by that, but it was difficult at times.

'It would have shown why you were so worried when he was missing, and why you visit his family whenever you can. Anyway, I ticked off those girls, so they might shut up now. Thought you'd like to know.' Pete stood up. 'Saw that piece by your brother today. He's good, isn't he?'

'Good?' Alice glared at Pete. 'He's brilliant!'

'Sorry, bad choice of words. He's brilliant, and so are you two girls. I'm going to miss you.'

'Where are you going?' they both asked together.

'Shipping out next week. Secret destination, of course.' He winked at them. 'But if I see Will I'll give him your love, shall I?'

'Don't drink too much wine.' Becky clasped his hand for a moment, sad he was leaving, because he'd been a staunch friend to her. 'You take care.'

'I will.' He lowered his voice. 'I hear there's a certain Brigadier coming along, and our first stop will be Rome. I'll expect letters from both of you.'

After promising him they would write, they watched him walk away.

'Here we go again!' Becky ran her hands through her thick dark hair. 'It's so hard being left behind all the time. This war has more ups and downs than a fairground ride. We just start to relax a little, and then we're back to worrying where our friends and family are, and what dangers they're facing.'

'And it's going to get worse,' Alice said. 'This country is filling up with troops and equipment. When the big push starts, everything and everyone we have will be thrown at the enemy. But before that it looks as if they want to drive the Germans out of Italy. That won't be easy.'

'I don't believe it will.' Becky stood up. 'But this is what we signed up for, and at least we're on the offensive now. I can't remember the whole speech, but what was it Churchill said? "It is not the beginning of the end. But it is, perhaps, the end of the beginning."'

Alice fell into step beside her friend as they left the mess. 'That's right, but we still have a long way to go, so let's keep smiling for the sake of the men in our lives.'

'Absolutely.'

A pang of sadness always touched Bob when he approached the house they now lived in. How he missed their row of terraced houses! Small and cramped they might have been, but they had been home. His mother had lavished care on their small garden, but the front of this house was just paving, and his mother never bothered with it. Still, it would be lovely to see them all again. He was sorry Helen had not been able to come with him this time, but he only had forty-eight hours' leave. He'd better make the most of it though, because goodness knows when he'd get home again.

'Bob!' His mother rushed out to greet him, quickly followed by his father.

'This is a wonderful surprise. How long have you got, son?' his father asked.

'Only forty-eight hours.' He placed his arm around his mother's shoulder. 'I'm gasping. Is the kettle on?'

'Of course.'

They were soon settled around the kitchen table and catching up with the news, when there was a knock on the front door.

'I'll get it.' Bill Adams left to see who it was.

Bob could hear Becky's father talking to someone, but he didn't recognize the masculine voice.

Bill returned, and one glance at the man with him sent Bob's heart racing. 'Are Will and Jim all right?'

The man smiled. 'As far as I know, they're fine. I'm not the bringer of bad news. You must be Bob. I've heard a lot about you. I'm David Hammond.' The Brigadier held out his hand for Bob to shake.

Ah, we finally get to meet this man Becky talks so much about, Bob thought to himself as he studied him. He was a tall man who carried himself with confident ease. His gaze missed nothing, and the lines around his eyes showed he was no stranger to laughter. He was impressive.

'Would you like tea?' Mavis asked.

'Thank you, Mrs Adams. I apologize for dropping in on you unannounced, but I would like a word with you and your husband.'

Bob's father and mother were immediately on their feet, and he did the same. 'We'll leave you then.'

'Perhaps you'd like to go in the front room?' Mrs Adams suggested, slightly flustered. 'We'll be more comfortable.'

'This will be fine.' David sat down.

'What can we do for you?' Becky's father asked.

'I've come to deliver an invitation to have lunch with my parents next Sunday, twelve o'clock, and they hope you will be able to accept. Rebecca has talked about you often and they would like to meet you.'

'That's very kind.' Mavis glanced at her husband, and when he gave a slight nod, she said, 'We'd like that very much.'

'Good.' David handed them a card with the Hammonds' address on it. 'I also wanted to introduce myself to you as I have asked Rebecca to marry me.'

'Oh!' Bill frowned. 'She hasn't told us that.'

'She has refused me,' David continued, sitting back and watching their faces intently. 'However, that was my fault. I tried to rush her into a hasty marriage, but she's a sensible girl and would have none of it. I have no intention of giving up, but I need time, and that is something I don't have. I'm off on another campaign, and when the invasion of France begins I shall be in the thick of it.'

'You must find it hard to keep leaving your daughter.' Mavis gave him an understanding smile.

'Very difficult, and I know it upsets her when I keep disappearing for long periods at a time. I should have remarried after my wife died, but I didn't consider it until Rebecca came into my life. My parents are approaching retirement, and I'm unhappy about leaving them with the responsibility of bringing up a young child. My mind would have been easier if Rebecca had agreed to marry me without delay, but she believes marriage between us would not work.'

'Why?'

'She has many reasons, Mrs Adams, and I do not agree with any of them. I came here today because I want you to know that no matter how long it takes, I do want to marry Rebecca.'

Bill and Mavis looked at each for a moment, and then Bill said, 'We appreciate you telling us this. We have brought our daughter up to think for herself and accept the consequences of any decisions she makes, whether they are right or wrong. We trust her, and if she does eventually agree to marry you, then you have our blessing.'

'Thank you for being so gracious. I can assure you that I mean only the best for your daughter.'

'Becky's told us very little about her feelings for you, and we have been concerned that an officer was taking an interest in our daughter. We are relieved to have met you at last.'

'I understand, Mrs Adams, and that's why I'm here. No doubt

I shall be as concerned about my daughter when she's older, and view every man who comes near her with suspicion.'

'You will.' Bill smiled. 'But by talking to us so frankly, you have put our minds at ease, Brigadier.'

'David, please.' He stood up. 'Would it be possible to talk to Bob, perhaps over a drink?'

'I'm sure he'd be delighted.' Bill left the room and returned with Bob and his parents.

'The pubs should be open now, so would you all join me? I'd enjoy a pint before shipping out again.'

'Good idea.' Bob grinned at the officer. 'I'm on my way again, too. I wonder if I'll be your escort?'

David turned to Mavis and Sally. 'You'll join us as well?'

'Oh no,' Mavis shook her head. 'You men go.'

After shaking hands with the two women, David left with the men and headed for the pub.

Bob was bursting with curiosity as they walked the short distance to the local pub, and he kept giving the Brigadier sideways glances. Will and Becky had both talked about him, but he could see how inadequate their descriptions had been. Even Will with his mastery of words had not quite got it right. The physical description fitted, but they had failed to mention the air of authority coming from him. This man was sure of his own abilities, and Bob could imagine how determined he must have been to get out of France after Dunkirk. Failure was not something he would accept easily.

The pub was crowded, but when David made for the bar, people smiled and moved to give him room.

'What did he want?' Bob asked Bill quickly while he had the chance.

'He wants Becky.'

'And he came to ask your permission first?'

'No.' Bill gave a wry smile. 'He *told* us. And we told him Becky would make up her own mind, and we trusted her to do the right thing. If she accepts him, then we will as well. He told us she has refused him, but he has no intention of giving up.'

Bob studied the man standing at the bar with his father. 'No, he won't give up, and Becky could have a fight on her hands.'

Bill gave a quiet laugh. 'It seems strange to hear him call her Rebecca in such a well-educated accent. We've been invited to lunch with his parents next Sunday. I could almost hear Mavis trying to work out what she could wear. We gathered, from the way he spoke, that his family are very fond of Becky.'

'I'm not surprised at that. She did give them her support while he was missing. But it's not straightforward, is it? He's got a daughter, is older than her, and is definitely upper class.'

'The age difference is no more than between Mavis and me. And our Becky would cope in any situation,' Bill said proudly, 'as long as she's got an engine to take to bits.'

They were grinning at each other when David arrived with a tray of drinks.

For the next hour or so they talked as they drank their beer. Bob was impressed with the ease with which the Brigadier mixed with them and others in the pub.

By the time they saw David Hammond to his car and watched him drive away, Bob understood why Will and Becky thought highly of the man. There were no airs and graces about him, and he had a dry sense of humour.

Bob liked him.

Thirty-Two

The letter from her father had Becky gasping in surprise. Usually very forthcoming, this time her father had said little about David's unexpected visit and their lunch with his family, except to say that they had all got on very well. He had added a couple of funny stories about the dog and Sara, but she had the feeling that there was something he wasn't telling her.

Sighing, she put the letter back in the envelope. She wasn't due any leave at the moment, so a trip home to question her parents would have to wait.

'Oh dear, who's upset you?' Alice asked, as she joined her for breakfast.

'I'm not upset, I'm puzzled.' Becky explained, and then said, 'He was preparing to ship out, so why waste his time delivering the invitation personally? It could quite easily have been sent by post.'

'I would say he is drawing your families closer together. You have refused to marry him, but he hasn't given up, just changed his tactics. And whatever happens he's trying to make sure you stay interested in Sara.'

'I would never abandon her. He knows that.'

'He just wants to make sure,' Alice said gently. 'Did your parents enjoy the lunch?'

'Yes, they said they had a lovely time.' Becky cast her friend a worried look. 'This war makes relationships so difficult. I wish I could sit down with David and talk everything through, but we never seem to have enough time. I can't rush into something I might regret later just because there's a war on. I know it's happening a lot now, but I'm not like that. It's a big decision, and I'm not sure exactly what his feelings are for me. I couldn't go into a marriage with doubts like that.'

'This has got to be settled between you, Becky. Neither of you are going to be happy until you do, and it isn't wise to leave things unresolved in these uncertain times. You could regret it for the rest of your life. I was glad I'd promised to marry Anthony because that brought him a little happiness in his short life. But the difference between you and us is that we both loved each other. While you have doubts about David's feelings, you are wise to wait. You've got to get the man to talk.'

'I know, but I've no idea how long he'll be away this time, or how long he'll stay when he does come home.'

'Why are you girls looking so serious?'

They both spun round at the sound of the familiar voice, and were immediately on their feet to welcome Pete.

'When did you get back?' Becky asked, smiling with pleasure.

'Just now. Did you miss me?' He sat down and took the mug of tea Alice had rushed to get him.

'Of course. Nice tan you've got there.'

He pulled a face and sipped the tea. 'What have you girls been up to while I've been chasing the enemy around Sicily?'

'Just the usual,' Becky told him. 'Are you back for a while?'

'Hope so.' He smiled at Becky. 'I saw your Brigadier out there. Is he back yet?'

'No, he's still out there.'

'Ah,' Pete said as he gulped down the rest of his tea. 'Poor bugger's in Italy now, I expect.'

'My brother's out there as well.'

Pete nodded. 'I read one of his reports in the newspaper today. I've met a couple of War Correspondents, and like the padres they are always in the thick of the fighting. They're damned brave men. You can be proud of your brother, Becky.'

'I'm proud of you all. In my eyes you're all heroes.'

Pete snorted in amusement and changed the subject. 'You girls want to go to the pictures tonight? I'm paying.'

'My goodness, you *are* pleased to be back. Of course we'll come,' Alice laughed.

'Good, that's a date then.' He stood up. 'See you both later.'

Becky and Alice followed the Italian campaign closely and were delighted when Italy surrendered. By the beginning of October the Allies had liberated Naples, and Italy declared war on Germany. With the Germans in retreat in Russia and heavy raids being carried out on Berlin, Hitler was facing defeat on many fronts. It was encouraging, but no one was under any illusion that the war would soon be over. There was still much bitter fighting ahead.

* * *

This fact was apparent to everyone in Italy, including Will, as he jumped on a tank to get closer to the battle.

'Hey, Press!' one man shouted. 'You'll get shot up there. Walk with us, it's safer.'

At that moment all hell broke loose and the men dived for cover as heavy artillery opened up on their position. Will ducked as low as he could and stayed where he was. It was deafening as the tanks returned fire, concentrating on the wooded area ahead of them.

Will looked down and saw the man who had shouted at him running behind the tank. 'What was that you were saying?' he called.

The answer he received certainly wouldn't be appearing in any of his reports.

The battle to clear the woods was long and hard. Will focused on recording it, steeling himself against the death and suffering all around him. If he allowed himself to become overwhelmed he wouldn't be able to do his job, but when things became too bad he jumped down to help get the wounded to the medics. He made no distinction between Allies and Germans; all were young men fighting for their lives. It was madness.

By late afternoon the position was secure and Will went to the command tent to send his report.

'Message for you, Press.' The Major in charge of communications handed him a note. 'They want you back in London.'

'Damn!' Will swore. 'I wanted to be with you when you reach Rome.'

'I'll send you a postcard,' the officer joked. 'If we can get you transport quickly enough you'll be home in time for Christmas.'

'So I will.' He brightened at that thought. 'Any chance of that?'

'Leave it with me. I expect they're recalling you to cover preparations for the invasion of France.'

'When do you think it will be?'

'Next year for sure. Spring, I should think.'

Will nodded in agreement. 'Do you think 1944 will see the end of the war?'

'Impossible to say, but let's hope so, eh? Now,' the major said as he studied a map. 'I can get you to the airfield at Foggia and see if the USAF can give you a ride back home. Go and get your gear together, have something to eat, and by then I should have something arranged.'

'Thanks, sir.'

At first Will had been disappointed to be ordered to leave Italy, but now he was pleased. It would be wonderful to see his family again, and he might also get a chance to meet up with Alice. They had been writing to each other regularly, and it was clear they had a lot in common. He had liked her from the moment he'd seen her, and his feelings for her had grown into something more than friendship, but he'd been careful to keep his affection for her hidden. She had lost the man she'd loved and was about to marry, but that was some three years ago now, and he hoped she was ready to put that behind her and move on. He snorted in disgust at that thought. How did you put the loss of someone you loved behind you? Life would go on, of course, but that person would always be a part of you, just as Jim's parents were to his family. And why the hell was he daring to think that a lovely girl like Alice would fall for him? She was surrounded by men, and would have her pick when she was ready for another relationship.

By dawn the next day Will was at the airfield, and an hour later flying home in an American Transport plane. The weather was rough and it was a bumpy ride, but he didn't mind. And it was only as he settled down that he realized just how weary he was. No indication had been given for his return, but he hoped he would be able to have some time at home before being sent somewhere else. If Becky couldn't get home then he'd go to the camp and see her.

Resting his head back, he closed his eyes and drifted off, oblivious to the discomfort of hard seats and a pitching plane.

'Wake up, chum. We're here.'

Will shot awake to find the plane was on the ground and making for a parking spot.

'You sure are worn out,' the American said. 'That was a rough flight, but you slept all the way.'

'Can't remember when I last had such a good sleep.' Will stretched and grinned. 'Every time I dozed off in Italy, some daft fool would start shooting at us.'

'Yeah, there's some bitter fighting going on there.' The plane came to a stop and the airman began helping Will to gather up his gear. 'Off for some leave, are you?'

'I hope so.' Will hoisted his kitbag on to his shoulder and carried the camera equipment in his right hand. 'I'll know more when I've reported in and found out why they've brought me back in such a hurry.'

'Hey, let me carry some of that for you.' The airman was studying Will, frowning when he saw he was taking most of the baggage on his right side. 'You been injured?'

'No, my left arm is weaker than the right. I was born like that.'

'That right?' He helped Will out of the plane. 'Well, it sure don't stop you doing anything.'

'I've never allowed it to. Fortunately I was also born with a determined nature.'

They walked across the airfield together in friendly conversation, and the airman said, 'This country of yours is beginning to burst at the seams with men and equipment, and that can only mean one thing. We're building up to the big push.'

Will nodded in agreement as they entered the building to check in. 'It looks like it. Thanks for the lift.'

'Our pleasure.' The airman shook hands with Will. 'Good luck, and I hope you get that leave you obviously need.'

'Thanks.' Reporting in didn't take long and the airbase even provided Will with a lift to London, so he was soon on his way.

On arrival, it was as he had expected. He was to cover the preparations for the invasion of Europe, travelling to various camps the length and breadth of England. None of it would be used at the moment, because secrecy was of the utmost importance. The Germans mustn't even get a hint of where the landings were to take place. Surprise would be vital. Once the operation was under way, then news would be released to the general public. The briefing was long, and Will was glad he'd been able to sleep on the plane. By seven that evening he was on his way home.

Lights were on downstairs as he quietly opened the front door, and he could hear the murmur of voices and laughter coming from the kitchen. He smiled, wondering why they had so many rooms in this house and only seemed to use the kitchen and bedrooms.

Keeping as quiet as he could he stood just inside the room, and his heart leapt with pleasure. Crammed into the kitchen were Bob, Jim, Becky, the parents, and the two Americans he had met on the *Queen Mary*.

Becky was the first one to see him and jumped to her feet. 'Will! Oh, this is wonderful!'

The room erupted as everyone gave him a boisterous welcome. It had been a long time since all of them had been at home at the same time. His mother was nearly in tears, Becky had gathered their foursome together in a huddle, trying to wrap her arms around all of them, and the Americans were slapping everyone on the back in delight.

'Gee, this is great!' Greg gave Hal a shove. 'Go and get that bottle of whisky. We've got to celebrate Will coming home. Boy, what a time we're going to have this Christmas. We want to know everything you've been doing, Will.'

'All in good time,' he laughed. 'This morning I was in Italy, then on an American plane, and after that I spent hours in London. No one thought to offer me any food. I'm starving.'

A space was hastily cleared at the table for him as the women set about making a pile of sandwiches, and the kettle was soon boiling.

'Hope sandwiches will do?' his mother said. 'Greg and Hal have given us some real ham.'

'That would be perfect, Mum.'

'What's it like out there?' his father asked.

'Tough, Dad.'

Becky's smile faded. 'I think David might be out there, too. Did you see him, Will?'

'Sorry, Becky. If he's there then I didn't meet him.'

Her disappointment showed for a moment, then the smile was back.

'How's Alice?' he asked, changing the subject. 'Is she on leave as well?'

'She's fine, but still at camp.'

'In that case I'll pop along to Aldershot and see her while I'm at home.'

'She'll like that,' his sister told him. 'She always looks forward to receiving your letters.'

'How long have you got?' his mother asked, putting a plate piled high with sandwiches on the table, and setting out the cups for tea.

'I've been given fourteen days, so I won't be going back until the New Year. And I'll be in this country for a while now.'

Relief flooded across his mother's face. 'That's lovely. Perhaps we'll be able to see more of you.'

Will nodded, bit into a sandwich and sighed with pleasure. 'I'd forgotten what real ham tasted like. Tell me how you're getting on,' he asked Greg and Hal.

They talked well into the night, and when the parents went to bed they finished off the bottle of whisky Hal had brought with him. Will's tiredness had vanished as he enjoyed being with his sister and friends again – and he counted these two Americans as friends. Becky was the only girl amongst them, but she was used to that and fitted in easily, as she had always done. Bob was relaxed, and Jim was more like his old self. It did Will good to see all was well with them.

He settled back and enjoyed the fun as each related amusing tales of the things that had happened to them. Greg and Hal made them roar with laughter as they told of some of the scrapes they had got into while adjusting to life in Britain.

At one time he glanced across at his sister and read the expression in her eyes. She was thinking the same as him – this might be the last time they were all able to meet up like this. He gave a slight nod of his head, and her smile was tinged with sadness for a brief moment. They had always had a close rapport, and that hadn't changed.

The house was full and Becky had her own room, and the Americans another. That left the boys to share one room. There was only a single bed so they tossed a coin for it and Bob won. Jim made do with two chairs pushed together and Will slept on the floor. He didn't mind; he'd slept in far worse places.

Tomorrow he'd slip away and see Alice.

Thirty-Three

With his War Correspondent's papers, Will had access to almost any camp, and through his film reports he had become quite well known. The guard on the gate even called him 'sir' when he asked him who he'd come to see.

'Could you direct me to Colonel Brent's office?'

'I'll escort you there myself. Is he expecting you?'

'No, I only arrived back in this country yesterday.'

'Ah.' The guard nodded as he walked beside Will. 'I saw one of your news reports from Italy, and it looked a bit rough where you were.'

'It was, but that's where the stories are.'

'Of course.' The soldier opened a door and gave Will an admiring glance. 'You blokes are doing a good job. Up the stairs and it's the second door on the left.'

'Thank you.' Will followed his directions and rapped on the door.

'Come in,' a female voice called.

He stepped inside the room. 'I've come to wish you a happy Christmas.'

'Will!' Alice leapt to her feet and rushed to greet him. 'Where did you come from?'

'Italy,' he laughed as she hugged him, planting a gentle kiss on his cheek.

'Oh, it's good to see you.'

'I arrived back yesterday and found the house full with Becky, Bob, Jim and the two Americans. Everyone's there except you, so I thought I'd come and see you today. Have you got any free time?'

'I'm sorry, Will—' She stopped when Colonel Brent walked in.

The officer looked at Will for a moment, then held out his hand. 'You must be Will Adams. I've heard a lot about you from Brigadier Hammond. It's a pleasure to meet you.'

'And you, sir.' Will shook hands. 'I hope you don't mind me coming to see Alice?'

'Not at all. It's quiet around here today. In fact there isn't much going on for a couple of days.' He took a form out of the desk and wrote on it, then handed it to Alice. 'Three days is all I can let you have, but that will allow you to spend Christmas with your friends.'

'Thank you, sir.' Alice's face lit up with pleasure. 'I haven't seen Will for such a long time.'

'Grab your things and come home with me. Everyone will be so pleased to see you. The house is crowded, but you can share a room with Becky.' Will gave her a little push. 'Hurry. I'll give you fifteen minutes.'

With a bright smile on her face, Alice sped away.

'That was good of you, sir. We both appreciate it.'

'My pleasure.' The officer indicated he should sit. 'Now, tell me what's really going on in Italy.'

Alice was back quickly as promised, but finding the two men in serious conversation, she waited patiently at the door.

Will cast her an apologetic look, and when she indicated that he should carry on, he turned his attention back to Colonel Brent.

After another fifteen minutes the officer stood up. 'I mustn't keep you any longer. Thank you for putting me in the picture, Will. Can you drive?'

Will nodded. 'It's necessary in my job.'

The officer scribbled on another form. 'Take this to transport and they'll give you the use of a car. Alice will show you where it is, and you can bring it back when Alice has to return.'

'Thank you, sir.' Will could hardly believe his luck. He'd come here hoping to be able to snatch some time with Alice, and had ended up with a pass for her, and the use of a car!

Will and Alice hurried out, eager to make the most of their unexpected good fortune.

The car they were given was old but it sounded sweet when Will turned on the ignition. 'Nice,' he said to the soldier who was leaning on the open window.

'It ought to be.' He grinned. 'Your sister was the last one to work on it. I swear she's only got to approach an engine with a spanner in her hand and it wouldn't dare misbehave.'

Will roared with laughter. 'That sounds like my sister.'

The soldier smirked. 'Who else?'

'Pete!' Alice scolded. 'You're making her sound like a bully.'

'She is, but only where engines are concerned.' His smile broadened. 'Apart from that she's the nicest girl on the camp.'

'Oh, thanks,' Alice said in a hurt voice.

'Correction. She's one of the two best girls in camp.'

'Too late.' Alice tried to keep a straight face, and failed. 'Come on, Will, let's get out of here, or my leave will be over before we get through the gates.'

Pete tapped the top of the car and stepped back. 'Take good care of her.'

As they drove away Will said jokingly, 'I wonder if he was talking about you or the car?'

'Oh, undoubtedly the car.' Alice shook her head in amusement, and once through the gates, she asked, 'Are you quite sure it will be all right for me to come home with you?'

Will reached across and briefly squeezed her hand. 'They will all be delighted. Greg and Hal have brought enough food with them to feed half the street. Mum told me that includes a turkey, and you know how scarce they are.'

'A turkey? Where on earth did they get that?'

'We didn't ask.'

'No, best not to, I suppose.' Her expression turned wistful. 'I haven't had anything like that for a long, long time.'

'Nor me. I seem to have been living on army rations for years. It's surprising what you'll eat when you're hungry.'

They drove for about half an hour when Will pulled over and stopped. He turned to face Alice. 'Do you mind if we talk?'

'I thought that was what we had been doing, but you look serious. What is it, Will?'

'You realize that 1944 will bring the invasion of Europe, and the push to defeat Germany?'

She nodded.

'Well, the next few months are going to be busy for me, and I want to tell you something while I have the chance.' He took a deep breath. 'I've become very fond of you, Alice. In fact I fell for you the first time I saw you.'

She started to speak, but he stopped her.

'No, don't say anything. I know you lost the man you loved and are probably not interested in anyone else at the moment, but I want you to know how I feel. I don't suppose I stand a chance, do I?'

'Oh, Will, I do care for you very much. But I'm frightened to make a commitment again. You're always in the thick of the fighting, and I couldn't face that agony again.'

'I understand.' He leant across and kissed her gently on the lips. 'Will you promise me something?'

'If I can.'

'Keep writing to me, then when this war's over we'll talk again, and until that day comes I'll continue to hope. Promise me that what I've just told you won't change any thing between us.'

'I promise, Will.'

'Good.' He started the car again and they resumed their journey, talking about things that interested them. Will breathed a quiet sigh of relief; he'd taken a chance by revealing his feelings for her, but it had not appeared to damage their easy relationship. This year was going to be a dangerous time, and it was sensible to take things cautiously, but he knew he loved her, and was prepared to wait. He felt happier now he'd told her how he felt, and she had moved across the seat closer to him, so that was encouraging.

Laughter was coming from the front room when they arrived at the house, and Alice smiled at him. 'Sounds like they're enjoying themselves. Thank you for coming for me, Will.'

'I'm glad your boss was so generous.' He opened the door and stood there for a moment until there was a lull in the chatter. 'Look who I've found.'

Giving a cry of delight, Becky was the first one to reach Alice. 'How did you get away?'

'That was all down to Will,' she said, as everyone crowded around her.

'This is wonderful!' Will's father declared. 'Put the kettle on, Mavis. Sit down, my dear, and tell us how long Will managed to wangle for you.'

'Three days.' Alice looked at the parents. 'I hope it's all right for me to descend upon you unannounced?'

'Of course it is. The more the merrier.' Becky's mother was smiling happily as she headed for the door. 'I think this calls for some of those lovely biscuits Greg and Hal brought with them.'

'Cookies, ma'am,' they said laughing.

'Sorry, cookies it is, then.'

'Gee.' Greg couldn't stop smiling. 'This is going to be a great Christmas, and let's hope it's the last one during wartime. What do you think are the chances of it all being over by this time next year, Will?'

'It could be, but don't bank on it. The Germans won't let us walk into their country unopposed, and only total surrender will do.'

'Yeah.' Greg sobered for a moment, and then the easy smile was back again. 'Let's make the most of this time together, because none of us know where we'll be next year.'

Everyone agreed with that just as Mavis and Sally returned with a trolley of teas and snacks.

'Let's not talk about the war for a few days,' Bob's mother scolded as she handed round the cookies.

'Good idea.' Becky got up to help serve the tea.

Hal was looking out of the window. 'Will, did you come in that army car?'

Will nodded. 'Another little gift from Alice's boss.'

'How much gas you got?' Greg was also gazing out now.

'Not much, but we could take a short ride somewhere. Anything you particularly want to see?'

'Richmond Park,' they said together.

'That isn't far from here so we'll definitely have enough petrol to go there. That's if we can get in?' Will wasn't sure about that, but it was worth a try. 'If the gates are closed we could go to the Terraces on Richmond Hill. There's a lovely view of the Thames from there.'

'That's great! We've got our cameras with us and want pictures to send back home. We've done London and now we want some views of the countryside.' Greg glanced around the room. 'And we want pictures of all of you.'

'Let's do that now while it's still light.' Hal tore out of the room and could be heard running up the stairs. He was soon back. 'The sun's trying to come out, so let's all go into the back garden.'

Everyone grabbed their coats and filed outside. Hal and Greg knew exactly what they wanted, ushering them into different groups, and then one including them all.

'Mr Adams, will you take one of us with Will and Bob, as a memory of how we met on the boat coming over?'

When they were satisfied they had enough snaps, they returned to the front room to warm themselves by the log fire.

Will spoke quietly to his sister. 'As the trip to Richmond is just up the road we'll have enough petrol for London and perhaps a dance.'

'That would be wonderful. But are you sure we can do that?'

Will grinned. 'I saw Pete slip a couple of cans in the boot.'

'Good old Pete.'

'Seems like a nice bloke.'

'He is, and we often go for a drink with him, or sometimes the pictures. He's a happily married man with two children he adores, and he treats us like friends, which suits us fine.'

Will nodded, and took a biscuit from the plate on the trolley. 'Right, I suggest we go to Richmond in the morning while the women are cooking that wonderful turkey. I can only cram five in, so who's coming?'

'Bob and Jim should be the other two to go,' Bob's father suggested.

'All the young men together,' Mavis agreed. 'But I want you all back by three o'clock at the latest. I don't want our meal to spoil.

It turned out to be the best Christmas they'd had since the war began. Greg and Hal came from large families and were happy to be with their adopted family, as they now called them. The trip to Richmond had been very enjoyable, and many pictures had been taken. They had even managed to fit in a dance.

Alice was the first to leave, and then the Americans, but the rest of them were able to see in the New Year together.

On the stroke of midnight, Becky's father held up his glass. 'Welcome to 1944, and may you all be safe and with us at the same time next year.'

Thirty-Four

Over the next few months Becky was able to catch up with her brother quite a few times, and also Jim, who like Will was still in Great Britain. She only saw Bob once, but apart from that they didn't manage to get home at the same time. Christmas had been the only time they'd all been together, and it had been such a special time.

On a beautiful day in May, Becky was playing in the garden with Sara and the dog, when the girl gave a squeal of delight, and rushed to her father's waiting arms, calling, 'Daddy!'

He swung her high as she showered him with kisses, and the scene brought a lump to Becky's throat.

Mr and Mrs Hammond were standing watching with smiles on their faces, and Becky joined them.

'Hello, Rebecca.' David bent and kissed her cheek. 'You look lovely, and I'm very pleased to see you here.'

'Rebecca comes all the time,' Sara told him. 'And sometimes she brings a car and takes us out for a ride. It's fun.'

'I'm sure it is. That's very kind of you, my dear,' he said gently.

Becky nodded. 'When did you get back?'

'Today. I came straight here, but I can't stay long.'

'I suppose you're back to prepare for the invasion,' she said, knowing this was on everyone's mind now. 'Do you know when it will be?'

'Soon,' was all he would say.

After only fifteen minutes David gave his daughter a huge hug, said goodbye to them and left again.

It seemed as if the entire country was on the move. Becky drove past lines of lorries packed with men, and there were tanks and all kinds of vehicles. The Major General and two other high-ranking officers were silent in the back of the car, and she couldn't help wondering what their thoughts were at this momentous time. The invasion of France was imminent, and it was an enormous undertaking.

Her mind turned to her brother, the boys and David. They had all been preparing for this moment for months, and they'd seen very little of Greg and Hal. It was exciting and frightening at the same time. With the combined forces of all the Allies they were now ready to launch an attack. She prayed her brother wouldn't go in with the first wave ashore, but knowing Will that's where he would want to be.

She had hoped David would be in the car as well, but he had sent her a message saying that he would be travelling with his regiment. Being an artillery unit they were almost certain to be amongst the first troops.

'Damn the weather,' the Major General muttered. 'The forecast is not good, but we can't delay too long. With troop movements on this scale it's going to be a miracle if we can keep it a secret. Blast it! They mustn't know we're coming.'

The column of lorries stopped, and Becky had to do the same as tanks rumbled out of a wooded area where they had been hidden. She drew in a deep breath. They were Canadian. Were some of the men they'd danced with amongst them?

Everything started to move again, slowly, and she could almost feel the tension coming from the officers in the car. She made a decision, and said, 'Major General Villiers, I could make faster progress if I left the convoy and took some of the back roads.'

'Do it, but don't get us damned well lost,' came the tense reply. 'Get us in front of this if you can.'

'Yes, sir.' Becky took a sharp right turn and put her foot down, praying she didn't make a mess of this. The signposts had all been removed long ago, so she would have to trust her sense of direction.

Fortunately it had always been good, and two hours later she was pulling in to the port with the convoy behind her. It was only when her passengers had hurried away that Becky looked around at the amazing scene. Some ships were being loaded with men, others were already full, and the sheer number of ships was incredible, not to mention the thousands of men waiting to set sail. The plans had all been put on hold because the weather forecast was not good enough. She felt sorry for the men already crowded on boats. The waiting would be agony.

'Becky!' she heard someone call, and she turned to see her brother running towards her.

'Will, how did you manage to see me in this crowd?'

'Easy, I just watched for any officers arriving and hoped you might be driving. Are you staying for a while?'

'No, I'm going back to camp right now. Are you sailing with the troops?'

'Yes, but second wave.'

She breathed a quiet sigh of relief. 'Have you news of any of the others?'

'I saw Jim a few days ago and he's parachuting in, but I don't know the date. He might already be over there. And as far as I know, Bob's with the naval ships.'

Tension knotted her stomach. All three of the boys were going to be in the thick of it. 'I believe David's here as well. You haven't seen him, have you?'

'No, he's probably already on a ship, but they can't go in this weather.' Will glanced around as more troops arrived. 'I've got to go.'

'Take care, Will. I'll be thinking of you all.' She would like to stay a while, but this was not the place for her to be, and she had been ordered to go straight back to the camp.

The roads were nearly empty now, and so was the camp by the time she reached it. It was strange not having Pete and the other men around, but transport was important and every available man was needed. She stood by the car for a moment, feeling rather lonely, and wishing she could take a more active part in this operation.

'All we can do now is wait and pray,' Alice said as she came and stood beside her.

'You should have seen it, Alice. There are thousands of men being packed into boats, not knowing if the invasion is going ahead or not. How on earth can they keep such a huge movement of troops a secret?'

'Seems impossible.' Alice shrugged. 'But whether they go or not is up to those in charge. Have you got time for a cup of tea?'

'Hang on a minute while I find out if I'm needed.' Becky checked with the transport commander, and finding she was free for an hour she joined Alice again. She fell into step beside her friend. 'What will you do now Colonel Brent isn't here?'

'I'm to help any officer who needs a typist. I'll miss him; he was lovely to work for. Are you going to visit David's family soon? I expect they're feeling anxious, like everyone else.'

'I'll go as soon as I can. I saw Will today, by the way.'

'Oh, I do hope he isn't sailing with the invasion fleet.'

'He told me he's going with the second wave. Jim's being dropped in, but Will didn't know any more than that, and Bob is with the navy ships.' Becky ran a hand through her hair in agitation. 'We knew this was coming, but I don't think I fully appreciated the enormous undertaking it would be.'

After a short delay the weather cleared enough, and on 6th June the huge armada sailed for France. Becky had not yet been able to see the Hammonds as no one was allowed to leave the camp.

'I don't like the look of that.' Alice frowned when she saw the lines of ambulances waiting to be called upon. 'Will you be driving one?'

'I've been asked to stand by. With most of the men gone drivers are in short supply. The hospital is on full alert to receive casualties.' Becky was worried sick. 'I don't think I'm going to get much sleep tonight.'

'Nor me. Has Will told you he's asked me to marry him?'

'No, but I guessed he's in love with you. What did you say?'

Alice sighed. 'I couldn't commit myself. I already wear one ring around my neck, and I didn't want to make it two. Think me foolish, Becky, but I felt it would be bad luck to think of the future, and by doing so I would be putting Will into danger.'

'I don't think you're foolish at all,' Becky said gently. 'I understand, and so would my brother.'

'He did, and I do hope the war is over soon so we can all get back to a normal life. Have you decided what you're going to do when it's finally over?'

Beck shook her head. 'Like you I can't make a decision at the moment. All we can do is wait and pray that all those we love come through this. Then perhaps we'll be able to sort ourselves out.'

'You're right. Fancy a drink?'

'No thanks, Alice. If you don't mind I think I'll try and get some rest.'

'Good idea. See you tomorrow.'

Sleep was elusive, but Becky did manage to doze fitfully on and off, until they were roused at four o'clock in the morning. She tumbled out of bed as the sergeant yelled, 'All drivers assemble at once!'

They soon found out that the waiting ambulances were about to be put into use, and every available driver was needed. Nurses and doctors were streaming on to the camp from the nearby military hospital. The vehicles were manned in grim silence. Becky followed the ambulance in front of her as they made their way to the ships bringing in the wounded.

Over the next three days she made many journeys, struggling all the time to remain detached from the suffering so she could do her job. It was the hardest thing she had ever had to do in her life, and she thought she was managing quite well until the end of another gruelling day. She had returned to the camp to get the ambulance filled with petrol for another trip, and was fumbling with the cap when the sergeant stopped her.

'Get something to eat, and rest,' he told her.

'I'm not hungry, and I'm not tired. I can do another trip.'

'Look at your hands, Corporal Adams.'

Glancing down she saw that her hand was shaking badly, and fought to control the tremors, but without success.

'Get some rest, and that's an order. Someone else can take over for you.'

'I'm sorry, Sergeant.' She felt ashamed.

'Don't be,' he said kindly. 'Report back in twenty-four hours.'

'Yes, Sergeant.' She turned away, not sure what to do or where to go.

'You're not the only one to be feeling the strain,' he told her. 'I'm standing you all down in shifts so you can rest, but I need you back here at the same time tomorrow, fit enough to drive.'

'You can count on me.' Her mouth set in a determined line as she spoke, determined not to let her exhaustion show too much.

It was late afternoon and still light, but Becky wandered aimlessly. Eating was out of the question, and sleep would be impossible. It was as if every nerve in her body was jangling. She just wanted to be alone; not even Alice's company would help after what she had seen, so she walked until she found a deserted area right on the edge of the camp.

The sun was shining as she sat under a large tree. Giving a shuddering sigh she closed her eyes, then doubled over to rest her head on her knees. The emotions she had struggled to keep under control would no longer be denied, and her slender body now shook with wracking sobs.

So much suffering. Young men injured, dying. It was terrible. The cruelty of war, and the heroism shown by those involved, was enough to make anyone cry. And all those she loved were out there amongst the carnage. Had she transported some of the Canadians they'd danced and laughed with? And what about the Americans her family had befriended? Would they ever see them again? Would Pete's children lose their father? Will, Bob, Jim, David . . .

She gripped her knees, ashamed of the breakdown she could not control. It was clear now that her stupid worries about her relationship with David were of no importance. In the light of what was happening it didn't matter. He was an officer – so what? She loved him, and deeply regretted not being able to put his mind at rest about his daughter before the invasion began.

Time lost meaning, and all her silly little worries faded into insignificance as she sat there, allowing the tears to flow. It was dusk when she finally lifted her head, dry-eyed, calmer, but utterly drained.

Dragging herself to her feet she went back to her quarters to wash and put on clean clothes. That made her feel better, and she wished the awful memories could be washed away as easily, but she doubted if this experience would ever leave her.

People were coming and going at all hours so the mess was serving food whenever it was needed. Becky knew eating was the last thing she wanted to do, but it was vital she had something or she would make herself ill. She had to be fully fit for duty tomorrow.

There were a few of the other drivers already in the mess, and Becky joined them.

'Hello, Becky,' said one of the men, James, as he moved over to make room for her. 'Have you been relieved of duty as well?'

She nodded and sat down, viewing her plate of sausages and mash with distaste. 'Until tomorrow.'

'Same as us.'

No one said anything as they concentrated on getting some food inside them, and she saw that not one of them had been left untouched by recent events.

Becky's stomach was telling her not to attempt putting anything in it, but she chewed determinedly. It took quite a while to clear most of her plate, hoping it was going to stay down.

James put a mug of tea in front of her, and pulled a face. ‘Well, we’ve managed to eat, and now all we’ve got to do is get some sleep.’

‘Yes, that’s all.’ She gave a dry laugh, drained her mug and stood up. ‘See you tomorrow.’

It was only when she crawled into bed that she realized how mentally and physically exhausted she was. *Sleep*, she told herself, *because tomorrow it starts all over again.*

Thirty-Five

'Wake up, Mavis!' Bill Adams was shaking his wife.

She sat up, disgruntled. 'What's up? And what on earth is that racket?'

'We don't know, but we'd better get downstairs. We can hear explosions. Sally and John are already up.'

Mavis scrambled out of bed and grabbed her dressing gown. 'Don't say the raids have started again?'

They found Bob's parents in the garden, looking up at the sky.

'Any idea what's going on?' Bill asked.

'We just saw a plane nosedive and explode.' John had a pair of binoculars to his eyes. 'They're not ordinary planes though. Here comes another one; you have a look, Bill.'

Every gun in the area opened up, and Bill watched the plane explode in the air. 'It was impossible to get a good look at it before it was hit, but damned if I know what it is.'

When nothing else happened, Mavis gave a sigh. 'We invaded France a week ago, so perhaps this is Hitler's way of getting back at us. It's nearly dawn and no point going back to bed. Let's put the kettle on, Sal, and get something to eat.'

It was only when they listened to the news later that they discovered that they had seen V-1 flying bombs – Hitler's secret weapon.

The V-1s continued to come and were quickly nicknamed Doodlebugs. They all hoped their threat would cease as the Allies advanced in Europe.

Two weeks after D-Day a telegram arrived addressed to Mr and Mrs Adams. All colour drained from Mavis's face as she turned it over and over in her hand. She handed it to her husband. 'You open it, Bill. I can't.'

Bob's parents knew full well that these telegrams brought terrible news, and they stayed in the kitchen ready to support their friends. There was an air of dread in the room as they waited for Bill to read the telegram.

Finally he said huskily, 'It's Jim. He's been killed in action, and they've informed us because he gave our names as next of kin.'

'Oh, dear God!' Mavis and Sally had tears running down their faces. 'The children are going to be devastated.'

Bob's mother put the kettle on for a comforting cup of tea. She dabbed her eyes and blew her nose before filling the teapot. 'He was like a son to us, and it's hard to know he won't be coming back when this dreadful war's over. Do you think we'll be able to bury him with his parents?'

'No, my dear, he'll be buried out there.' John placed his arm around his wife's shoulder. 'We can put a stone with his name on it at Pat and Harry's grave, though.'

'That's a nice idea.' Bill stood up. 'I'll go to Aldershot and see if I can tell Becky in person. It will be kinder, but if she's not there I'll have to leave a message.'

The hospital runs became less frequent after the first few days of the invasion, but a ship had docked today and they had been busy. Becky was refuelling the ambulance in case it was needed again, when the sergeant called her.

'You're wanted at the main gate. Look sharp about it.'

She hurried, wondering who had come to see her, and when she saw who was waiting there she broke into a run, knowing that this day was about to get worse. Her father would only have come here if something had happened.

He reached out in sympathy when he saw the dark circles of strain under her eyes. 'Oh, my darling.'

She hugged him. 'Tell me, Dad.'

'I'm so sorry, but it's bad news. Jim's been killed.' There was no easy way to tell her that one of her lifelong friends was dead. He gripped her arms as she swayed with the shock. 'We've just received the telegram and I didn't want you to read this in a letter.'

'Such a terrible waste of a young life.' She bowed her head, grief ripping through her.

'Dreadful.' Bill studied his daughter with concern. 'Are you still driving ambulances?'

She nodded. 'I'm a good driver, Dad, and that's what I signed up to do. Any news of Will and Bob?'

'No, but no news is good news, isn't it? What about David?'

'Nothing. I must go and see his family, but I haven't had the time. We've been too busy.'

'Would you like me to go round now and let them know you'll visit as soon as you can?'

'Thanks, Dad; they'd be pleased to see you. How are you all coping with the Doodlebugs?'

'We're managing.' Bill frowned. 'Don't hold your grief inside, darling. Jim was precious to all of us. No one will mind if you shed a few tears.'

'I'm drained dry of tears. All I feel at the moment is pain, anger and regret for things I should have done.'

'I know, sweetheart. A great deal is being asked of everyone. Too much in some cases.'

She nodded. 'Far too much. I've got to get back, Dad, but thanks for coming.'

Her father hugged her, and then stood back. 'This nightmare will end, Becky. That's what all the young men and women are fighting for.'

'I know. Give Mum my love, and tell Sara I hope to be able to visit within the next week.'

She watched her father walk to the bus stop, then turned away. She hadn't believed she could hurt any more, but she had been wrong. The horror and pain of losing Jim was devastating. She couldn't get the picture of his laughing face out of her mind.

The sergeant took one look at her white face and asked, 'Bad news?'

'Yes, Sergeant.'

'I'm sorry.'

'So am I,' she said, and automatically picked up a spanner.

'Take a break.'

'No, Sergeant.'

'Are you arguing with me, Corporal?'

She looked up, her mouth set in a grim line. 'Thousands of people are in the same position. I don't need special treatment.'

He gave a brief nod, turned on his heel and marched away. Becky didn't know if she would be on a charge for insubordination, but she didn't care. At this moment nothing seemed to matter.

Alice was waiting for her at the end of her duty. 'You've got to eat, Becky.'

'Everyone's telling me what I should do,' she grumbled as she fell into step beside her friend. 'So don't you start as well.'

'Sorry.' Alice looked harder and didn't like what she saw. 'You've [illegible]

'Awful.' There was a catch in her voice. 'I'm sorry I snapped at you, Alice, but I'm so angry! Dad came today and told me Jim's been killed.'

'Oh, I'm so sorry. I liked him.' Alice took a handkerchief out of her pocket and wiped her eyes.

'We were all so close. It was as if we were one family, and it was hard enough when Jim's parents were killed, but this is too painful.'

Placing a hand under Becky's arm, Alice kept her distressed friend moving towards the mess. 'We have to keep going and defeat Hitler, or all this suffering will have been for nothing. I won't allow myself to believe that Anthony and all the others have died in vain.'

'It isn't that easy though, is it?'

'Damned hard.' Alice gave a tired sigh. 'We'll do it though, won't we?'

'Of course, what choice do we have? It's either stay positive, or crumble under the strain.'

'Exactly, and meals mustn't be skipped, Becky; you're getting too thin. People are depending on us to do our jobs.' Alice seated her friend at a table. 'What do you want?'

'A large steak, medium rare, followed by strawberries and real cream.'

Alice gave a nod of respect, well aware how much the loss of Jim was hurting Becky, and on top of the difficult job she had been doing, the burden must be almost intolerable. 'They've run out of steak, so I'm afraid it will have to be Spam or vegetable pie.'

'In that case it'll have to be the pie.'

They managed to clear their plates, and instead of strawberries and cream, they finished off with a cup of tea and a cigarette. Neither girl had smoked before joining the ATS, but they had soon started, finding it relaxed them.

'They're showing a Laurel and Hardy film this evening. Fancy going?' Alice asked, hoping a distraction would help her friend.

'Might as well. I've been relieved of duty until tomorrow

morning.' Becky stubbed out her cigarette. 'I really must give up this habit when the war's over. I'm smoking far too much. I've got a couple of letters to write first, so I'll see you around seven.'

The next day Becky was given the job of driving an officer. When she received the orders she was furious and stormed up to the sergeant, suspecting this was his doing.

'I'm quite capable of driving the ambulance, Sergeant.' She glowered at him.

'I know you are.' His mouth twitched at the corners. 'The trouble is, not many other drivers are capable of driving an officer around London. Major General Villiers has asked for you.'

'Oh, I used to drive him quite a lot.' The steam went out of her and she gave the sergeant an apologetic look. 'Sorry, Sergeant. I thought you considered me unfit to continue transporting the injured to hospital.'

'Then you were wrong. I tried to keep you here, but I can't argue with a Major General.'

Becky's smile was the first genuine one she had managed since the invasion had begun. 'Not a wise thing to do. I'll need the best car we've got.'

'Help yourself.' The sergeant looked her straight in the eyes. 'And it isn't wise for a corporal to argue with a sergeant, but I'll overlook it this time.'

'Thank you, Sergeant. It won't happen again.' She hurried away to check over the car she wanted, glad he'd been in a good humour.

Over the next few weeks Becky became a permanent driver for different officers. Doing something she really enjoyed gave her a chance to try and come to terms with Jim's death. It was hard to believe that the four of them wouldn't be together again at the end of the war. There had been short notes from Will, Bob and David, and she was relieved to know they were still all right. Will had told her that he'd come across Greg and Hal in France, and that also helped to lift her spirits.

The Allies were moving through France, and when Paris was liberated on 25th August, everyone hoped the war would be over by the end of the year. But as winter set in it became clear that wasn't going to happen.

The Doodlebugs were less frequent now, but explosions had

been taking place across south-east England, and it appeared that Hitler had another secret weapon, the V-2 rocket. Unlike the V-1, this could not be heard until it exploded on the ground, which gave no chance to take cover.

'Damn the man,' Becky muttered when she heard that another rocket had dropped on the outskirts of London. 'He's beaten, so why doesn't he give up?'

'It won't be long now.' Alice blew on her cold hands.

'That's what everyone keeps saying. This bitter wind is enough to cut right through you. I wish they'd let us in.'

'It'll be worth queuing, Becky, to see if there's a newsreel from Will.'

'He's done a marvellous job, hasn't he?' Becky smiled proudly. 'And do you know, I think he's enjoyed himself. When the war started he was disappointed because the forces wouldn't take him, but just look at what he's achieved.'

'Anyone can shoot a gun, but not many have his talent. He found the right job, but my goodness, he's given us some worrying times.'

Becky chuckled. 'Hasn't he just! Is he still asking you to marry him?'

'He puts it at the bottom of every letter. Just as a reminder to me not to forget, he says.'

'Any idea what you're going to do about him?'

There was silence for a moment, then Alice said, 'What do you think about having me as a sister-in-law?'

Becky's squeal of delight made people in the queue turn and stare. 'Oh, Alice, we'll all be delighted.'

'You mustn't tell Will or your family yet. We have to wait until he comes home, because I'm going to let him propose properly, then he can tell everyone the good news.'

Becky couldn't stop smiling, so happy for her brother and Alice. 'I promise to keep my mouth shut.'

'What about David?'

'I'm going to talk to him when he gets back. When I was driving the ambulance the suffering I saw tore me apart, but it also helped me to put things into their proper perspective. The wounded on those ships are all ranks, including officers. They're all out there facing the same dangers. I've been worrying too much about the class difference and the fact that he is an officer.'

'And now?'

'I don't care any more, and I don't believe David ever did. I just need to be sure of his true feelings for me. Once I know that I'll be able to decide what is the right thing to do.'

'Thank goodness. You're talking sense at last!'

They were both happy as the queue finally began to move into the cinema.

Thirty-Six

It had been a sad Christmas and New Year, with Becky and her family feeling the loss of Jim deeply, and not one of the boys at home to help cheer things up. Everyone was waiting for the weather to improve, and praying that 1945 would see the end of the war.

The months dragged for Becky, but finally spring arrived, and as the trees burst into life they seemed to trigger new hope. It couldn't be long now.

Becky looked up when she heard shouting and saw Alice tearing towards her, waving her arms frantically, and hugging everyone she came near. Not a bit like the dignified Alice she knew.

'It's over!' Alice threw herself at Becky and hugged her as well. 'The bugger's killed himself and Germany has surrendered. The eighth of May is a date we will always remember.'

'At last!' Becky cried as she lifted Alice off her feet in excitement. 'They'll all be coming home! I must go and see David's family.'

'Come on,' a group of soldiers urged. 'There's a party starting in the mess.'

'Er . . .' Becky glanced around, hesitating.

'Go on.' The sergeant was beaming, and that was not a sight they came across very often. 'Everyone's excused. Go and celebrate the end of the war in Europe. But while you're doing that we mustn't forget there's Japan to deal with, and a lot of our boys are still in Burma.'

'Oh, Lord.' Alice grimaced. 'I hope Will doesn't decide to go out there now.'

'He'd better not,' Becky declared. 'He's got two of us to deal with now.'

It was three months later when Japan surrendered, and everyone's thoughts began to turn to the future. Troops were pouring back and eager for demob. Alice had already said she was leaving at the earliest opportunity, but Becky was holding back until she had seen David. He might not feel the same now that the war was over, and if that turned out to be the case, she was still toying with the idea of staying in the army. She liked the life, and wasn't sure she could settle down to working in a shop again – in fact she was positive it would be impossible to readjust to that kind of life.

David was still in Berlin, and there was no sign of him returning yet, so she would have to be patient. Will was already home and Alice had gone to meet him, but there was no sign of Bob.

Becky walked up the drive to the Hammonds' house. Before she reached the door, it opened and the dog made for her at speed. The animal was quite a size now and Becky managed to sidestep just in time to avoid being knocked off her feet.

'Aha! You thought you had me that time, didn't you?' She bent down to make a fuss of the dog, and was sure the animal was laughing.

'Rebecca.' Sara joined them, her smile as wide as it could get. 'The war's over everywhere, and Grandma says Daddy will be coming home soon.'

'Isn't that exciting?' She let the little girl pull her into the house.

Mr Hammond was not at home, but Mrs Hammond was pleased to see her. 'Let's have tea in the garden, shall we?'

It was a pleasant day and so peaceful in the garden. While Sara was playing with the dog, Mrs Hammond turned her attention to Becky. 'We're expecting David back within the next couple of weeks. He couldn't say exactly when.'

'I don't suppose he knows, but it will be such a relief when things are more settled and we can start planning for the future. We've spent years not looking past the next day or the one after that.'

'Yes, it's been hard.' She stared into space, and then back at the girl sitting next to her. 'What are you going to do now, Rebecca?'

'I haven't decided yet.'

Sara had stopped running around and was now standing next to Becky, looking up at her with a worried expression on her face.

'If you leave the army you won't stop coming to see me, will you?'

'Not if you want me to keep coming. I wouldn't like it if I couldn't see you any more.'

'Please keep coming, Rebecca.' She was leaning on Becky's knees and gazing up at her. 'We went to your house yesterday for a party.'

'Really? I didn't know about any party.'

'Your parents kindly invited us,' Mrs Hammond explained. 'It was arranged unexpectedly to celebrate your brother's engagement to Alice. Your father came for us himself.'

'Oh, that's wonderful!' Becky was so excited. 'I wish I could have been there, but I expect I'll get a letter tomorrow telling me all about it.'

'They were sorry you weren't at home, but I believe they're planning a huge party when they can gather you all together.' Mrs Hammond smiled wistfully. 'It was such a happy occasion, and we were honoured to have been included.'

'I like your mummy and daddy,' Sara told her. 'They're nice. There were two American soldiers there, and they made me laugh and they danced with me. One of them threw me right in the air, and everyone joined in. It was a lovely party.'

'Greg and Hal were there?' Becky asked Mrs Hammond.

'Yes, that's right. They'd only just arrived and had come straight round to see your family.'

Becky clasped her hands together tightly in an effort to control her emotions. 'I'm so relieved they're back safely. Will told me he'd seen them in France, so I knew they had got off the beaches all right, but I've still been worried about them. In fact I seem to have spent this entire war worrying about everyone.'

To have received two lots of good news had made Becky's visit to the Hammonds a very happy one, and she returned to the camp absolutely delighted. She had missed that impromptu party, but they would have another one later. Alice wasn't due back yet so she would write to her and Will tonight.

Two days later Alice arrived back at camp and Becky pounced on her, demanding all the details. She also received a letter from Will and her parents. They said that the Hammonds had been invited on the spur of the moment, and they had really enjoyed themselves. The dog came as well and had been very excited at all the attention she was given. Hal said he had a dog at home and couldn't wait to see him again, as well as his family and friends. Her father said Greg and Hal appeared war weary, just like all the returning troops, and a boisterous gathering was just what they needed.

Alice and Will planned a Christmas wedding because Will would be going back to Berlin for a few weeks. Then he said that he had a couple of offers for broadcasting and would be considering those at a later date.

A week later Alice was demobbed, and Becky bid her a sad farewell, knowing she was going to miss her being around the camp. But she would soon be her sister-in-law, so that was a happy prospect.

She had just driven into the camp after taking an officer to the London HQ when she saw a tall officer talking to the sergeant. Her heart leapt with pleasure when he turned and smiled. There was no mistaking David, and she was overjoyed to see him home at last.

With a few long strides he was beside the car and opening the door for her. She jumped out eagerly. 'Oh, you're back! It's so good to see you. Have you been home . . .?'

In her excitement she had momentarily forgotten where they were, and she snapped to attention. Before her hand could lift in a salute, he caught hold of her arm.

'You don't need to salute me.' He turned his head to speak to the sergeant who was watching with avid interest. 'You know what to say if you're asked. And thank you, Sergeant.'

'My pleasure, sir.'

'Come with me, Rebecca. We can't talk here.'

David's MG was a short walk away and he opened the passenger door for her. 'I'll drive.'

She got in. 'I haven't got a pass, David. Where are we going?'

'We're going somewhere quiet, and you don't need a pass – you're with me.'

'Ah, of course.'

He cast her an amused glance. 'No argument about my unprofessional conduct?'

'Not a word.' She was far too happy to be concerned.

'That is progress. When are you leaving the ATS?'

'I don't know yet if I'm going to. I'm still trying to make up my mind, and I've got another two weeks to make my decision.'

He let out a pent-up breath, but he said nothing, which surprised her. Then she noticed he was gripping the steering wheel rather tightly and suddenly realized that he was nervous. Then her pleasure evaporated. He was going to tell her that he had changed his mind, and wouldn't be seeing her again. Perhaps he had met someone else he considered more suitable. Neither of them spoke for the rest of the journey.

He took her to Virginia Water where they had once had that lovely picnic, and after parking the car they got out and began walking. There were few people around, and those they did see smiled at them, all enjoying the warm sunshine and the fact that the long war was finally over.

When they reached a secluded spot, David stopped and turned her to face him. Becky took a silent deep breath and waited, sure this was the moment he was going to tell her he had changed his mind about her.

'When I met you at the recruitment office I thought you were lovely, intelligent and lively, but so young and innocent. Just over five years of war have changed you into a beautiful woman. All the way through France and into Berlin, I have cursed my stupidity for the clumsy way I proposed to you. When I told you that my feelings for you were attraction, and that I didn't want to love again, I was lying, not only to you, but to myself as well. I tried to tell myself that I was acting for the benefit of my daughter, but that was nonsense. She couldn't have more loving grandparents to care for her, and I know they would have been very willing to bring her up if I hadn't survived the war.'

When she started to speak he stopped her.

'No, let me finish. I've loved you from the moment you smiled at me the first time we met, and I don't want to spend the rest of my life without you. Please marry me, Rebecca. I love you so much.'

It took her a brief moment to take in what he had just said, and then with tears of joy in her eyes, she nodded. 'I've also been doing some hard thinking, and I realized that my worries about you being from the officer class were silly. Once I had come to my senses about that, all I needed to know was that you love me. So yes, I will marry you, David.'

She was swept into a fierce embrace, neither of them caring that they were in a public place and might be seen.

'Thank God,' he said, his voice husky with relief. 'I felt sure that I had ruined any chance I might have had.'

They were both smiling now, and Becky admitted, 'I also thought I had lost my chance with you, and that you were about to tell me you'd changed your mind.'

'We both nearly made a terrible mess of this, didn't we?' he said wryly. 'Thank heavens we came to our senses in time.'

'I would have regretted it all my life if I had walked away from you and Sara. When I was driving the ambulance and saw so much suffering, I was filled with regret that I had let you go without telling you how much I loved you.'

'Well, that's all behind us now, my darling, and we can start planning for the future. We'll go and tell Sara and my parents first, then straight round to your family.'

Sara had been attending school for the past two years, and had grown a lot since Becky had first met her. She was beginning to look like her father now as she ran to greet them when they arrived.

David ushered everyone into the lounge, and then stooped down to his daughter. 'We've got something to tell you, sweetheart. Rebecca has just agreed to marry me.'

Becky was shaking with nerves. How would Sara take the news? Would she object? They got on well together, but how would she feel about another woman being in her father's life? Would she be jealous?

'Umm . . .' Sara was looking from one to the other. 'Does this mean Rebecca will be living with us all the time?'

'It does, sweetheart, and when I move around, you and Rebecca will be able to come with me and live in the officers' quarters.'

Suddenly the girl was hugging her father, and then rushing to Becky to do the same. 'You won't have to leave us now. Whoopee!'

Becky sagged with relief.

'I think she approves,' David laughed.

'And so do we!' Becky was kissed and hugged by David's parents, then Mrs Hammond said, 'This is what we had hoped for, but my goodness you two really did keep us waiting.'

Mr Hammond took a bottle of champagne out of the sideboard and placed it by glasses already laid out. 'We've discussed what we would do if you did marry Rebecca, David, and we're giving you this house as a wedding present. We shall be moving out.'

'Oh, but you mustn't!' Becky was alarmed. 'This is your family home.'

'Rebecca's right. We shall be away for long periods; you must continue to live here.'

'No.' Mrs Hammond shook her head. 'We've made up our minds.'

'But where will you go?'

Mr Hammond filled the glasses and handed them around. 'Have you forgotten, David, that at the end of the garden is that parcel of land my father bought, and we've never done anything with it? We're going to build ourselves a new house there. The plans have been in place for some time, and now would be a good time to go ahead.'

David's frown smoothed out. 'I had forgotten that. Well, if you are determined to do this, then we will accept your very generous gift, won't we, Rebecca?'

She nodded, quite overcome. 'I don't know what to say. Thank you seems so inadequate.'

'Thank you will do, my dear.' Mr Hammond appeared to be very satisfied.

'However, we insist you stay here until the new house is ready for occupation,' David said.

'Agreed.' Mrs Hammond smiled and held up his glass. 'We are delighted at the news, and we wish you both a long and happy life together.'

'I'll drink to that.' David touched his glass to Becky's, and placed an arm around her waist.

Sara had been given a glass of orange juice so she could join in the toast, and she watched her father and Becky over the rim of her glass. 'Will I call you mummy now?' she asked Becky.

'Only if you want to, but it's quite all right for you to carry on calling me Rebecca if you prefer.'

'Hmm, I'll think about it. What will your brother be to me after you've married Daddy?' Sara was clearly thinking this all through.

'He'll be your uncle.'

Her face lit up with a smile and she turned to her grandmother. 'I haven't got one of those, have I?'

'No, darling,' Mrs Hammond told her. 'And Rebecca's mother and father will be more grandparents for you. We're going to have a lovely big family.'

'Oh, isn't this exciting! Have you told them, Daddy?'

'Not yet, but we're going there right now, and we think you should all come with us.'

Mr Hammond went back to the sideboard. 'I've got another bottle of champagne here.'

'Good, I need all the support I can get. I'm not sure if your father approves of me, darling. Though I did tell him I intended to marry you. He said he trusted your judgement, but I got the feeling he was sure you would keep on refusing me.'

'Well, he was wrong about that.'

David nodded. 'Thank goodness he was. Now, Dad, we're going to need the Rolls, so how's the petrol situation?'

'I haven't got much, but there's some in your MG. Can I siphon it out?'

'Go ahead.'

'I'll do it.' Becky had already turned towards the door when David caught her arm.

'We can manage that little job while you discuss wedding plans with Mother. October at the latest,' he said as he left the room with his father.

Mrs Hammond gasped. 'That doesn't give us enough time!'

'October,' came the reply.

Now Becky was worried. 'We can't have a huge wedding, Mrs Hammond. Mum and Dad haven't got much money, and there will be my brother's engagement and wedding to think of as well.'

'We know your family lost everything in the bombing, my dear, so don't you worry, we'll work it out with them. You and David discuss it when you have a chance, but it would be lovely if you had a military wedding. And the guest list would, of necessity, be rather long.' She gave Becky an understanding smile. 'And talking of engagements . . .'

When the men returned, Mrs Hammond said to her son, 'David, haven't you forgotten something?'

'No, I wanted to do this when you were all here.' Pulling a small box out of his pocket he stood in front of Becky, and took hold of her left hand. 'I hope you like this. It was my grandmother's.' He slipped a beautiful solitaire diamond ring on her finger. It fitted perfectly.

Becky gazed at it in wonder, speechless.

'We can get something else if you don't like it.'

'It's stunning, and I love it. I'll be honoured to wear your grandmother's ring.'

'It looks lovely on you. Now let's go and break the news to your family.'

Thirty Seven

They had chosen the right time to call on Becky's parents because everyone was there except Bob. Alice immediately noticed the ring on Becky's finger and smiled her approval. With so many of them there the front room was crowded.

David was ready to tell them about the engagement but stopped when it was obvious his daughter could no longer contain her excitement, and was about to blurt it out. He bent down and whispered in her ear, and she grinned, nodding vigorously.

He stood up again. 'I'd better do this quickly, as our daughter is bursting to tell you herself. I am proud to tell you that Rebecca has today agreed to be my wife.'

Becky's parents hugged her and shook David's hand, obviously delighted with the news. But something David had said was ringing in her ears and nearly brought tears of joy to her eyes. He'd said 'our daughter'.

'I'll take good care of her,' David assured them.

Bill nodded. 'The most important thing is that you love her, son. You make sure you do.'

'You can have no fears on that score, Mr Adams.'

Mr Hammond was already pouring out a small amount of champagne for everyone to have a little for a toast when Sara launched herself at Becky's parents. 'Can I call you Grandpa and Grandma number two now?'

Everyone laughed at that and Becky's parents readily gave their permission.

'And I'll be your uncle and Alice will be your aunt,' Will told her.

'Ooh, will you come and visit me?'

'Of course,' Alice told her. 'We'll all be family soon.'

Sara spun round to face Mrs Hammond. 'I'm going to have an auntie as well, Grandma.'

Bill tapped the table for silence. 'Let us raise our glasses and wish both couples a happy and long life together.'

When the glasses were drained, Bill turned to his wife. 'Mavis, put the kettle on and let's all have a nice cup of tea.'

Mrs Hammond walked out to the kitchen with her mother, and Becky guessed they would be talking about the wedding. She was quite happy to leave this with them for the moment. They could discuss the details later.

'I wish Bob could have been here,' Becky said to his mother. 'Have you heard from him?'

'Yes, he's staying in the navy, and seems quite settled with Helen. He said they will marry one day, but are in no hurry.'

'I'm not surprised. He loves the sea, and I'm very happy for him.'

Everyone was moving around the room talking to each other, and finally Alice was able to catch up with her friend.

'After all the ups and downs of the war years, it's good to be able to look to the future, isn't it?'

Becky nodded. 'We can never know exactly what the future has in store for us, but the uncertain years are behind us and we can move on with our lives at last.'

A week later, when Bob and his girl, Helen, had also arrived home, they held a proper party to celebrate the engagements. Greg and Hal were still in the country waiting to be shipped home, and they were also able to join them.

Bill Adams once again took on the role of toastmaster. 'We have already wished the happy couples the best for the future, but today I would like to propose another toast. Please raise your glasses to everyone here, and those sadly no longer with us. Friends and heroes, every one.'